LUCY CHRISTO

AISE FOR LUCY CHRISTOPHER'S BOOKS

*Marvellous and magical . . . A weird, wonderful
ride into an unforgettable tempest.*
DAVID LEVITHAN

As a teen, I would have adored this book . . .
MAGGIE STIEFVATER

A vivid new voice for teens.
MELVIN BURGESS

A stunning, scary and beautiful book.
JOHN MARSDEN

Tautly written and hard to put down.
INDEPENDENT ON SUNDAY

*Original and thrilling, this is another cracker
from an author to watch.*
THE SUN

*gripping, heartbreaking, emotionally substantial look
at war wounds and the allure of danger.*
KIRKUS STARRED REVIEW

I always think that Lucy Christopher's writing has a kind of sorcery: through it, she conjures her own distinctive weather. In each of her novels' unique landscapes – from the mesmerizing desert heat of her award-winning *Stolen*, to the bird-filled wetlands of *Flyaway* and to the dangerous and windswept forests in *The Killing Woods* – the weather is a character in itself. Now, in *Storm-Wake*, the weather is truly a force of magic. Strange storms wrack the island setting, while violent tides draw the characters' fates in startling new directions. Here, a young girl grows up and faces choices about what is real, who she loves and where she really belongs. Here's a story relevant to all our lives, at once startlingly real and blissfully dreamy – and surely a classic in the making.

BARRY CUNNINGHAM
Publisher
Chicken House

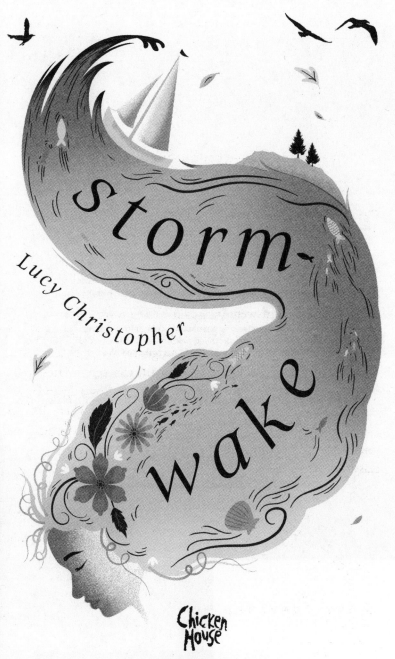

Lucy Christopher

storm-
wake

Chicken
House

2 Palmer Street, Frome, Somerset BA11 1DS
www.chickenhousebooks.com

Text © Lucy Christopher 2018

First published in Great Britain in 2018
Chicken House
2 Palmer Street
Frome, Somerset BA11 1DS
United Kingdom
www.chickenhousebooks.com

Cover design and interior design by Helen Crawford-White
Typeset by Dorchester Typesetting Group Ltd
Printed and bound in Great Britain by CPI Group (UK) Ltd, Croydon, CR0 4YY

The paper used in this Chicken House book is made
from wood grown in sustainable forests.

1 3 5 7 9 10 8 6 4 2

British Library Cataloguing in Publication data available.

ISBN 978-1-906427-73-3
eISBN 978-1-911077-59-6

For Dad and Barb, with love.

Also by Lucy Christopher

Stolen
Flyaway
The Killing Woods

Be not afeard; the isle is full of noises,
Sounds and sweet airs, that give delight and hurt not.
Sometimes a thousand twangling instruments
Will hum about mine ears, and sometime voices
That, if I then had waked after long sleep,
Will make me sleep again: and then, in dreaming,
The clouds methought would open and show riches
Ready to drop upon me that, when I waked,
I cried to dream again.

William Shakespeare, *The Tempest*

CONTENTS

ACT ONE
SPRING

The Scene: An Unnamed Port

Nine Years Previous

ACT ONE. SCENE ONE.

This story starts with a dream, and its dreamer.

He was younger then, rolling in the belly of his boat, on rougher waters than expected inside those harbour walls. The first day of spring, but he felt at the end of the world. And still, the storms stayed.

In fever dream, he turned in his bunk, his hand splaying to the side and hovering in mid-air. He pressed his finger and thumb together, so gently, as if he were picking a flower. Careful, careful ... he couldn't rush it, couldn't *crush* it, either. The flower was so little, more precious than any jewel. He breathed lighter, stretched a little further. *There!* He touched it. Just *there*! It left a tingling in his fingertips.

'Stormflower,' he whispered.

He ran his fingers down its stem – smooth, smooth, a little wet, so tiny and firm – more sparrow's leg than plant. And, soon, the feeling came, the happy rush into his veins. No pain now. All fading back – the sharp stabs in his mind, the confusion, the anxiety when he thought about the darkness washing over the world. He could drown in darkness like that; anyone could.

Not him.

He'd met that sailor in the port's bar – fate, perhaps? – and he'd watched the old man's face, candle-bright as he'd talked of that land.

'*Alchemy . . . change . . . heal the darkness . . . a chance.*'

As the sailor's words had tangled inside him, there'd been urging and rough magic and dreams in the old man's eyes. Then the flowers he'd sketched on the napkin between them. The map.

And then, every night while the rains got worse, came the dreams.

So.

The young man did what he always did in those dreams. He snapped the flower's head from its stem and put its petals inside his mouth.

And he chewed.

ACT TWO
SUMMER

The Scene: An Island

Eight Years Previous

ACT TWO. SCENE ONE.

For Moss, storms had a smell: churned-up salt water and seaweed, damp wood on the tide, even the far-off burn of lightning . . . but this storm had something else. It was sweeter. *Wilder.* Moss pushed her hair sideways and looked up at the cliffs. Tiny pieces of colour were everywhere, as if the rocks held gemstones. She growled as her hair flew back in front of her face, tangling in a hundred different sailor's knots.

But she'd seen right.

Stormflowers.

Opening.

Again, she shoved her hair clear to see where the flowers grew thickest, all around Pa's cave. Wind was pulling their petals, rattling their stems. The storm's sweetness was *this*. There were pink ones, white, others gold – petals floated from the rocks to settle on her shoulders. She heard a high-pitched singing sort of sound too. Pa had always said the flowers would sing. When they wanted to. When they were ready to open full.

She tried to see Pa at the cave entrance. *Now* she knew why he wasn't down on the beach with her, exploring for wash-up. He was doing this. Somehow he'd opened the flowers, made them work!

She dropped the collecting pot and ran. Fast, fast, faster, leaping the sharp stones on that part of the beach. Quick, quicker, she skidded through their camp, then took the well-used path up to the cave. She was huff-puffing before she was even halfway. As she spread her arms wide so that she was almost touching the wild-moving pine trees, she was imagining how, later, beside the campfire, Pa would dance and sing and swirl her. Would tell stories till the fire went low, of the world where they had come from, of where they would go back to, also, one day. His smile would be broad beneath his bird-beak nose, his blue-grey eyes soft.

Now she felt lighter. Now she ran faster. She went quick-spinning and leaping beneath those petals, all swirling and falling. Until, flinching, she saw the sky smash.

'Lightning,' she whispered, savouring the word like a treasure. 'Sky's on fire.'

Was what Pa would say. She spread her arms wide till her wrists brushed pine needles and felt their cool zing.

Sky's!

On!

Fire!

She loved Pa's sayings and how his voice tilted as he spoke them; she liked to test how they felt in her mouth. A bigger, second flash came, but she didn't lie flat on the ground like Pa had taught her and wait for it to pass. She stood still, feeling the wind claw, smelling the petals, hearing the sea moan above the reef. And, still, that singing – that high-pitched, sweet-pretty singing! From beyond the volcano, at very toppest of the island, she thought she heard the wild dogs howl in answer. Perhaps even the lizards hissed in their caves. Today, everything on the island cried out.

At Pa's cave, the heavy cloth across the door was half pulled back. Inside, the wind was not so firm. When Pa turned, his teeth caught the light from the candles and glinted like the petals did. He held out his arms and she ran for them.

'How did you make the flowers full-open, Pa?'

'Luck?' He shrugged, smiling. 'Maybe it was just the right time.'

She breathed in, there was smoke and earth; the smells always in Pa's coverings no matter how hard Pa washed at them. She crouched to Jess too, and breathed in running and rabbits. The dog licked her ear. Then Pa took Moss's hand and pulled her to the table to see the glass vase. She reached to touch it, thinking, as always, how special it was that something so fragile had survived their rough journey across the sea so long ago. Underneath its lid, a mixture swirled.

'Opened petals?' she asked. 'All crushed up?'

Pa nodded. 'Mixed them with salt water and sand. I told them dreams and stories! When they'd had enough, they opened.'

'Island feeds on stories.' She repeated the words he'd told her once when he'd been crouched close to the fire.

'Clever Moss.' He tapped her on the nose. 'I found these ones on the volcano. I sang for them. Perhaps I got the song right; perhaps they were just ready to work.'

He winked, then hummed for Moss. It sounded more like a bird's song than the rowdy-loud sailing songs Pa sang beside the fire after palm wine. Two notes, up and down, getting faster and higher in pitch until it was like a finch's trill. He put the flowers he'd picked on the table, in a line. Before, when the island had had storms, the flowers'd only opened a little, and she and Pa had

9

peered inside the closed-up petals to see their yellow hearts. But today their centres shone, and their petals glinted vivid-bright as fish scales.

'When I felt this storm coming,' Pa continued, 'I knew the flowers would open – I felt it core-deep! Now we can send them out to the world.'

'Heal the floods,' Moss murmured, repeating other words she'd read in his book.

'Fix the darkness,' he added.

'And then we'll go back there, yes?'

But Pa didn't hear her words. Instead, gentle-slow, Pa picked up one of the smallest, most orange flowers and held it out. Glow-bright, it was.

'The pollen,' Pa explained, 'making it glint.'

But she knew that; Pa had told her a thousand times.

Healing pollen.

Magic pollen.

Pollen to change the rest of the world and make it safe again.

Pollen to heal Pa, too.

When she breathed in, the pollen's sweet smell tickled the back of her throat.

'Try it now, Pa,' Moss said. 'See if it heals anything! See if your brain feels better!'

He ruffled her hair, got fingers caught in it. Careful-slow, he took the flower between finger and thumb. Snapping the flower's head from the stem, he put it inside his mouth. His eyes widened, and he chewed.

Moss squinted as she watched him, waited for his Adam's apple to bob down his swallow. Did Pa look any different? Could one flower make him better?

Pa laughed at her expression. 'Do you want to try?'

She took a pink flower. Closer up, its smell was sweeter than the honeycomb she fetched from the hives. It wriggled in her fingers and felt almost . . . alive. There was a sound like giggling. Was it coming from the flower?

'We can't eat something that laughs!'

Pa's eyes went crinkle-kind. 'Sing to it. Let it know you mean well.'

She copied him – those two bird-trill notes – moving her mouth in the same way he did. Jess barked. The flower went still in her hand, almost as if it were listening too. She turned it this way and that, seeing its million shades of pink.

'It's too beautiful,' she said. 'It giggled!'

'So? You giggle too! What six-year-old wouldn't when I do *this* . . .' He reached forward to tickle her ribs and she squirmed away, giggling louder than the flower. She wanted to spin and spin with the whooshing feeling inside.

When she opened her palm and looked back at it proper, it seemed to buzz on her skin. Something felt different inside her as she watched it, like her pulse beat faster and stronger.

'Like magic,' she whispered.

'It likes your stories,' Pa said. 'It gets energy from them, wants to be inside you to hear them better.'

She laughed again, and the flower seemed to move – just a little – towards her.

'See?' Pa said.

Quick-fast, she put it in her mouth. Chewed. Got an explosion of sweetness on her tongue. It made her teeth tingle. Made her want to laugh and laugh and spin and swirl. Made her want to sit beside the fire and tell stories with Pa, read from his book. Draw pictures with sticks, dance in spirals. Pa had been right: these flowers were full-magic. Now she felt full-magic too.

Pa tipped rock-pool water from a scallop shell on to the table. 'Watch this, Moss.'

On a breeze from outside, the flowers moved towards the water, their petals darkening as they soaked it in.

'They drink it?'

Pa nodded. 'They'll make the floods go down.'

But how would little flowers drink in all the great big sea?

He laughed loud, his noise all startled-bird. She jumped. She felt the zing of petals against her cheeks, a sway inside her. Had the flower changed her, too? Healed her of something she didn't know she had?

'But what do I know about flowers like this?' Pa continued. 'What does anyone? A new species, Moss . . . a new chance. And we're the explorers!'

She saw hope and happy in his face. She dug her fingers into Jess's fur to go steadier. The flower's taste was strong. Now it made her want to shut her eyes and do nothing but dream.

When a gust of wind tried to pull petals from the table, Pa caught them quick.

'If I can just get the mixture right, maybe we'll make the world better without even leaving our island,' Pa said. 'Later, we'll send my book back to show them what we did!'

There was glinting in Pa's eyes, as if pieces of pollen were caught there. He picked up the vase and tilted it. Inside, the mixture glinted too, buzzed like a million fireflies pressed tight. 'Perhaps whoever first discovered the healing given from poppies or willow felt like this too. We could be about to change . . . everything!'

Moss looked back towards the cave's mouth to see ocean swirling and storm clouds coming. 'If the Experiment works, will we see the other land?'

'You remember it?'

Moss frowned to think of that other island, smaller than theirs, so far away on the horizon line. Had seeing it been a dream instead?

'It disappeared,' she whispered.

Pa smiled. 'After we came. When the waters rose to cover it.'

She was thinking hard. 'Maybe when that land comes back we'll know . . .' she shrugged, trying to decide what they'd know, '. . . we'll know it's safe to return, back to the rest of the world.'

'Maybe.'

Pa took the lid from the vase, and such sweetness came into the air that Moss wobbled again.

Pa put his hand out to steady her. 'Easy, my bird.'

His hand was warmer than before. He squeezed her shoulder before picking up more flowers from the table. He crushed them in his fist and dropped them into the swirling mixture, which turned a deeper shade of orange. He licked his fingers, not wasting a driblet of flower juice, then spat into the vase. The mixture swirled harder.

'What now?' Moss asked.

But she knew. Hadn't Pa told her enough times as they sat around the fire? Hadn't she read it in his book? Now, he'd push this mixture out to the storm, and winds would take the healing pollen back to the rest of the world. But would anything change? Would land return? Would darkness go away? She licked her lips, tasted sweetness.

Pa carried the vase to the cave entrance where the wind was racing-fierce, dragging Moss's hair over her eyes again. Pa pointed the mouth of the vase towards the storm clouds, his clothing flapping in the wind.

'Change,' Pa whispered.

They watched the mixture swirl up out of the vase and hang in the air as a bright puff, humming and fizzing. Moss's eyes watered. She wanted to stick her tongue out to taste it, keep it with her. But she also wanted to help Pa send it away. If that air went back, the floods would go down. Maybe then they would've fixed the world.

As she thought it, the orange mixture swirled and dived, darted towards the storm clouds.

'Take it,' Pa said. 'Fix us all!'

ACT TWO. SCENE TWO.

The Scene: An Island
Seven Years Previous

The winds continued, and the flowers stayed open. Each morning, Moss watched Pa crush more stormflowers and send them away. Each night, she sat close to him outside their reed-thatched hut and asked about the rest of the world.

'Only we escaped?'

'Only us to this island.'

'But it's safe here?'

Pa nodded. 'Safe for as long as we need.'

Beneath star-glow, Moss waited. She remembered how Pa woke at night as if surfacing from a deep pool, gasping for air, and she tucked closer to him, listening to his watery tales. First, Pa told her about the selkies that teased fishermen from their boats. 'Those girls are so pretty, Moss,' he said, 'even if they are half seal!'

She giggled when he winked at her. He told stories about mermaids and mermen. Of sea serpents that lived in deep-darkest waters but might show themselves again, one day. Sometimes, as he

15

spoke, he threw petals to the fire and made tiny images from his stories live in the embers. Mini mermaids swam through flames. Small serpents curled around coals.

And then, as always, he told her of the kelpies – horses formed from the actual sea itself.

'Water-spirits,' he said. 'Legends say that when there are floods, waterhorses are born from oceans.'

Moss snuggled closer to Pa's chest. 'Maybe that's what happened to the rest of the world. Was it kelpie magic that ruined it? Made it flood?'

From tight against him, Moss felt Pa's laugh in her own body, and she smiled too. They liked making up new theories for how the world went bad.

'I wish it were that.' Pa shook his head sad-slow. 'But humans ruined the world . . . using too much, being too greedy. Making the darkness.'

'Were *we* greedy back then?'

Pa's body went still. Perhaps he could not remember it well, either: their time before. He didn't talk of it much.

'Not you, Moss-bird,' he said. 'Other people.' His fingers stroked her left ear, then reached to the battered pot resting on the embers. 'This is cool enough now.'

He took a sip and licked his lips; he handed the flower-brew to Moss.

'Fire-water,' she said when she drank. 'It zings.' After she swallowed more, she added, 'Tell the story about us . . . the one you wrote in your book.'

Pa hugged her tight. 'Once there was an island,' he whispered. 'And it didn't feed on water and light, like other living things did, it fed on dreams ... on stories! Sometimes, if a person wanted something desperately enough – wanted a story – the island made it happen. Its flowers made things change ...'

Moss took another sip of flower-brew and held it in her mouth like Pa held his, containing the tingle behind her teeth. She felt like a dragon – something else from Pa's stories – ready to breathe multicoloured flames.

'Our very own legend,' Pa said. 'Flowers that heal; that slip along the wind and alter the air ... We are so lucky to see it, Moss. One day you and I may be legends too.'

He took his book called *Scrapbook* from out of the hut, ready to read more. She traced her fingers over his joined-up letters.

'Cursive writing,' he said, explaining. 'Linking letters together until they make words, which then make stories.'

Forming stories from scratches: that was magic too.

She turned the pages of the book so gentle, so as not to damage them. As he spoke, she traced a map he'd made of the island: the place for the wild dogs at the top, the long Western Beach stretching down the right side, their cove and hut at the bottom, the rocky coast where their boat had wrecked ... then, in the middle of the island, the triangle volcano. When her fingers paused over *Lizard Rocks*, Pa watched her close.

'Too much danger there, Moss,' he warned. 'Never go there alone.'

He waited for her to nod before continuing.

'Do you remember what I told you once?' Pa said. 'That this island's not on any proper maps? Whenever someone leaves it, they forget. It no longer exists. Only in dreams do people remember. It's a secret land – the greatest secret. And to imagine, some people didn't think the world *had* any more secrets!' His eyes were wide as he looked at her. 'There are always secrets, lurking beneath. Remember that, Moss; you cannot ever know everything.'

Moss rested her fingertips on one of his drawings of a storm-flower. It was so very nearly the same as the real thing, only missing its sweet smell.

'I drew that one just from dreaming about it,' Pa added. 'Long time ago. That dream came real.'

Each day, Moss walked their crescent cove to check for washed-in treasure. Often, Pa came with her. If they were lucky, some days brought wood and storm-drowned fish, plastic bags and bottles. Other times, they walked far to check Western Beach also, or climbed halfway up the volcano to see the horizon. They never saw the other island, and rarely any decent wash-up, either. Though Pa sometimes went off on his own, beyond the volcano to Lizard Rocks, and came back with different treasure, sometimes even fresh books.

'Too dangerous,' he'd remind her, each time she asked to come too. 'Lizards might eat a sweet-tasty chick like you.' Then he would tickle her ribs until she squealed happy.

Moss had grown used to the full-flower sweetness in the air, and to how it made her light-stepped as a flutterby. She'd grown used to seeing dabs of flower-colour everywhere: in the dirt and sand, in the rocks and branches.

But one day, the air was fizzing . . . as it'd been when the flowers first full-opened. This day, again, she felt the storm proper. In her bones and skin. In the pressure in her skull. She pulled her coverings close.

18

A skull storm.

Another of Pa's sayings. She'd never heard Pa say it to describe the weather, though; only himself. The fierce-swirling pain in his head. She shook off her own ache. The wind was pulling her to the sea, and she felt swirling too.

'Could petals change a person to a storm?' she'd asked once, as she'd watched him at the Experiment.

Pa had picked up more petals, squeezed their juice inside the vase, licked his fingers. 'Who knows what they can do? We're only beginning to find out.'

'Could the flowers make me a friend, then? Another dog, or person? Family?'

'One day, maybe.' Pa had knelt close. 'But I'm your family, Moss-bird. Me and Jess. Me and these stories.' He'd pointed around the cave, at the books he'd rescued from their boat and the sea. He'd tapped the end of the dog's nose and then smudged that wetness to Moss's. 'We have to be patient for more.'

'Patient is boring.'

He smiled. 'Jessie will be making more dogs soon.'

It was true: Jess had a belly swollen with puppies, half-made from an island dog. But maybe Moss didn't have to wait that long for something new.

She dug her toes into the sand, and looked again to the swirling sea. This was the kind of storm that brought in whole forests of treasure. She skipped to the tideline, spinning and stretching her arms, making her skirts fly and her skull-storm head throb. She was dizzy with the thrill, the storm inside her now too. When she stopped, the whole world spun. Their whole island.

She watched waves begin on the horizon line, saw how they

grew. Maybe she was being silly. Maybe, out there, was only more water. Maybe the flowers hadn't soaked up any floods: the rest of the world was still dark ocean.

But maybe not, too.

She sneezed as a petal landed on her nose. Then blinked. Because, just then – *out there* – something had changed. Hadn't it? The horizon line moved. A little. There was a kind of . . . arch. Moss sank her toes into the water's edge, squinted. Far out, the water arched again. But there were no reefs right there for water to break on. So what was it?

She remembered a picture from one of Pa's books of a boat, sinking and rolling, drowning its passengers. She thought about how their own boat had smashed. Could a shipwreck be happening again? She started forwards fast into the choppy water.

Then stopped.

She was crazy. The horizon only held back more ocean, a few storm treasures, birds at sea, stingers, and sea snakes. It would take time for floods to go down. Take time for someone to build a boat and sail it here. But, still, Moss thought she saw something bobbing. Not big enough to be a boat, but . . .

She watched to see where it might come in. Was it driftwood or scraps of material, a bicycle tyre? They'd made good use of those washed-in things before.

That curve in the wave came closer. From how it moved, it looked – almost – like something alive. Moss watched so serious she didn't notice colder seawater come smashing at her calves. But she did see lightning flare far away, heard thunder a few moments later. It wouldn't be long until the storm was full here. She would stay until the rain came – at least until then. Until storm mist swamped everything.

From far up on the cliff behind her, she heard Pa singing his bird-trill tune, sending flowers out. The sea hissed back, churned harder. Petals swirled and settled in the water, bled colour before they sank.

The waves grew. And Moss saw it again, this time a bigger, frothing white wave, rising above the others. It arched again until, now, it was no longer a wave but a neck. With a . . .

. . . long nose.

Hair.

It was a creature before her! A beast in the sea.

Swimming?

A monster from one of Pa's stories?

Perhaps she was dreaming, drowsy from the flower-scent in the air. Moss kept her eyes steady, looking so careful. It had two flicking, pale ears. Eyes and a mouth. Did Pa or the flowers make this come? She was buzz-flying, but she did not run to him for answers, not yet. Instead, she opened her arms wide in welcome.

The wave-creature raced closer. She saw its eyes; its long, straight back; how it arched its neck. That creature shouldn't be able to do this. She knew this, even if she could never remember seeing one of these creatures before. Because . . . this was a horse. She'd only ever seen them in Pa's books, heard about them in his stories. Somehow, here, in front of her – a pale, powerful, swimming horse.

She shook her head. The horses in Pa's stories lived on land, were covered in leather and buckles and ridden by humans. This horse seemed part-sea. Hadn't she just seen it rising from the waves?

Then she realized. Pa's stories, told beside the fire.

Waterhorses.

Kelpies.

Magic spirits.

They'd come real. *One had.*

It stepped from the water, glistening and smelling of seaweed; so bright against the sun, almost like it had fish scales all across it. It snorted, pawed the sand. Moss was not proper scared, but she stepped backwards all the same. It seemed as if the creature might run right over her if she did not. It kept its eyes on hers – huge eyes, dark with a thousand watery secrets. When Moss breathed in, the horse's sweat-salt air came inside her. She could touch it; it was close enough. It watched her and waited, almost demanded something with its bold stare.

'You are welcome,' she whispered.

She did not know if the creature understood. 'Course Pa had taught her that animals could not speak, but it was not just animal: not just any one thing. Her hand moved towards it; she could not fight the urge any longer. She had to feel if it was warm and real.

The horse bent its neck, tilted its head. She rested her fingers on its glinting pale shoulder, felt it flinch. There was hair there, soft and warm, not scales like it had first seemed. The animal did not disappear like she had half expected it to. Instead, she felt muscles, taut and stringy beneath the hair; she felt strength.

Moss saw the whites of its eyes as the horse looked to something behind her. When she turned, she found Pa had climbed down from the cliff and was striding towards them, his clothes and hair rising with the wind.

'A horse?' He stared at it, wide-eyed too. He looked back at the water. 'A real one?'

'It came from the waves.' She paused. 'Or maybe from the flowers?'

Pa nodded. 'I saw them swirling down to the sea.'

'They made a companion!' Moss smiled at Pa's frowning. 'From the water! Of course, Pa!' It was what she had asked for in the cave: what she'd wanted. The flowers had listened! 'It's a water-spirit, like from your stories. The flowers made it!'

Pa reached to touch it too. There was flower juice on his chin, caught in his beard hair. He laughed sudden-sharp, grabbed Moss's hands, and whirled her to the wind. She spun so fast the beach blurred.

'The flowers work!' he said. 'I don't know how, but they . . .' the wind caught his words as he spun and spun, '. . . they make things change, make things beautiful that were swirling-dark before!'

They slowed, and he pulled a hand away to tame Moss's tangled hair, the excitement still bright in his eyes. Moss knew why. With the flowers, Pa could bring winds. Could bring waterhorses! Pa could change a sick world.

She stretched out her calves to feel light rain. Slow-cautious, she touched the edge of the horse with her toe. The horse skittered. 'Are you scared of it?'

'*Her*,' Pa said, his eyes running over the horse's body. 'She's too beautiful for being scared, no? Besides, we created her. Or the flowers did – created her from our stories. Why be scared of our stories?'

'*Your* stories,' Moss said, soft.

The horse jigged on the sand as if she wanted to run.

'Everything is starting to shift,' Pa murmured. 'To change.' Pa tilted his pale eyebrows at Moss's expression. 'It's like I pull something in, *will* it to be different. It's like something responds. Flower-magic!'

'She's so pretty,' Moss said. 'Wonder-bright.'

Pa's eyes were soft as he watched her. 'Pretty like the sea aster, don't you think?'

Moss remembered the grey-purple stormflowers that grew near sea's edge on Western Beach and lived only on salt water, the stormflowers that made flutterbys dance-happy.

'Sea aster,' Moss said, tangling her fingers in the horse's mane. 'Yes!'

It was the perfect name!

The horse's nostrils widened, and again she pranced back. When Pa made to touch her too, her muscles strained through the skin on her neck, rippling through her body. Moss grabbed Pa's arms as the horse reeled away.

'Maybe she's not to be caught,' she said. 'Not full-caught, anyway.'

Moss saw the pollen-spark in Pa's eyes as he watched the horse go.

'A sea spirit,' he whispered. '*Our* storm-woke sea spirit.'

It was only now the horse was gone Moss saw something else had come in. This something else lay on the wet sand where waves still washed at it, next to a clump of kelp. It was dark and crumpled, still moving with the beat of the waves, still covered in seaweed. Maybe it was a black plastic bag, still half full of old rubbish and covered in weed – plastic bags had washed in before and had been useful. But as she stepped closer, she saw that it moved different than that. As if it were almost . . . breathing. As if it were a creature underneath the weed: another wonder-strange sea beast!

'Pa, come quick, there's something more!' She drew him away from staring after the horse. 'And it's alive! Here, something more here that's storm-woke!'

She pulled back the seaweed fast.

Gasped.

It was so much smaller than the horse! It was crouched over itself, all spine. She moved closer still. As she saw it proper, she realized . . . it looked like them. A human!

'Someone from the Old World?' She grabbed Pa's arm and pulled him forward. 'Someone's come!'

'No, can't be.' Pa held her shoulder, frowning. 'It's something stranger, Moss – look closer. His skin is stranger than ours!'

When Moss looked again, she saw it too: this new creature *was* different. So much darker and slicker. This creature looked as if it really were covered in scales.

Pa bent, urging Moss to take another look. 'Not like us.'

Now she saw it proper. It wasn't exactly scales this creature was covered in; rather, he had the *pattern* of scales threaded through his dark, shiny skin.

'And his fingers, Moss! Look-see!'

Moss saw it – the faint blue webbing between his fingers, right up to the first knuckle. His scale-patterned skin pulsed like an ocean ripple. He gurgled up saliva, struggling to breathe, as if he'd almost been drowned.

'Another sea spirit?' Moss asked. 'Like from your stories? What is it this time?'

Pa frowned. 'No, I think something even stranger than that.' He looked to the sea. 'How did it come? From what?'

Moss flexed her fingers. 'Maybe I made it this time.'

Maybe this was her own special treasure. Made from her dreams. Was it possible she had the calling-magic like Pa too? Possible the flowers might listen?

The rain fell. It felt soft, too soft, after the wild winds that came before. Moss heard the raindrops drum gentle against the sand, but it was only when water slid down the back of her neck and made her shiver that she felt it true. The sea spirit, or whatever it was, shivered too. She knelt beside him. He looked so thin, like he might break, like he might even cry.

Pa knelt next to her. 'Maybe he changed from a fish in the sea?'

'Or the flowers made him too?'

Pa shook his head in wonder. 'A mystery!' Again, Pa stared towards where the horse had galloped-gone. 'I always knew this island would be full of secrets, but this . . . these things . . .'

Slow-gentle, Moss brought her hand to the new creature, and he uncurled a little. It reminded Moss of the stormflowers she'd seen uncurling in rain. He smelt of the ocean, something wild and deep – like the black sea bass that came on spring tides. But he could *almost* be human, couldn't he? Like them? He shivered and hissed, dropping stringy saliva near Moss's leg. She moved away, scraping her feet on the tiny beach stones.

'What does he want?'

'He can't speak, I don't think. But you could teach him, maybe.' Pa watched Moss with a smile playing about his lips. 'Don't think he will eat you.'

Moss slid further away.

Pa touched the top of her head, nudged her back towards the creature. 'It's good to be wary, Moss, but I've also taught you to help others.'

'You said there are no others yet!'

'There's this.'

26

When Moss looked at the fishboy once more, she searched for his eyes. At first, he would not give them to her; he shied away by pointing his head to the stones. Moss wondered if the creature was scared, like how she had been when they had first arrived on the island. She could remember that feeling, just.

'I will teach it.' She tried out the words. They felt fine.

The fishboy jerked when she said them. Maybe he did understand something after all.

She crawled forward until she sat direct in front. He still would not look at her. She reached to touch him again and, this time, she kept her hand against him and felt his spine, hard through his skin. There were solid bones there, real enough. He looked so human; there were just those little pieces of him that were different: his scale pattern, the webbing, the glint of his skin . . .

'I will help you,' she said.

He looked at her then; she caught the flint in his gaze. His eyes were dark like his skin, but there were flecks of gold inside their centres. They caught her breath with beauty.

'Will you name this spirit too?' Pa said.

'What if he already has a name?'

'A spirit with a name?' Pa shrugged. 'If he does, he cannot say it.'

Moss was still looking at the new creature's eyes – they were such strange eyes, glinting like sun on water.

'Callan,' she said.

She had read the name in one of Pa's storybooks and remembered it. *Powerful* was one of the words she paired with it in her mind. His body seemed so shivery; perhaps a name like this might make him as strong as his eyes were bright.

'Fine choice,' Pa said. 'In another part of the world, there was

27

once a mountain range called Callan.'

And that seemed right too.

She pressed Callan's wet, cold skin, left her fingers against it until they turned damp.

'Maybe you will be another new species,' Pa told him. 'A fishboy made from flowers, to join a mare made from waves . . .'

Callan's teeth chattered, like his mouth was full of tiny, sharp knives. He didn't look like he was going to run off like the horse had.

'We should find him coverings,' Moss said.

Pa nodded. He pulled Moss to her feet. 'Go back to camp and get the fire going. The storm is all but stopped.'

He was right. Now there was sunlight piercing the swollen clouds, stopping the rain almost as quick as it'd started. Often when Pa smiled, the weather did too.

Moss hurried across the beach towards the hut, but paused to look back at Pa and the fishboy. Pa crouched over him, his arm across the boy's back. He was talking to him gentle-soft, saying he would come to live with them and that they would look after him.

She did a cartwheel just for fun, then laughed to see seabirds quick-diving for fresh storm-drowned fish. Moss stretched her fingers and pointed them to the ocean, made them how Pa made his when he sent the flowers out.

'A companion,' Moss whispered. 'A gift!'

It didn't seem real, after so long, after thinking there was no one else.

ACT TWO. SCENE THREE.

C al copied how Moss's mouth moved and the sounds she made. Quick-fast, Cal copied the sway and flow of how she threw nets from the rocks to the waters where the fat-bellied fish liked to breed and linger. Not long, either, before he was digging, with Moss's same short, sharp movements, for razor clams in the wet, hard sand when the tide went back. Some days, Moss thought of him as her shadow.

Night-times, Cal slept deep, tucked tight between Pa and her and Jess in the new-made bigger bed in the hut. It was more than once when Moss had to prod him to check he was still alive. More than once, too, when he'd woke confused.

'You're on the island,' she reminded him. 'You came out of the sea.'

He looked at her with glazed eyes.

'The flowers made you. Remember?'

He shook his head. '*You* did.'

She liked it best when she slept with him curled tight around her.

'Like yin and yang,' Pa said after she'd roused-sleepy one

29

morning and Cal unfolded from her. 'Curved together like that.'

Moss laughed and flicked Pa's arm. 'Like nonsense talk, you mean. Yin-yang, ding-dong.'

As Pa taught Aster, Moss taught Cal. At first, she treated him like Jess, clicking her tongue for him to follow when she went out treasuring, tapping him on the nose when he didn't catch a fish quick-fast. When that happened, Cal's eyes glinted.

After treasuring, they sat tight-close, like birds on a branch. And when the winds whipped fast and Pa was up in the cave bringing them in, they'd sit full-closer. At night, Pa still read and told stories – told his dreaming to the island – but each day he spent longer away.

'But you're so much more patient with Callan than I am,' Pa said when Moss questioned it. 'And it is good for you to have a task.'

'Like you have with the flowers?'

'Like so.'

Pa was always up in the cave now, perfecting the Experiment, making notes about it in his book. But no more spirit-creatures came magicked from the sea. No land appeared. No boats sailed in. The often storms were just full of rain.

'You have to wait for change,' Pa said when she asked. 'Maybe it's not the season.'

His eyes darted always to the sky, then back to the wide ocean. Moss wondered about the signs he waited for. As long as the rain fell, the flowers stayed open, and Pa sent his potion out on the winds. But now there only ever seemed to be more water, not less.

When Pa wasn't in the cave, or finding stormflowers, or check-ing the weather, he worked on taming Aster. Gentle-slow, he'd come closer to her, till he was walking beside, then sitting on top, and then moving with her across the sand. Some days she did not leave his side; other days she disappeared and there was no sight of her glinting-bright coat till the sky was fast-dark again.

There were days when Moss did not see Pa much, either.

'Stay by the fire a little longer,' she would urge. 'Don't go to the cave. Come treasuring with us instead.'

'But you have Cal now,' Pa would say.

One morning after Moss had watched Pa walk up to the cave, she turned to Cal with a new plan.

'We should sit on Aster. Go on her to the top of the volcano.' Moss had seen how Aster danced and swayed under Pa like a wild wind, and how Pa whispered in her ear to calm her steady. She'd seen how fast and far the horse could go. Wonder-fast, fast as the flying fish. Faster.

'We can do it, same as him,' she said.

But Moss knew that when the horse was calm it was only because she chose to listen. Would Aster listen to them too? Cal's face was a frown.

'Come on,' Moss pressed. 'We've already collected all the decent treasure from last storm.'

'Not many decent.' His eyes flashed in the sun.

'Anyway, don't you want to see the whole island?'

'Yesss.' He said it like a wind gust. Sometimes his words still shivered and hissed.

She grinned. 'Knew you wanted a proper look-see. We'll climb the volcano proper. On Aster it'll be easier.'

Whenever they had tried before, plain-walking, they'd gone puff-red with the thin air and only reached halfway.

Careful as she could, Moss scrambled messy on to Aster's back and held her hand down for Cal. While the horse skittered like a crab, he took her wrist and leapt up behind her. Beneath, Moss felt Aster's muscles wound up as a nautilus shell, spiralled tight. Perhaps sitting there was mad-thinking. Still, Moss whispered into Aster's ears the way she'd seen Pa do; then she pressed with her legs like Pa did too. She told the horse where they wanted to be. She imagined the top of the volcano and let her longing of being there be heart-strong.

'Think about going there,' she said to Cal. 'She'll listen.'

Aster did – it was full-magic how the horse moved at her thinking! Moss giggled, sunlight-happy; she felt Cal's laugh against her back too. Maybe Pa would be angry if he knew they were Aster-sat. But Pa was on his own adventure. And this were theirs.

Cal gripped tight around Moss as Aster stepped across the sand and into the pine trees. When the horse went faster still, they clung with muscled thighs taut from swimming and hunting. When Moss unbalanced, the horse moved to steady her.

Cal howled like the wild dogs did at the moon. 'So quick-fast!'

Moss, too, gave her best wild shout to the wind. The horse went quick as their thinking – quicker!

They climbed, until the route became so steep that grass turned to rock; Aster arched, shrimplike, digging her hooves in. Up to the volcano gases and the thin-tightest air was where the stormflowers grew thickest.

The most magic place, Pa always said. *Alchemical. The centre.*

Up here flowers were everywhere, covering the rock like a different kind of colourful ocean. The air was sweeter than the heart-core of honeycomb.

Cal leapt down to get at them, and Aster skittered from his sudden movement. Moss placed a hand on the horse's shoulder, tried to soothe her like she'd seen Pa do: thought calm thoughts. If the horse went speeding back down the route they'd come with her still on top, she'd be tumbled to sharp rock.

'Gentle,' she whispered. She thought an image of a midday sea in sun, and wondered if the horse saw it too. Was this how the connection between her and Pa worked? When Aster stilled, Moss slipped off after Cal. She had fast-little breath from being so high – almost top-highest they could get.

Moss did not try to stop Aster when she left – the horse always wanted to be closest to Pa most of all, and besides, it would be easier to get down the volcano on feet than up. Not so puff-hard.

Cal had fingers gentle under a stormflower's opened petals, curious as a dog pup. She came to him and crouched beside. She never understood why the flowers did not zing hard in Cal's mouth like they did for her or Pa. Cal ate them, sure, as flavour in tea and stew, but he never sought them out like she or, more often, Pa did.

'These ones grown here are the best,' she said. 'Look-see.'

She pushed Cal down to sit on the sun-warmed rock, then pulled one of the larger flowers straight up from a crack, its thin, dirty roots twisting in the light wind.

Cal flinched as she held it to him. 'Pa does singing to it first, Moss.'

'Not always. Not so much now.'

Even so, she did a quick bird-trill of the notes, just as Pa had taught her. Then she tore off the five perfect petals and placed them in the palm of her hand. The gold pollen smudged on to her skin. She remembered watching Pa do this not so long ago.

'She loves me, she loves me not,' Pa had said, in time with each petal he tore. Each time, *she loves me* always finished his chant. Five petals gone always equalled love.

'Old rhyme,' she said to Cal now to explain it. 'When people were uncertain of who to love back, they pulled petals like this.'

Cal frowned. 'Sounds risky.'

Moss, too, thought the rest of the world must've been very strange if it took tearing off flower petals to know something like love.

She gave the fifth, most special petal to Cal. 'The sweetest one,' she lied, for they were all equal-sweet. 'Try.'

'I watch you first. Maybe I do it wrong.'

She laughed and took another petal. 'Fine.'

She held out her tongue and placed it on top. She waited for that sweetness to settle down into her, for the zing that followed, waited for the ease in her chest. Cal watched her close.

'You think they make true healing?' he said. 'Think they work as the Pa say?'

Moss swallowed and felt the petal tingle down her throat. 'It makes breathing easier, I know that. And Pa does not get Blackness when he has them.'

Cal stared back steady. Perhaps he did not remember Pa's Blackness. Pa's moods were thicker before Cal came, before the flowers opened full.

She reached forward to touch Cal on the nose and spread a little pollen there, like how she'd do with Jess, but Cal caught her fingers fast. He held them inside his own, and she felt his webbings against her skin. There was glinting in his eyes, and she knew what he was thinking: that he was not Jess, and do not treat him so.

But what was he? He looked like the boys in pictures from Pa's books, but some things were different. There was his scale pattern. And his eyes, so big and dark and glinting-bright. There was glint-magic inside him too.

'Eat a petal,' she urged.

She looked at his smooth-skinned face, at his high cheekbones. If Cal had once been a fish, then he had been one with a wide, clear face. With a knowing eye. With a fast spin in his tail. She wondered about the most beautiful fish in the world, and whether he had been it.

Cal put the petal in his mouth and chewed. His eyes moistened and squinted. He shook his head. 'Too strong-sweet.'

'But tingles nice?'

He shrugged.

'Makes breathing better?'

'I breathe fine.'

'You hiss.'

His eyes flashed.

'What?' She raised her eyebrows. 'Sometimes you do!'

'And sometimes you growl at night like the wild dogs!'

Moss placed the next petal in her mouth. She pushed out her tongue for Cal to see.

'Can you not see it zing?' she said. Or tried to. The words came out muffled and slippy.

Cal smiled, teeth bright as pollen, square and straight as hers.

She swallowed that petal too. Now she could feel the buzz Pa talked of, the one he used to bring in storms, to bring in Cal and Aster. How many flowers must he eat to feel so full-strong for that? If Moss ate more than one whole flower, she always felt a little sleepy.

In time, Pa had said.

In time, Moss would bring the storms, then send the flowers out on their winds. She'd make the land rise and the boats come. She'd do it proper. Better than Pa. She'd do it till the floods were full-gone.

'Try again!' she said to Cal.

When he shook his head, she made a grumble-noise. 'Look-see, take it right from my tongue where it tingles hard. I'll hold it out, then you take it and see.'

He raised a dark eyebrow. She put another petal on her tongue. She wanted to suck it clean of its sweetness straight away, but she made her mouth stay still. Even when saliva formed in her cheeks.

'Take it,' she said again, her voice thick and clumsy, a little like how his sounded still, sometimes.

He leant forward. He was watching her, checking, and that frustrated her too. She needed him to take the petal fast-quick before she ate it too!

He touched his tongue to hers. She saw his eyes widen huge and he flinched back. But he had not taken the petal! Quick-fast, she pressed her tongue back against his until he had it. She closed her mouth, watched.

'Feel it?'

He rolled the petal about behind his teeth and up around his gums, his eyes still wide.

'Tastes different when it come from you.'

She smiled. 'It zings?'

'It zings.'

Later, they climbed to the toppest they could get on the volcano and looked out. There was sea and sea and sea. No land. No boats. No nothing but water. Moss slumped down – perhaps Pa's Experiment hadn't worked at all and dark waters still covered all the rest of the world. Cal stared long at the sea beyond their cove like he was looking for messages written on it.

'Thought you wanted to see the whole island?' Moss took Cal and spun him to the rest. No storm mist today, so all was clear-viewing.

'Western Beach,' she pointed out, turning him to the left. 'Then, Lizard Rocks – where the hiss-slitherys are – and the Point. But you know them places.' She turned him left again. 'There's another pine forest there, like the one at the back of our cove but a bit bigger. And over there on the north-toppest side is where the wild dogs are . . .'

'Where Jess goes for her babies?' Cal grinned sideways.

Moss caught it with her own grin. 'Well, she don't go to the Lizard Rocks, does she?'

Cal shrugged, and she pushed his shoulder.

'OK, or maybe she does! If any of her babies ever stuck around camp long enough for us to examine them, we'd know if they were half reptile!'

Cal kept turning left, now looking to the side Pa called the east.

'And there,' Moss indicated with a sweep of her hand, 'is where the sharpest, deepest rocks are, where our boat wrecked, in the storm after we landed.'

'Wrecked?'

'Broke into pieces. Pa told us about it, remember? Where he saved our books and useful things from.'

Cal nodded. 'Special storm treasure.'

She turned him left again to complete the circle. 'And back to our cove!' She swept her hand over the view as if she herself were making it appear. 'Our hut, the beach, the reef, Rocky Point, pine forest . . .'

Cal spun and looked at the whole island a second time, then a third time too. Then he stopped, staring out at the sea beyond their cove again. 'But no more land.'

Moss nodded. 'No more.'

He was frowning like he was thinking hard. 'Was once?'

'Was once. Another island out there at least. And where me and Pa came from too, of course.'

Soon, they clambered down from the volcano, skidding on skitter-rocks and sending flint bouncing, grabbing at clumps of grass to steady themselves. Moss was looking out to the horizon line, and Cal was following her gaze.

'Someone could swim to there,' Cal said.

'To the horizon? You think?'

The waves were not choppy today, so perhaps . . . maybe. Beyond the reef, it did not look so far.

'What would someone do once they got there?'

'Go past the line.'

'You know the horizon is not actually a proper line, Cal; it just looks like one. Once we got there, we'd just find more water – endless water, like we've seen from the top of the volcano just now.'

'Maybe no.'

'Maybe *yes*!'

They clambered down further.

'Then . . . we make a boat,' Cal said. 'Like in them stories Pa tells.

Like the one you came in. With a boat, we go further and see. Find land.'

'And how do you think we make a boat?'

'With wrecking treasure! With there being so many storms these days,' he grinned, 'there be so many treasures!'

ACT TWO. SCENE FOUR.

The wood was wide and yet light: driftwood saved from many tides. Moss dug through it, pulling out the drier pieces. Cal laid them in lines on the sand.

'You know it won't look like a proper boat,' she said.

'Don't have to. Just has to float.'

Moss frowned to remember her own boat from so long ago – it was getting harder to do so. Harder, also, to remember the trip Pa and her had taken from their old world. She thought she could remember being curled up cosy, somewhere warm. Three or four year cycles had passed since then, though, hadn't they? Or more? So hard to be sure. She pulled at the biggest, heaviest piece of wood, trying to shift it clear.

'Anyway, Cal,' she said. 'Remember, our boat smashed out there.' She pointed beyond the reef and Rocky Point, over towards the east. 'So even if this thing does sail . . .'

Cal shrugged, moving the biggest, heaviest piece easy. 'That were long time past. And Pa been sending them flowers since.'

'That doesn't mean the water will be less rough, or the rocks less sharp.' Moss chewed her lip. Pa was always full-sure they shouldn't leave the island to check for other land, not till they were certain there was some. 'And if we forget?' she asked. 'If we can't get back?' She reached over to Cal's arm, stopping him from shifting more wood.

Cal drew himself up straight and made his mouth go long, exact-same as Pa's could look. 'Remember, Small Things, once we go beyond the reef, beyond the line out there,' Cal paused in his impression of Serious Pa to wink at Moss, 'then we forget the island. When that happens, the island no longer exists.'

He widened his eyes in the way Pa did when he said something important. Moss smiled; Cal always got him so right. Moss never had the nerve to do him quite so good.

'Remember,' Cal continued, booming his voice like Pa's. 'The island and its magic become just dream then.'

Cal reached across to tickle Moss like Pa did. Moss caught his fingers on her ribs, drew them up to her mouth, and nipped them.

'Enough of Pa now.'

Because what if Pa's warning really happened? What if there really was a *forgetting line* out there? What if she and Cal were stuck out in the floods for ever?

Cal shrugged as he watched her. 'We only look-see. Not go far.'

She nodded careful-slow. Just a look-see was all right, just a little way beyond the reef, not so far to forget. And if they did see anything new, Pa would be dancing-grateful, wouldn't he?

Then they could plan.

She took out the twine she'd made from spinning reed. Cal came to help, eyes glinting like fish tails. *There* – like that – she saw the sea in him: fast-quick, then gone.

'Fishboy,' she whispered, smiling.

'Lizard Face.' He pulled his lips back and darted his tongue out at her.

Cal and Moss got the twine tight around the planks, made a platform big enough for them both to sit on. They picked two of the lightest pieces of driftwood to use as paddles to push the raft forward.

'We'll swim it to the reef, then carry it over through the sand channel; after that we'll sit on it to . . .' She could not finish. She did not know to where.

'Till we know,' Cal said.

'Just a look-see.'

They carried the raft between them. It was heavier than she'd thought it would be, but Cal was stronger than she'd thought him to be too. He'd been growing – soon he'd be taller than her.

At the shoreline, they placed their raft in the water.

'Well, it floats,' Moss said.

Cal frowned and pressed the wood as if daring it to sink. Moss looked up to the cliffs, picked out Pa's cave. The cloth was still across the entrance; Pa wasn't out watching the winds. Maybe they should've done this on Western Beach, to be sure he wouldn't see them and scold them. Too late now.

Moss took Cal's cool hand. 'Ready?'

'Yesss.'

They stepped into the water; it was warmer than it had been. They pushed the raft with their knees, then with their hands when the current slapped against their waists. When they passed Rocky Point, they flopped forward into the sea and moved the raft by kicking. Cal pulled himself up on to it soon enough, left her to swim alongside.

42

She smirked up at him. 'You should practise your swimming, you know.' She spun around, ducked underwater, and came back to the raft. 'It's fun! See? I can move my legs like a mermaid!' She showed him. 'Like a dog, too!'

But his eyes didn't follow. They darted to the water far out near the horizon, then back to the shore. She remembered how Cal's skin had stayed bloated for days after he'd washed in; remembered, too, how he'd shook with fear when Pa first made him bathe. But that was a long time ago. Was Cal still so scared of water?

'Full storm-bashed,' Pa had said about him. 'Half drowned.'

That first day, Moss had traced the silver sheen of the scale tattoo pattern on Cal's skin and called him 'storm-woke' instead.

'Woken by the waves,' she'd told Pa. 'Something special brought for us.'

Now Moss watched Cal extra careful. In deeper water, could he turn back to fish and swim gone, away?

Soon, they got to the reef and hauled the raft up. Moss flea-jumped till she found the smooth sand channel through the sharp coral and showed Cal, making sure he followed it and didn't damage the reef. Cal shifted the raft high to his shoulders and took most of the weight. As they started the slow journey across, Moss saw Aster in the cove behind them, spinning in circles and pawing the sand. Unlike Cal, she had never been back into the water. But Moss often thought she wanted to from how she watched the waves.

Again, Moss looked up to the cave entrance – still no Pa. Though she felt a wind pick up, coming at them from the horizon. Maybe Pa was calling it in: his daily attempt at a storm.

On the other side of the reef, the water was rougher and deeper, the colourful coral gone. They lowered the raft to the sea again. Moss held it steady while Cal got on, then gave him the wooden paddles. When she leapt aboard, she smiled, feeling the freedom of being just them on a raft. Since she'd first arrived there, she'd never been so far from the island.

'How do we know when we at horizon line?' Cal said.

She frowned. 'It's not a real line, remember? And we'll just go for a little while, just until we see.'

'See what?'

'See *something*.'

But a part of her wanted to go further: as far as they could, until they proper knew, with no doubt, if there was anything else out there.

'This island sits in a kind of bubble,' Pa had said. 'The storm-flowers keep it like that. Here, we are safe. Beyond, I do not know any more.'

Away from the shelter of the cove, the wind picked up. They rocked on the waves, uncomfortable.

'See anything yet?' she asked.

'Water.'

'Anything now?'

'More water.'

'Anything below the water?' Moss peered over the side. 'Like land? Like countries hiding, ready to come back up?'

'More water.'

It was the same as they'd seen from the top of the volcano: more and more of the same. Beneath them, the water got darker. Deeper. She could no longer see the seabed, not like in the shallower water before the reef. Anything could be down there: sea serpents and mermaids from Pa's stories, or, just as easy, sharks and stingers.

Maybe they'd been stupid to come. She looked towards the horizon. No land. No boats. No people. There weren't even any birds. Just a darkening sky. Just water. She'd thought there'd be something: a sign of life, at least. Something under the sea.

A raindrop slithered down Moss's neck. It was getting colder, too. Soon, a current took them, gentle-teasing, spinning them, and Cal's fingers gripped the raft. She sighed.

'We should go back,' she said. Clouds were forming, as deep and dark as the day Cal and Aster came. 'Let's paddle.'

But when they tried to turn the raft, it kept going out, moving even quicker towards rougher waves, caught by a wind. Pa had taken a long time to learn how to sail a boat; why should they think they'd be able to sail mere planks of driftwood? Why had she let Cal convince her this was a good idea? Harder now they tried, but the currents beneath them were stronger.

'We've no control,' Moss said. 'Should we swim for it instead?'

Cal frowned as he watched the swirling water, the growing weather. She did not want to swim in that, either, not all the way back to the reef, but perhaps there was little choice. She touched the water, feeling it. Shock-cold.

Then, quick-fast, she turned back to the horizon. Had she seen something – there, in the corner of her eye? For a second, then gone. That other island? *Something?* She turned as the raft tossed, trying to see it again. What was it? Just a bird? A rock? Treasure?

She prodded for Cal to look too. She was still trying to make it out when the raft moved rough-quick, sharper than before.

She clung.

Now she had to pay attention. One moment they were steady;

then they were almost tipping to the water. Wind raced around them as they spun. Gripping the edge of the raft, she tried to grab Cal too, but he was limpet-strong to the wood, still trying to look out to where she'd pointed. When she followed his gaze and looked again, there was nothing. Just a trick of the light, maybe; a bigger wave than usual.

When the rain came, it got harder to see.

All she could do was cling on and hope that the wind was pushing them back towards the island, not further away. The waves got rougher. And here came the lightning. She saw it rip the sky. They'd get hit if they stayed. She pushed her hair out of her eyes and, final-true, saw the cove – there – behind them through the mist and rain! She shouted to Cal to show him. He nodded, pointing out a way towards the reef, paddling again.

But already there was a wave behind him, getting so high. It took her breath as she looked. Building higher. Getting nearer. Turning into a dark cliff. It was about to fall.

The ocean drew them back, closer. The raft tilted up into it. Only when his body tilted too did Cal turn. She saw him open his mouth when he saw it. Shout something.

Then it hit.

Moss was flung from the raft. She felt its pieces hit her cheek as she heard it smash. She felt the cold, rough pull of the water. She couldn't see Cal, but she heard him shout again. Then all she heard was the roar of the ocean. Pounding blood in her ears.

She took a gasp, heart-tight, when she found the surface. Then back, over and over, she turned in the waves, getting dunked. Dragged. Something was breaking – cracking! She stretched her arms and legs wide, but did not touch Cal. Felt only water. How close was she to that horizon line? Was she about to forget, like Pa had said would happen if she went too far from the island? She'd be stuck in dark floods for ever. She would lose Cal. Pa. Everything!

She bobbed up to snatch a mouthful of air before being dunked under again, twisted and forced in whichever direction the sea took her. She could not fight it. She opened her eyes underwater, tried searching for Cal. Had he gone, slipped back into the sea? Was he fish again?

She gasped another breath at the surface, was taken under. She spun and turned and thought she touched seabed. Then something hard hit her elbow. The reef? Something soft brushed her face – seaweed? Her chest ached. She couldn't keep under for so long with so few breaths. And it was darker now. Colder. Quieter.

Breathe me in, the water said. *Taste.*

She shut her mouth. Looked for Cal.

Taste me, it said. *Let me inside.*

No Cal. No air. But . . .

Lights! Dots of colour.

Schools of fish? Or flower petals! Swirling all around, leading her. She reached out to touch them, and the colours darted away.

Darkness again.

Spinning.

Then another current of light. Like something alive. Like Pa's flower-air. She followed it.

But now there was another noise too. A human sound. A voice?

It was coming straight from the black water. Somewhere close. She tried to look around. Saw only the sea. Blurred colour.

Was it Cal? Pa? Down here?

No!

47

She curled away when she heard the voice again, her ears throbbing. She pushed a hand over her left ear, cradling it. She burrowed into the seabed, away from the sound, dug her fingers into the sand. But her heart pounded, her chest on fire. She needed air. Needed to go up, not down. Couldn't hide here! Thrashing like a hooked fish, she looked towards the surface.

And saw him.

Someone stood over her. Here, in the water. A tall shadow man. But he was made from the sea. That's how it seemed. He moved with the current. And, like that, he pulled her. Pushed her. Was this another of Pa's sea creatures? A spirit?

No! This was something worse. She felt it, bone-deep.

She looked away, then back.

He was still there.

Then, sudden-fast, he moved. Clawed through the water towards her, opened his mouth to shout. He held his hands out and shoved the sea her way. The water came inside her lungs. Choked her! And now there were hissing noises everywhere. Angry swirling waves. She couldn't see! Couldn't look back at him!

She pressed her hands harder against her ears; shut and opened her eyes. She focused on the water swirling, seaweed writhing, a shell in the sand.

She was dying. It had to be that! This is what it felt like.

One breath. Could she just take one? Could she get to the surface?

But that man was still there. She heard him. She dug at the seabed to escape. She could hide here, stay tangled.

Drown.

But she couldn't wish it . . . quite.

48

This time when she opened her eyes again she saw blackness and debris, weed and . . . those lights. Those glorious glowing lights!

Eel-fast, she followed them.

Away from the shadow man. She did not look at anything else till she were sure. No watery man. No angry figure above her.

Had she imagined him? Another sea creature dreamt from the deep?

She swam.

Until her knees and shins were scraping over coral, and the water was warmer. Until there was softer sand beneath her fingertips and she could drag herself along with it. Until she was being pull-pull-pulled through the shallower water, away from the deep cold . . . towards land. Safety.

And she was spluttering.

On a shore.

Gasping.

Air.

Air.

Air.

Breathing.

No watery angry man. Not now. No shoving or shouting. Only coughing and coughing. Brown water spewing.

Air.

Breathing.

And hands on her. Steady and soft, holding her. Soothing. Someone was talking. Not the same frightening voice from under-water, not him. This voice was quieter, gentle-firm. She coughed and gasped.

Air.

49

Breathing.

Sweet-good, it came inside. Whole big lungfuls.

Someone was pulling her from the sea. Wrapping her into him and making her warm. Safe. Dry.

Giving air.

Breathing.

Pa.

He had pulled her back.

Had he pulled Cal back too?

But where had that man from the sea gone?

She shivered hard. She was like Cal when he'd first come from the ocean. Quick-fast, she checked over herself, but she was still *her*. Not a fishchild like Cal. Not ... changed.

She turned to search for him on the sand.

'Cal?'

'Be still now.' Pa's voice. 'You've been half drowned!'

Had Cal been too? Had he seen that angry man down deep also?

She turned her head. Where was he?

She had to know. Had to see he was still here. Still Cal.

Then cold, webbed fingers touched her arm and took her hand, and she gasped again. She crawled to him – behind her all this time! – and he smiled weak. Not disappeared. Not fish. But he was bleeding and shaking. Like her.

What – she tried to say – *what happened?*

Her mouth would not work.

Cal's eyes were wide as he looked over her, as he touched the tips of his fingers to blood on her wrist. There were red bloody stripes going down her arms too.

She turned to the sea. Was the angry man there, somewhere?

Was he coming out from the water?

'What were you doing?' Moss heard Pa's voice behind her. He almost sounded as angry as the man down deep. 'Were you trying to leave?'

'No,' Moss said, she tried to. 'Only trying to find . . .'

She coughed again. Quick-fast, Pa laid his hands on her back, pressing her calm.

'Was this Cal's idea? Did he take you out there?'

She was sudden-scared of the tone to Pa's voice. She blinked at the sea. Where had he gone, that watery figure? Had Pa seen him too?

'Was us both who went out there,' she said, staring to the waves.

There were stormflower petals, streaming from the cliff, swirling around Pa, settling on his shoulders. He looked magic-fierce, like a creature from his stories, like he could be made from the sea too. The wind turned his hair to a mane.

'Come back to the hut.' Pa led her from the water, clicking for Aster to follow close. Cal stumbled to his feet behind them as Pa squeezed Moss tight.

'That adventure could have killed you,' Pa said. 'You might have left, might have forgot everything. Do you know the risk—?'

He looked over his shoulder at Cal. It was in a different way than before. His eyes narrowed, his lips pressed tight. Like he thought Cal was the only one to blame.

When Moss stumbled, Pa picked her up and placed her on to Aster's back. But he left Cal to walk alongside. As Moss sank down into Aster's soft mane, she heard Pa talking.

'We'll build another shelter,' Pa said to Cal. 'A hut only for you. Maybe it's time you slept away from us, no longer in the same bed . . .'

Cal stayed silent. But Moss knew he wouldn't like his own

51

shelter – not in the dark, alone; not without the warmth of her tight beside him, and the knowledge that, if he woke, she would be there to soothe him back to sleep.

'You are different from us,' Pa said. 'A spirit. Maybe you should be more separate.'

Still, Cal did not speak back. But as Moss closed her eyes and leant her cheek against Aster's mane, she felt his cold, bleeding hand meet hers once more. She clasped his fingers tight and drew them to her lips, breathed warm air on them. *I'm sorry*, she tried to breathe there. *I do not know this Pa either.* Though she'd seen glimpses of him – hadn't she? – in his Blacknesses, when he'd stayed dark for days. And those Blacknesses had been coming more often.

'It's not time to leave the island, Moss,' Pa said firm. 'At least this adventure has shown you that. Maybe it will never be safe now. Never be time.'

He glared at Cal. Like Cal had ruined everything. Like it was his fault if Pa's flower Experiment never worked and the floods stayed. Like it was Cal's fault the whole world went bad in the first place.

'No, Pa,' Moss said. 'Was me that did this too, I wanted to see as much as he did.'

But Pa shook away her words. 'From now on, Cal sleeps in his own hut. No more being the same. You're not to be so close any more!'

When Cal flinched, Moss gripped his hand harder. She saw in the tight line of Pa's jaw that something had changed inside him, and it was not a light-giggling change. This was a change made from shadows. This was his Blackness, back.

-SIX YEARS PASS-

ACT THREE
AUTUMN

The Scene: An Island
Several Weeks Previous

ACT THREE. SCENE ONE.

One dark eye cracked open, then the other.

Careful, careful, Cal woke. He did not want to scare it away – this dreaming. He must keep his head with it, half in.

'Specially so if the dreamings wake him.

If they flicker.

If they hurt.

There were meanings here. Knowings. But already the images were slipping fast-gone.

He blinked in thick dark, seeing enough to know he was in his hut, on his beddings, where he should be at this time. A moment earlier, though, he had been staring at ocean. He had been watching, waiting . . . *seeing*.

He'd had this dreaming before, glimpses of it. And again, now, teasing him . . . gnawing. It were not bad dreaming. Were more . . . curious . . . than that. Again, he tried to catch at it with his mind. And – *there!* – for a moment, he saw.

Dark water.

A shape.

Something in the waves.

Something in *their* waves.

These images were like weaselmice, biting at him, not letting go. Yet they were slippery-fast when he tried to take hold.

He could not lie in the dark with only glimpses.

He held his fingers to his head as if pushing back escaping brain bits. Then he shut fast his eyes. The ache! The flickerings! He turned his head sharp as if to catch them flickerings. He hissed to himself, tried to comfort his sore brain. Then he crawled out from under the blankets, rolled on to the floor. He had somewhere to be. Something to know.

But the pain! He swore as he dressed. Moved with eyes near closed. Air. He needed that. And water. The cool kind. Maybe he would wake Moss and they would wash this pain from his brain together. Maybe they would jump inside the sea and he would flush himself clean that way. Then the flickerings would stop. Then he would see the images clear. The sea would help. Her leaf-green eyes would help. Her hand on his as they stepped to the water.

Then – after – he could give her his Birthday Surprise. He could say it to her as they walked, tell what he had found in the rocks far away. Then, soon, he would show it to her real.

He slunk to the door. Outside was black and star-full. Midnight. Cold and bitey. The weather was gnawing at his skin too, like another pissin' weaselmouse. The recent days been getting colder, colder than Cal had known. He spat. Something was turning the place rotten and pinched-tight.

But there was a hook in him. He felt it, in his chest. Leading him. Could not fight a hook like that.

He clambered down the hill. At Big Hut, he paused. Should he get her? When Moss was by sea at night, her eyes shone back the moon. She still laughed when her feet found water.

But the Pa was making noises like the growlings of wild dogs – dream, dreaming – he was deep in. Cal had seen him yesterday, pushing petals past his lips. The Pa had not thought anyone were watching. But Cal knew. Cal always knew. Cal thought of Moss beside the Pa, but only enough to imagine her down-soft skin the colour of damp sand, and the smooth-cool of it. Her leaf-green eyes and her dark mess of hair.

Then he was gone again, lumbering on, into that cold darkness on silent, silent, quick webbed toes. He went for the cove, the sea.

He loped 'cross sand, slithered over slick rocks to get closer to the water. Was so black tonight, pit-like black, endless black. But . . . there was something there, on its surface, far out on that horizon line. Something . . . flickering. Like that flickering at the edge of his eyes. Like the image in the dreamings.

Dark water.

A shape.

Something in the waves.

Something in *their* waves.

Out there. Flickering. Solid. Then flickering.

Almost like . . .

Land?

Could it be?

Another island, like this?

Come back?

He'd heard Moss and the Pa tell the stories, had read Pa's book. But for long time now he did not think Pa's Experiment was anything more than a man throwing flowers to the wind.

The hook inside dug deeper, forced him to stay and squint at waves. Each time he thought he had it, the shape disappeared. Was it land? Or just treasure on tides?

His toes gripped round the rocks and he waited. Concentrated. He licked his lips, tasted salt in the air, and . . . something else. Earth? Sweetness? He shook his head to get a clear nose on it. Smelt harder. Something was out there, sure.

But the pain!

Again, he placed his fingertips to his head, as if to hold the thoughts in – or now, maybe, as if to tease them out. There were images, coming at him – memories from his dreamings. If he could hold these thoughts and see them . . . He shut his eyes, dug his toes into knife-rocks until he felt that pain and knew it was real.

When he had the courage for it, he pulled at the images, in the way he pulled fish from the nets. Slow-careful. So as not to damage them. So as to keep them whole and beautiful in their scales, glinting. And there – another image. Hiding firm in his brain. A memory.

He'd dreamt of a human, darker than Pa and darker than Moss. Dark like him. A stalker to his brain. A watcher. With mind's eye, he saw.

Then Cal felt it – something in his hand. Skin. It was not the way Moss's hand felt. This new hand were pulling him away.

Cal opened his eyes, looked down. There was nothing – no hand in his. He shook his head, making his vision dance. Could he be walking in sleep? Again, he dug toes hard on rocks beneath – *this* was where he was. In the cove. Night-time. This was real.

But when he shut his eyes again, he felt it. A sort of . . . hand. In his. Pulling him to the ocean. Pulling him beyond. And this time, a sound. Whispers. They came at him in a rush of hissing.

Not sounds he knew, but they felt known . . . still.

He curled his tongue to copy. Then opened his eyes quick.

And – there – again.

Dark water.

A shape.

Something in the waves.

Out there. Flickering. Solid. Then flickering.

Almost like . . .

Land.

Right there. He had seen it.

He turned quick for Moss.

ACT THREE. SCENE TWO.

Moss sat up fast, though not so fast as to wake up sleeping Pa beside her. It came again – the shriek of a gull. Once. Twice.

At this time of night?

She crawled across the bed and slid out from the coverings, avoiding poking the dogs: they would only growl. She needn't worry; Pa was too deep in fever dream, and nightmarish with it, to wake easy. She noted the sweat on his wrinkled brow, saw how his arms flailed: did Pa ever dream soft any more? Perhaps it was the oysters from earlier, causing this night-stirring. She, too, felt paining in her stomach. They had been nice, though: those fifteen oyster shells across the sand in a line, each to mark her new year. Earlier, she'd felt guilty that she had not left Cal one.

'He's not here, so what does it matter?' Pa had said. 'He can find his own, anyway. You don't need to mother him all the time.'

Perhaps, with this tummy-paining now, leaving no oysters for Cal was a blessing.

Pa had carved her a knife out of flint and given it as a present. He had given her fifteen bird-beak kisses to the top of her head.

Now was Cal's turn to give. It would be just like him to wait till Pa was sleeping. To wait till dark.

Moss listened to the snuffle of Pa snoring, and to a soft growl by Adder because she'd been woken by it. The shriek came again. It was more urgent now, like there was a gull about to batter the very hut down with its beak. From the beddings, Adder raised her head.

'Quiet, girl,' Moss told her young dog, warning her with her eyes.

They both knew there was only one creature making that shriek outside, and it was not any sort of bird. Pa snored louder, Adder grumbled harder. As Moss picked up the flint knife and tucked it into her clothing, she thought of Cal's hut up the hill and how she could sleep there instead; how one night, soon, she might, curled tight to Cal like she used to be. Yin-yanged.

Last year, Cal's birthday present to her had been a perfect-round, fat lizard's egg. The year before, it had been the knowledge of where the wild dogs lived. And the year before that, a red ribbon found on the tide; she'd tied that around her wrist. Each year as he'd given, Cal had grinned like the sea under moonlight – silver-sharp – knowing that she liked his gift best.

Moss tiptoed to the door, throwing on a rabbit-pelt covering before opening it a crack. Cal's eyes were glinting, level with hers. Even in the tiny space between door and wall, Moss saw the gold in them.

'Well, what is it?' she said. 'Pa's in dreaming, and you're making a racket.'

She saw his gold-flecked eyes roll then.

''Course he is,' Cal said soft, the lisp of his words on his lips.

He waited for her to open the door some more. She placed her hands on her hips. When he didn't speak, she prompted him.

'Is this my Birthday Surprise? Being woken in the middle of the night to stare at your fish features?'

She was smiling at him, teasing him. He frowned before he shook his head.

'Birthday Surprise coming still. Promise. But this . . . is something else. New surprise. In water. In waves. Bigger.'

She opened the door wider. 'Wash-up, then? Storm treasure?'

She checked the sky for clouds. Cal was gone before answering. Already, Moss was searching for boots, for skirts to go over sleep-wear. They'd not had wash-up for many moons, supplies of all sorts were running short: they needed this badly. But the weather wasn't moody enough for wash-up, was it?

She called soft to Adder, who reluctant-slow stepped from the bed, stretching out one leg at a time as she made her lazy path to Moss. Yawning, she butted her head against Moss's legs.

'Come on, you're not too tired to go running in moonlight, not too old like your ma.' Moss rubbed her dog's silky ears. 'Come on, my wild dog girl.'

Moss glanced over at Jess, still deep in sleep and snoring in tandem with Pa now, thick in whatever old dogs dream about, one foot twitching. Moss would leave her there: company for Pa if he woke. Besides, it pained Moss when they had to wait now for the old dog to catch up.

'You're not allowed to get old,' she told Adder, lifting her dark ear to whisper the words inside. Moss lifted her dog's white ear to add, 'Eat stormflowers! Run! Have babies at least!'

Adder licked her full across the face, her breath like dead mice. She stared back, steady as a challenge: there'd be no babies for her. Adder would be the only baby dog in their hut, even if she was a full-grown one.

'Well, Jess ain't having any more,' Moss said. 'And if she did, you'd only eat them again. Wild bad girl!'

Moss pulled on Pa's old boots, stuffed with rags at the toes. She stepped out from the hut and closed it quiet-quiet-quieter behind her. She found Cal leaning against a tree, over behind the still-smoking firepit, his dark, shaggy hair falling over his face. Perhaps she should cut it for him: it was as long as when Cal had been a Small Thing. Longer than the day he'd washed up.

Aster snorted, ghost-pale in the shadows.

Moss came to the horse and placed a hand against her. As always, Aster's warm breath smelt like flowers. When she snorted, sparkle-air hung before her. 'Didn't see *you* giving me any Birthday Surprises,' she whispered. 'Though I bet you know of some. Bet you know every spot where the flowers grow sweetest.'

Aster shifted from her touch. Moss looked away from her big, knowing eyes, found Cal's eyes instead.

'This better be good,' she warned him. 'It's cold tonight.' She stuck her hand out for his, like how they'd walked as Small Things. He hesitated, frowning at her fingers.

'If you're looking to see if I've cleaned my nails,' she began, 'you'll be looking a long time.'

Cal grinned and took her hand easy then. Like Small Things. Like always. She felt his fingers interlace with hers and the shock of his cold webbings against her knuckles. His hand was bigger than hers now. Weren't they both once the same size? Wasn't he once smaller?

'You will not believe,' he said, quiet. 'Maybe the Experiment worked. All these moons he been right.'

'What are you meaning?'

'Wait-see.'

Adder was already racing ahead, spinning in circles and chasing things invisible. They followed her, leaving Aster where she always seemed most happy: closest to Pa. As they walked, Moss looked over at their cove – the fingernail of sand that was their beach, the foaming sea at its edge. There was a wind, pulling and pushing them, harder than she'd expected. Was it enough to draw in treasure? Cal yanked on her hand.

'Come on. Go fast now.'

They ran down the trodden grass path, with Adder spinning and racing around them. They clink-clinked over the pebblestones at the start of the cove, skittered over the seaweedy rocks, then soft-footed on to the damp sand before the sea. At the shoreline, Moss took off Pa's boots, tied them by the laces, and hung them around her neck. She let the cold, dark water nip her feet. The sand was cold too, but she dug her toes into it all the same, never could help herself. She looked across, expecting to find Cal grinning at her, but he was still as he stood, looking at the far-water.

'You not see?' he said. 'Out there?'

He took her head between his fingers, moving it to look in the same direction he'd been looking.

'What you found?'

'Look harder. Out near the line. Far.' Again, he pressed his fingers to her head until she moved.

Moss looked. There was nothing but sea and black and moonlight; Cal's cold fingers on her neck behind her ears. A shiver was starting from those fingers and winding down her spine.

'You're freezing me,' she said, pulling away. 'Some surprise!'

Cal frowned harder, shoulders rolling forward. 'Told you, this is not your proper Birthday Surprise. This is new one . . . better.'

He was moody Cal now. She reached for his hand again, but he kept it for himself.

'You really not see?' Cal said, soft.

Moss scanned the water, the shore. No storm treasure anywhere. She watched the silver water at the tips of the waves, looking for changes, just as she had on the day Aster and Cal had come.

'What am I meant to be seeing?' When Cal did not answer, she prodded him. 'Come on, what?'

He coiled away. Rubbed fingertips to the sides of his head like he did when he was hard-thinking. 'Dark shape in water. Big!'

Again, Moss squinted at Cal, but his eyes weren't glassy, not drowsy from too much sleep. He was seeing clear.

'Maybe your eyes are better at looking?'

Cal rasped a laugh. 'Had not thought of that. We get closer, then. Rocky Point.'

'Now?'

He nodded. 'There you'll see far out.'

'The water will be cold.'

Cal shrugged. 'I can make fire after. Warm you.'

Cal was pushing her with his eyes. She loved his fires best, and he knew it. He could even get them going with damp wood in a storm, had a kind of magic like that.

'What makes you so brave now?' This time when she reached for his hand, he took it. She rubbed at a scar on his skin, tracing his tattoo scale pattern not even from looking.

Cal watched the ocean, considering. 'Dark shape may be gone by day. Besides,' he looked at her sideways, 'you will like.'

'Then tell me what this is before we get ourselves so cold!'

'Land.' Cal said the word so quiet that Moss was not sure, at first, if he'd spoken at all. He nodded at her, slow.

Moss stepped to him. 'You see ... *what*?'

'Dark shape. Out in the waves. Land.'

'Where?'

Again, Moss squinted at the horizon. She checked the tidemark to see if that had fallen back like Pa said would happen when the floods began to go. Nothing looked any different.

'Pa has not said anything ... And he would know!'

Cal shrugged. 'Maybe it comes back. Maybe is time.'

'You are dreaming, Cal. Trying to tease me.'

He pulled on her hand. 'I see.'

Still, though, he paused at water's edge before dipping toes in. She felt trembling in his hand. Still not too brave with the water then.

'If I am wrong, I find elvers for you each night,' he said.

Moss grinned. Cal knew elvers were her favourite snackling, even better than the sweetberry fruits at the base of the volcano.

Adder was already chest-deep, tongue lolling with its tip in the sea; she lapped at salt water, then spat it out.

Moss took Pa's boots from around her neck and placed them on the sand. 'You have to promise something else. Two something elses.'

He nodded.

'You can't change. Can't merge back to water, or fish, or whatever it was you were before you came. You stay here with me, as Callan.'

He stood very still as he looked at her. 'Don't know how to change like that.'

And she knew this, but it was night, after all, and darkness was tricksy. Darkness was when the lizards roamed wide, and when stormflower scent was sweetest. It was often darkness when storms came.

Again, her fingers were running across the scars on his hand, remembering how she had tried teaching him to swim that first summer, and how he had trembled too hard to learn. She loosened her rabbit-pelt covering and dropped it on Pa's boots.

'You sure? All the way to the Point?'

'Till you see.'

The cold against her calves made her gasp, but soon the water wrapped her up, gave her that second skin she loved. Cal only paused a moment before stepping in after. Moss looked to the black ocean. Was Cal making this up? On days when Pa was feasted-drowsy on stormflowers, or had drunk palm wine till his cheeks went red, he'd say that Cal would tell her lies, one day – lies she'd want to believe. Were these the lies Pa meant? But Pa never remembered his harsh words about Cal in the morning-clear.

As she waded out – her skin already numb and carefree – she kept looking for the land. If it had come, maybe Pa would smile like he used to. Maybe they would even . . . leave? Was that full-possible now, after so long?

Soon, the water went moon-full, shining silver to their faces. Adder's seal-slick head was beside her, proper paddling dog, panting cold. Moss called over her shoulder.

'What does this land look like?'

'It comes up and it goes down. It . . . flickers.'

'That doesn't sound like land.'

Cal shrugged. 'Maybe is something else.'

Moss moved faster then, near-swimming. She didn't want what Cal had seen to be *something else*. Land, more than anything, might shake Pa from Blackness.

Cal caught her up, laced his hand tight in hers.

Moss shivered, and not from the cold of the water. She thought of Cal falling back, disappearing in a tide. She remembered when they both near-drowned.

'We rest here,' she said, pointing at a rock jutting from the water – the beginning of Rocky Point.

They scrambled up, Cal only letting go of her hand when he was secured tight, grasping the stone. Moss pulled Adder from the waves and held her on her lap, even though she was too big, and wet, and her legs draped everywhere. On the rock, Moss was warmer. Even here in sea, at night, these rocks stored the heat of the volcano. She brushed the back of her hand against the petals of a tiny stormflower, growing even there; felt it zing her skin. Cal wriggled closer, sapping her warmth.

'Follow where my eyes go.' Again, Cal pressed his cool fingers against her cheeks, moving her stare.

She leant back into him, sharing body heat. And – *there!* – just for a moment . . . had she seen it? Was there something that had *flickered*? Just at the edge of her vision. Solid, then gone. If she did not turn her head too fast . . .

'At the side of my eyes . . .' she whispered, '. . . only for a moment . . .'

'Yes. Turn and it goes.'

Cal pressed close. Whatever it was, it seemed big, just like he'd said. It *could* have been land-shaped. *Maybe*. But now it was gone again. Land did not disappear like this. Did it?

'We must tell Pa,' she said, thinking about the stories, thinking how his Experiment maybe now had proof of working.

But Cal was frowning, and she could guess what he was thinking. These days, Pa near-never looked to the horizon, or spoke of what might be beyond it. He'd stopped the Experiment so long ago, why would land come back now?

She plucked a petal from the flower at her fingertips and placed it in her mouth. Perhaps she'd see land better with that inside her. She gestured to Cal to see if he wanted the same, but he shook his head.

Moss chewed on it, thinking. 'If there is land, did Pa make it come?'

'If there is land,' Cal said, 'we raft to it.'

She flinched. Last time they'd done that, they'd near-drowned. There'd been that angry man in the sea.

'This time we leave proper,' Cal said.

Moss watched his gold-flecked eyes shimmer as he laughed. This was not the husk of a laugh she so often heard from him, this was loud and high, had mad joy wrapped up in it. It made her laugh too.

'Maybe there are other people,' he said. 'Out there. Already other places to be.'

When Cal laughed again, it made him look so full like a Small Thing once more that it took her breath. She had forgotten, till then, how much they used to laugh – after games on the sand, during stories Pa told . . .

She reached out and touched Cal's laugh with her fingertips. Only, his laugh stopped when her fingers met his lips. He looked at her steady and she did not move her fingers. She had a memory of doing this when a Small Thing too; of trying to catch his laughings and smilings, of trying to hold them live in her palm like how Pa held flowers. She had a memory of him catching petals on her tongue. She moved her fingers to his cheeks; to where his laugh had gone.

'Tried to catch it,' she said. And there, for a moment, it appeared again: his smile pushing at her fingertips. His smile was like the land out there. Going, then coming. Flickering.

'Catch it proper, then,' he said. Her fingers fell from his cheek and touched his teeth as he spoke.

His eyes had challenges glinting.

So.

She leant towards Cal and pressed her lips to where his laugh was. It was like they'd played at as Small Things, all those storm-flowers taken from tongues, all those 'happy ever afters' from stories.

'Caught,' she whispered.

And proper this time.

ACT THREE. SCENE THREE.

Moss pulled away from Cal. Felt his quick-light breath. Tasted salt. Now every part of her was touching stormflowers – was that tingle-quick.

They'd done this before, but it felt different now. Perhaps it was the dazzle-bright moon on his skin, but Cal looked smoother, less fishy; Moss did not see his scale pattern. She grinned, squeezed his fingers. Then she dragged her eyes from Cal to see the land again.

'How can a land disappear?' she said.

'How can a horse come from sea? How can flowers make a storm?' He glanced at her sideways.

'We tell Pa,' she said.

He moved his head in that tilt of his that could mean *yes* or *no* or nothing at all.

They clambered, careful, from the rock to the pinching sea. Adder plopped into the water, all blubber-limbed, swimming round them with teeth glinting.

'You're more seal than dog,' Moss told her. 'More shark.'

Now it was as if Adder's father had been a bull shark instead of one of the wild dogs.

71

'Dog shark?' She turned to Cal. 'That's a *something*, isn't it?'

'Dog*fish*,' he hissed.

Moss flicked water towards Adder, watched her bite at it. Cal took a bigger stride until he was wading beside Moss.

'This all right?' she asked. 'The water?'

'All right.'

She squeezed his hand, thinking about how far he'd come since being so tremble-feared. 'We'll get you swimming proper in the warmer tides, you'll see.'

But she didn't hear what he said back to her, because Pa was on the shore. She saw him plain-clear, walking around without outer coverings, staring at them.

Her hand tightened around Cal's. 'What's he doing?'

Adder swam ahead. When Moss and Cal reached shore, Pa was wide-eyed. A sharp wind had come down with him too, swirling his night-coverings. Farther up behind him stood Aster.

'You're awake, then?' Moss went to him and took his arms – thinner these days, and stringy. 'Not sleepwalking?'

She hesitated, sudden unsure whether to tell him of the land they'd just glimpsed.

Pa shook away her concern, but she kept hold of him tight: though he was awake, he was not full-clear. These fevers were happening more often. If she didn't get him calm again soon . . .

'What were you doing out on that rock?' Pa's voice was dog-growl quiet. He stared at where the sea had soaked her coverings, then at Cal behind.

'We saw something, Pa.'

Pa's eyes widened.

She leant forward to rub his arms; they were colder than fish bellies. 'Let's get you warmed first, then we'll tell you.'

'*We?*' Pa looked out to sea, then switched eyes back to Cal, narrowing them. 'He was taking you away again? That it?'

Moss saw his dark look. 'Cal never *tried* to take me anywhere.'

Moss felt Cal's little finger wind itself to hers. When she looked over, she saw his lips had sand grains on them. She would've reached across to brush them off, but Pa's strange-dark manner stopped her. If Pa was fading to Blackness, perhaps it was better to wait before telling of Cal's land. But then . . . why hadn't he seen the land yet for himself? He'd been looking full out to the ocean.

Pa pitched forward, grasped Cal's shoulders. 'Remember, the sea punished you once . . . Why take Moss out there again? Why be so stupid?'

Moss shook her head at him; she did not want to start this argument up again, right-sure! But instead, Pa grasped tighter on Cal's shoulders. It was the Blackness, only that, building up inside Pa and changing him. Soon Pa would be out of this cycle and soft-sweet again. Always the same – a few days of bad, and then longer of good.

'Return to bed,' she said. 'You're half sleeping anyway.'

Everything else, including the dark shape in the ocean, could wait. But as she pushed Pa to go, Cal reached to grip Pa's arm, keeping him.

'There is land,' Cal said. 'I seen it. Moss seen it. It come up and it go down.' His voice rasped as if he had swallowed salt water.

'Land?' Pa frowned as if he was trying to remember what the word meant.

Moss widened her eyes at Cal in a way that said *We'll never get him to bed now!* Sure enough, Pa rushed for the shoreline, his feet quick-fast in the water. He reached back for Cal's shoulder and brought him close, till he was a clamshell's width away.

'Where is it?'

Moss came to stand beside them; even Aster stood a little closer to the sea, nostrils wide.

Cal did not move Pa's head to see it like he had with Moss; instead, he pointed. 'There,' he said, quiet. 'Almost do not look, then you see. Coming, then gone.'

'Flickering?' Pa said. 'Are you sure?'

Moss followed where Cal was pointing, and tried looking in that sideways way she had last time. But now there was nothing. No flickering. No land. Like Pa, she could not see it either.

Where had it gone?

Pa waded in, trying to pull Cal with him. 'Nothing!' he said.

Cal writhed away when Pa went deeper. Before Moss could stop him, Pa dug into the folds of his night-coverings, pulling out stormflowers. He tipped back his head and ate a fistful: if Moss ever had that many, she'd be quick-fast flying over the volcano, soaring with the bats. But Pa grew still. Stood like a heron about to strike. Moss reached out her hand to grasp his, to keep him tethered in case the buzz came quick, but he would not take it. Instead, he waded deeper, his fingers twitching with new energy, his head snapping side to side. Perhaps, like this, he would see. The flowers would heighten his senses, sharpen his focus.

But Pa turned and came back towards them, his expression certain-firm. 'There is no land. You lie, Callan! Didn't I say he would lie one day, Moss?'

'There is.' Cal had quiet sureness. Moss felt it in how he stood, in how he was not even flinching from the cold water pulling around their calves.

Pa frowned at Moss and Cal's hands, clasped together.

Callan will take you from me . . . he'll try to . . . he'll promise you lies.

Moss knew he was thinking it.

If she could make Pa see he was in fever, maybe he'd treat Cal as he used to, would be kinder. Maybe if Pa were calmer, he'd see the land. But why hadn't he seen it already?

Pa came closer. 'Can *you* see it, Moss?'

Moss nodded slow. 'I thought I did.' She looked out and, again, there was nothing but ocean and the far-off horizon, the moon's reflection on the waves.

Pa watched her. 'You believe Cal?'

She hesitated. 'Why shouldn't I?'

Cal stood straighter. With his shoulders rolled back, he was now taller than Pa. But there was fire in Pa's eyes. Moss saw it dancing there, orange-gold, like the flowers he'd eaten.

'But Cal changes,' Pa said. 'He grows further away.'

A tingling feeling was building in Moss's skin, in the crevices of her fingers. It was like she was holding her hand in front of the fire pit instead of in Cal's. She pulled at Cal, urging him back to the shore and away from this Pa, but he was like a limpet on a rock and wouldn't go.

'This is not the first time Cal lies,' Pa added.

Moss gritted her teeth. Pa was talking like Cal was not even there!

Even so, Moss was thinking of – *remembering* – some of the times Cal had not been full-true.

Hiding food for himself.

Taking Adder to hunt lizards when he said they were catching fish. Saying things about Pa that didn't seem right.

And now, this land.

Maybe.

But everyone said untruths sometimes.

Pa was blinking hard, like he did when he had skull storms coming. When he looked at Cal, it was like he was seeing right through.

'He will take you from me,' Pa said, his voice distant. 'He wants me gone and everything here for himself, wants you . . .'

Moss knew she shouldn't trust Pa when he was like this; he didn't know what he said. Cal turned from him quick-fast, striding up the beach.

'He the one who lies,' Cal hissed. 'Who keep secrets. You wait-see!'

Moss ran after, Adder barking at her heels.

'It's not a game,' she told her dog. 'Be still!' But Aster was stirring up the dog further, cantering beside them and tossing her head.

Cal stopped where the sand turned to pebbles, bold-staring at Pa. 'Land,' he said, pointing firm at the ocean. 'It's there. Maybe you're just too sick to see.'

For a moment all Moss could hear was the wind around them and a light stormflower song upon it. Then, lightning-quick, Pa scaled the space between them.

'I'm not sick,' Pa snapped. 'Do not say it again!'

Cal's stare was steady. 'But is true. Sick and forgetting. You know it well as me.'

Pa raised his arm and hit Cal in the face. It happened so fast Moss did not see it coming.

76

Cal fell.

His hand was up near his cheek, over his right eye. Moss bent to him. Her own cheeks stung-strange now too, as if she were the one who'd been hit. Her own ears throbbed! Like Pa had hurt her! Her eyes pricked tears. She blinked them down. For a second, she was back in the sea with that angry man from long before – this fear felt so wide! She shook the strange pain free, swam to the surface, looked for . . .

'Cal?'

But Cal was backing away from them both, hurt in his face, and not just from his eye. She wanted to grab him by his coverings and keep him from running. Wanted to tell him that Pa did not mean this and that soon he'd be calm again – that this was just the storm season coming, changing him. But she could only stare at the new mark on Cal's skin.

Cal backed further. And why shouldn't he? Pa had never been like this before, had never hurt them with hands. Cal uncovered his eyes, and Moss saw the swelling, how his skin were like a storm cloud building.

'Look how he does not see,' Cal hissed. 'Not land, not nothing. How he change and let no one else. He does not *want* to see.'

Already, Cal was turning. Loping away. Moss clutched her throbbing ears as she watched him go, disappearing fast to the pines.

ACT THREE. SCENE FOUR.

When Moss turned back, Pa was curled like a seed-pod, crouched on the sand. He held his shaking hand in front of him, staring at it as if it were not a part of him, as if it were a traitor. When Pa looked up, there were sudden tears on his cheeks.

'What did I do to him?' he said. 'To my boy?'

Moss could not remember the last time he had called Cal *his boy*; back when Pa still played games with them both, maybe. He shook his head, staring after Cal into the dark.

'You hit him, Pa.' She kept a harsh tone to her words.

His shoulders slumped forward and he breathed deep, like how he did when he was trying to think, trying to come back to the other part of himself.

'I forget,' Pa said. 'Sometimes I cannot even remember . . . not one thing.'

He had flipped back – sure and quick-fast; still, she did not want to hear his excuses. Moss looked towards the trees, but Cal was nowhere now.

Sick, Cal had called Pa.

He had talked about secrets.

Pa had made Cal's skin swollen like a bumble-sting.

'Why, Pa?'

He shook his head. Now in Pa's eyes she saw something deeper: fear hiding behind the fever. Did he even know what he'd done? He breathed out slowly. This was the real Pa, coming back. Moss saw it in the crease of his eyes and the gentle curlout of his spine. It had taken this shock of hitting Cal to do it, though.

'But there is no land,' he said, firm. 'There cannot be. You know that, don't you, Moss?'

And when Moss looked to see it again, she saw only black water, the swish and pull of the tide.

'Cal was lying,' Pa said.

She clicked soft for Aster, who stood a little distance away, and placed a palm on the horse's shoulder. 'Help Pa now, Aster-spirit.'

Pa stood and rested his right arm across Aster's withers. He laid his forehead to her neck and breathed her in. The horse blew warm flower-air to his face.

'I do not want to help you after what you did,' Moss said.

Still, she took his other arm and, together with Aster, led him across the cove. He felt so light, like a coco husk when the juice had spilled. Tears glinted bright across his cheeks. She would not be moved by them. She looked out to the darkness. She should be with Cal, touching fingers and flowers to his swelling eye. But Pa's head was heavy-bent with pain. If she left him here like this, would he even go back to the hut?

Adder was quieter now too, trotting slow beside. Even the sea was drawing back, leaving only sighs against the sand.

Jess was waiting for them at their hut, her milky old-dog eyes seeing little but her tail thudding all the same.

'Everything is fine, girl,' Moss murmured. 'Not worrying time.'

Though, looking at how Pa squinted and touched his temples –
thinking about the puff of Cal's eye – she could not believe it. Not
any more.

Pa had hit Cal.

The dog backed aside to let them through. When Pa leant down
to fondle the dog's ears, he stumbled and grabbed the doorframe.

'Should say sorry,' he murmured.

Moss pushed him inside. 'Sleep now. Apologize in the morning.'

Cal would not want Pa near him now, anyway. And it was how it
usually went: Pa got angry at Cal, Pa apologized.

But Pa did not ever hit him.

Moss lit a candle with an ember from the firepit and went inside.
After drying herself and changing, she found a book and opened
pages for Pa: shoved it into his hand. He called this book 'a classic,'
and he'd read it to her and Cal many times. She remembered its
tale of drowned cities and last hopes; Pa's stories of their own
drowned hopes sounded a little like it. He wouldn't read it tonight,
though; he would stare at the text for a while as if seeing pictures
there, then would fall asleep. No more bedtime stories for any of
them these days.

'Did you really see something out there, Moss?' Pa's voice was
drowsy-soft from their bed. 'It's just, there can't be . . . I would feel
it coming. I would know.'

'Shhhh. We'll look again in the morning.'

But what Moss true-meant was that *she* would get up first and
try to see the land. She would not excite Pa with this discovery
before she was sure this time. He'd be sleeping a good while

tomorrow, anyway. Sometimes, when he got deep in Blackness, he didn't get up for days.

Moss sang the sleep-song Pa had sung to her as a Small Thing.

'*Lu-lay, lu-lay . . . Sleep, little child . . .*'

Perhaps, if she could get him fast in sleep, she could go out to find Cal. As she sang, Moss tidied the books around the bed, putting them in a pile. So many thousands of stories Pa had told her and Cal – sometimes from books, other times making them up from his mind. Those making-up times were when his eyes had lit most. If he'd had more paper, Pa might've written down one long story for someone else, one day, to find – a story of them. He'd call it *The Island We Found*, or *Stormflowers*, or *Tempests*. With it, he'd make them famous and important, like he'd always wanted. Or like he used to want. She thought of his scrapbook, the one he used to write in each day. If he hadn't used up all its paper, would he still be writing it now?

Pa was snoring soft already, Adder curled tight against his back, the book forgotten beside him. Moss added it to the pile. She surveyed the thinning rugs, the wooden trunk filled with clothes falling apart, and, then, the sagging bed they still shared, still big enough for all three of them plus two dogs. She missed the shape of Cal there.

Jess whined her goodnight, then curled up in the space under the bed, the place she often slept for whole days now.

'That dog'll die there,' Pa had said yesterday. 'One day that'll be it. Sometimes I think the only thing keeping her alive is those flowers.'

Moss shivered to think it, glancing under. Jess's eyes glinted. Not dead yet.

Moss pulled back the blanket. She'd get in just for a little warmth, just till Pa was deep-sleeping. She blew out the candle. Pa rolled over in sleep, his fingers grazing her back. As a Small Thing, long before Callan washed in, Moss had lain curled and cocooned with Pa; now the space between them felt too little, Pa's breath too close, and his snoring kept her awake. She thought of Cal in his hut, all the space and silence he had. She could sleep there. She could go from these covers and curl up next to him instead. If Cal would still welcome her.

She turned on to her back, let Pa's hand drop. She reached under his pillow to check, and – yes – there were stormflowers, a dried-up wad of them, bound together with stem sap. These days, with his Blackness always so close, Pa was never far without them. She broke off a small corner and put a petal against her tongue. It fizzed there. She waited, letting it tingle.

Tell them what you wish for. They make things happen. Make things change.

She'd seen it. Many storm seasons ago.

Moss felt the burst of sweetness, the thrill of the flower-rush inside, the grin in her cheeks. The buzz in her chest was firefly-fast.

Tonight she wished for land. To see it. To know it was there.

As she did, the buzzing feeling changed, moved deeper inside her. Now the petals weren't making her relaxed, or happy, but queasy-strange. She took another dried petal and, after a short-quick buzz, the same thing happened. When it happened a third time, she put the wad of dried petals back under the pillow. Perhaps Pa had left them there so long they had gone full-flat. Then she had a further thought: maybe Pa had gone to Blackness so fast tonight because the flowers weren't so potent as normal.

Or maybe he was simply getting sicker – so sick now that not even the flowers couldn't work against it. She rested her eyes, just for a moment. Just . . . for.

One.

Dream.

And . . . as her breathing deepened . . .

She felt fingers in hers, a hand. A pulling forward.

In this fever dream, she went to the sea.

There were lights on its surface. Fizzing. Shooting across the water like stars. Gold flowers on Moss's skin, in her hair. The sea was writhing and swaying, wanting Moss inside. Beyond the reef, frothing wave tips grew.

Moss stepped into the water, and the sea made room. There was that feeling in her hand again, pulling her. Beyond the reef. Beyond.

Moss dived, and a shadow beside her dived too. She went down and the water bent from her movement. She and the shadow were made from the ocean now – they swam because it let them. Down there, Moss did not need air. She opened her skin and breathed sea instead. She felt it wash inside her, felt its salt rasp her ribs. Down there, the sun mixed with the blue and turned everything green. She could stay. She could dream.

But there was a noise. An angry voice. A watery dark figure down there with her. He was back. She curled away quick-fast . . . looked for the lights.

And she was swimming fast, aiming for the surface. She swam. Stretching her body out, her dark hair smoothed straight. Her skin hardened and her legs lengthened. Something like scales came. Around her now were flowers, swimming with her: a whole tide.

Moss moved with them, towards the lights and away from the angry man. Towards the surface. Until, when she rose up and gasped air, she knew there was land – real-proper land that she could see there solid. Direct ahead.

But when she turned to look back at the shore of her island and blinked in the sunlight—

Her island was gone.

She was bobbing alone in the waves.

Awake.

She blinked in the dark and spread her fingers wide. She could feel the blanket, the holes in it. She heard Pa's snore. There was rain, mouse-footstep light on their roof, and there was wind at their door, curling underneath. She felt it creeping towards her neck and chin, waking her skin. But there were no gull cries this time, no Cal. Only an uncomfortable fluttering of breath in her chest, like trapped wings.

Pa had hit Cal.

Cal had seen land.

Cal had not given Birthday Surprise.

None of this had happened before.

She sat up, moved away from Pa, and left the hut. The rain gentle-pricked her as she pulled her coverings close. She squinted at the sea for that land again, but it was too dark, with the moon no longer so high. But something *felt* different out there. She had seen land in her dreaming now, too.

Moss checked the tree line for lizards or wild dogs, wishing Adder had come with her. She puffed when she got to the steep bit, her breath hanging before her, half real. Cal's hut was a dark, brooding lump, crooked against the sky, built against the cliffs.

Slow-careful, she pressed open its door. Inside was sea-smell and darkness.

'Cal?'

She waited for her eyes to adjust before she moved further in.

'Pa did not mean it,' she whispered. 'Maybe the flowers not been working so well . . . I found dried-out ones under his pillow, working strange . . .'

No answer.

She recognized the bundle of softness on the floor that was Cal's bed. She crawled up close, stretching across until her hand found the edge of his blanket. She worked her fingers along. Any moment, she would touch his cool skin. Cal could grab her, even take her away like Pa had said.

In a boat, in a storm . . . take you from me.

He could kiss her again too. Let her sleep beside. Yin-yanged. He could talk of how they might reach the land he'd seen. She could clasp his hand tight as they ran, looking.

'I believe you,' she whispered. 'About the land. You have to be right.'

Her fingers touched where his head should be, felt down the blanket for the rest of him. But met nothing. No Cal. His hut was now as empty as her birthday oyster shells.

ACT THREE. SCENE FIVE.

Cal stood on slippery rocks, watching the going-back tide. Even with roaring waters, he heard them – throwing words like throwing rocks. Fierce-fast.

'You hurt him, Pa!'

'But he lies, don't you see? He is not who he was.'

'*You* are not who you were!'

Her voice was bird-flapping, all flighty-feared. Pa's voice unsteady.

But if they had trusted Cal . . .

Had listened . . .

Cal sniffed at sweetness. There were petals. He saw their colour, now and now again, trying to circle. He shut his mouth 'case they wanted to come in. Did no good to be trusting them flowers too much. Weather was brewing strange – up and down – them flowers maybe helping.

'Cal could be right,' Moss was saying now. 'Why won't you consider it another way?'

'There is no other way!' The Pa again. 'We wait until we know the floods are gone. Only then do we leave!'

But Cal knew things like other ways. He knew a whole egg clutch of other ways that Pa did not care to. He knew there was a secret in the Lizard Rocks, hiding deep. He should've told Moss when he'd had her close.

But he would not go near Moss while the Pa was beside her. Not now.

He dug his toes into the rock pool, searching for sea worms or limpets or other juicy snacklings – still listening. He had been watching Moss close these past two days, and still she had not found him.

And the Birthday Surprise were waiting.

'*Birthday Surprise.*'

Cal whispered the words on the air. Maybe Moss would catch them. Cal saw flowers open their petals and turn their heads to him.

'*Come find.*'

'*Soon.*'

He sent more whispers out. But still, Moss stayed with the Pa.

Darkness now. Might as well feed these snacklings to the lizards! Might as well jump to the tides and let the rest of 'em go pissin'! But he would get pulled back, oh yes . . . There'd be the jerk on his spine, the catching. There'd be the fear of going under.

He hissed loud, then went still-silent listening – they still bickered like seabirds in spring. He pressed a toenail to sticky sand; sea worms should be uncovering themselves. He dug, dug, dug, till he felt sea worms poke-tickling his foot. Though he could not find the strength to pluck one. Even when it would slip down his throat so long and soft and tasty.

Instead, he pushed his head to the wind and went loping 'cross sand. With her or no, he would see Birthday Surprise proper, go right through them tunnels till he knew for certain-true it were what he thought.

There was strong salt smell on this new wind, and that gave him memory of Moss from moons ago with salt-wetness on her face. As he ran, Cal pulled at the memory. When Moss had bad dreamings, there was often salt-wetness on her face. After one bad dreaming, Cal had pressed his tongue to her cheek and tasted her salt-tears. Licked them right inside him. And she had laughed then. And her tears had stopped.

Cal often thought about Moss's salt-tears – still inside him, still biting and moulding. Like how the waves cut back rocks and made caves. P'raps he was hollow from her.

Cal sucked air through teeth, kept loping. It would take so long to get there as for stars to come. But Cal was fast in rhythm, and his legs were longer now. He would see proper this time – go down-deep crawling in the dark to know what was true-there.

ACT THREE. SCENE SIX.

'**B**een ignoring us?' Moss said. 'Not seen you for three days.'

Cal tilted his head. 'You ignore me.'

Moss watched him from across the fire, cleaning fish. They both were tucked in close, sheltering under the woven palm covering and avoiding light rain. He stopped to sweep scraggle-wild hair from his face with the back of his hand.

'Still stewing-angry with Pa?'

He shrugged.

'You know he did not mean it, Cal.'

His shoulders pointed towards each other and his eyes watched the ground. Sideways, they watched her, too. There was something different about him, and it wasn't just the eye. He was curled over as if he'd been collecting heavy fish from a net, but maybe it were secrets he was collecting instead.

Moss dug her toes into the dirt, drew spirals. 'I keep going to your hut. You're never there.'

'Found new place.'

'Where?'

'Where these fishies come from.'

Moss squinted at the sandfish. It was late in their season. She did not know how Cal would have caught them in a net cast from rocks.

'Did you swim for those? Spearfish?'

She could not imagine it, not with how he trembled in deep water.

'I called and they came right in.' Cal rasp-laughed, not the same easy laugh she'd heard the other night on the rock in the sea. She risked a smile at him.

'I missed you,' she said, so quiet she did not know if Cal heard.

She drew spirals going out and then spirals going in, like the spirals Pa had drawn on the walls of his cave.

The shape of life. That's what he called them. *Shape of change. Never-ending, constant-moving.*

Spiral.

Spiral.

Spiral.

Nothing stays still . . . always spirals . . .

Drawing them always made Moss still, though. She drew patterns in the gaps between the curving lines. Cal watched her draw, though she knew he pretended otherwise by digging harder in the fish guts.

'You make stories,' Cal had said once. 'With only sticks in sand.'

'Just scratched lines.'

'But is real, too. You make it mean something.'

Then, the compliment had made her smile. He wouldn't make it now.

'Three days,' she said again.

Three days I've been thinking about the sand on your lips.

Wondering if you hurt.

If you hate.

'Not my fault.' Another shrug. Cal was full of the shrugs today.

The colours around his eye were spiralling from red to purple to blue to, almost, yellow. Moss had left aloe leaves for him on the stoop of his hut – ones she'd gone for 'specially – but he'd not used them. Did he blame her for the eye? Did he wish she'd followed him into the dark instead of staying with Pa?

'Pa's still sick,' she said. 'Sicker than I ever seen him. One moment he's shouting-angry, the next he's murmuring about how bad he feels about what he did.'

'He cannot help himself.'

'He was in fever, Cal.'

'He hurt.'

The weight of his words dropped heavy, made silence. Moss kept drawing spirals, kept looking up to watch Cal's long-thin fingers working on the fish: small and scrawny today, their bones delicate and easy to cut through. She didn't know why Cal had bothered with them, not when he could have found fat-bellied fish in their own cove pools. Tonight they'd be eating grit and skin, chewing on bone. Perhaps this was Cal's plan: to get one of those needle bones to stick in Pa's throat. She shivered sudden as she remembered that fierce look in Cal's eyes as he'd glared at Pa. Could Cal ever hurt Pa proper? Would he? These days she weren't sure of anything.

'Haven't seen your land again,' she told Cal. 'I've been looking.' She knew Pa hadn't seen it, either.

'Just 'cause you do not see,' Cal said, 'do not mean land not there.'

'Right. Just 'cause there's no tasty sea snail before me too . . .'

Cal dug deep-quick into the fish, plopped guts and clots of blood

91

to the dirt. He was doing it on purpose, teasing her with showing this fishy's most disgusting parts. Normal days, she wouldn't care – she'd show him something disgusting back – but today . . .

The pain in her stomach came again.

'Why you not believe?' he said, quiet. 'About the land. You saw it too. Why you go with Pa so easy?'

Cal's eyes flashed, surprising her even now. *Firesparks*, she'd called them once. She looked at his arms instead of getting lost there: his muscles now like taut sea kelp, stringy and tough.

'I been waiting for you,' he said. 'I got things to show. Birthday Surprise. Remember?'

Was this the pearl inside the shell – why he was so dark-angry with her as well as Pa – because she hadn't come to see her Birthday Surprise?

A corner of his lip curled. 'And if you tell me to hurry up with your fishy dinner, you can piss off.'

She grinned. 'You can piss off yourself. And take as long as you like with those sandfish; they won't take long to eat.'

'*Pissh, pissh, pisshh.*' Cal made a rhythm with the words that went in time with the slip-slip of his blade.

'Sometimes I wish I'd never taught you our language.'

'Sometimes I wish it too.'

She kept her grin. Her and Cal were still shy-fragile as skate eggs, but he was smiling back now, at least. He finished with the fish he'd been working on and sharpened his knife for the next.

'Why don't you, anyway?' she said. 'Why don't you try to get to that land you see?'

Cal held up a bloodied fish, thrust it towards her. 'Who'd clean your fish?'

Fish flesh fell on her leg, a little watered-down blood trickled over her calf. She smudged it away.

'You could make a raft again.'

'Need you to come with.'

Moss looked at the rain falling soft in the dirt beyond their shelter. 'And if I did come with and we went beyond the reef again? We keep sailing till a shark takes us? Or till we forget?'

He shook his head. 'There's land.' But there was doubt there, sure, in the creases of his forehead.

He lies, echoed the words in her head. Pa's words.

Again, she felt that dull rumble of an ache in her belly. Far off, the sky rumbled too.

'If there is land, we should wait till we see it proper,' she said, Pa's words again. She sighed. 'And you know I can't leave Pa long while he's in fever.'

Cal went back to the fish, and Moss picked up a pair of smalls she'd been making on and off. She bent her head, pushing the rusted needle through feather-thin cloth; it wouldn't be long before what little cloth they'd left would be full gone. She pushed the needle firmer when the cramping pains came again. Then pressed her fingers below her belly button, where the pain was worst, and tried to think of a calm sea; a tide rising like a soft breath. When Adder came, she settled next to Moss and rested her head on the paining place too. Moss tickled her ears.

'It's not sickness,' she said. 'Not like Pa got.'

Cal shrugged. 'Full moon this night. Elvers about.'

Quick-fast, Moss was thinking about those baby eels, slipping down her throat. Elvers would help sickness. Cal was on one of the larger sandfish now, his hands working quicker. She remembered those hands clasped tight around her on that rock in the ocean, when they'd curled her close. Again, she missed the curve of him.

She pricked her thumb sharpish, sucked at the blood. The sky, too, was bleeding colour. And stormflowers were opening; she could smell them. Another storm? She watched Cal shiver through his coverings. They always used to sit close before a storm, drawing heat from each other: birds on a branch.

Moss finished sewing the smalls, then tucked them into the waist of her skirt. They were sad toil today, and she'd have to do more of it tomorrow. Pa had smalls to be made too, and judging by how Cal was shivering, perhaps she'd make him something extra. When she saw Adder's legs twitching as they ran across dream-sand, Moss knew she had running to do too.

She stood. They needed seagrass for supper, and she had not searched the tide today besides. Now that they could no longer count on Pa's help, there were always more chores. She reached over Cal to fetch a pot, and he slunk from her.

'You're like an elver today,' she said. 'All slippery-spiralled.'

Cal grunted. 'And you're a chick who only listens to her pa.'

Moss narrowed her eyes at him: that one hooked.

'You're the chick.'

Hadn't Pa said that when Cal first arrived? *Still a baby with much to learn. We will teach him.*

But Cal was not a baby now. Now Cal's thick, dark hair was not only on his head, and he was muscled and lithe, slinky as a skate. Sometimes Moss thought Cal was turning into something like the hunters in Pa's storybooks.

Another cramp made her gasp. Perhaps it was the weather,

94

making her so deep in paining. Once this brooding had blown over, other things would calm. Then she and Adder would play. Then they would know for certain about the land Cal had seen.

She unthreaded the braids in her hair and let it go frizzy, stretched her spine. She was about to leave when Cal grabbed her wrist, his eyes on the sky.

'Weather turns.'

She sat back down beside him with the empty pot balanced on her knees. Like this, maybe Cal and her could talk, fix whatever had gone stormy between them. She placed her temple against his shoulder, turned her eyes to where the clouds scudded faster.

'They're darkening,' she said.

She felt Cal swallow. 'You said once you'd make the land come back. Said you'd do it yourself.'

She smiled against Cal's arm. She remembered, of course. Those dreams about being able to do the Experiment by herself! Sending out the flower-wind!

'Never happened, though, did it? Never proper learnt the Experiment before Pa gave it up.'

'You saw him do it, though,' he said, rasp-soft. 'Many times.'

She laughed. 'You did too.'

'Some.' He took one slow breath. 'So, what about if we try it again . . . if *you* do?'

Moss sat up to look at him. 'You want me to do Pa's Experiment? Now?'

He shrugged. 'Could try. Maybe see the land that way.'

Moss looked over at the hut. No movement inside, no sounds. Pa had been fevered-out since early morn and would most-like stay that way till eve. And the cave was just up the path, not so far away;

she could be back before the sun went down. Couldn't she? She turned the thought in her mind like she'd turn sea snails in glowing fire embers.

'If the Pa can do this, so you can,' Cal said, urging.

ACT THREE. SCENE SEVEN.

Cal was already walking up the path. Moss half ran to match his longer strides, Adder at her heels. The winds were stronger, already Moss saw petals dancing there. Could the flowers know what she was about to try? Were they expecting it? When Cal turned to her, new wind made his hair stand up like marsh reeds.

'What the Pa got, anyway, that different from you?' he said.

Moss looked aside, into the moving trees. Pa had everything – the dreams, the stories, the legends. He remembered what life had been like in their old world.

'Why do you suddenly believe in it, anyway, Cal?' she said. 'You've never thought Pa's Experiment worked before.'

'Not saying I do now.'

'You'll have to help. Like I used to help him.'

She thwacked a branch sideways at some wayward vegetation, and then flinched like the plant did. She thought of what Pa might say if he knew what they were doing. The Experiment was what he'd dreamt up. Would it even work without him?

'Autumn winds,' Moss murmured, watching the swaying trees,

their leaves departing like birds from a roost. 'The beginning of winter storms.'

Maybe this new island weather was just that. Not flower-magic. Not connected to Pa or any of them. She thought of the bruise around Cal's eye, the angry words shouted the other night. Things changed in autumn. Wild winds stirred up.

Cal held out his hand and, cautious, she wound her fingers in his.

'Just a look-see,' she said. 'Just a try.'

Branches moaned on either side of them, and Moss got a memory-flash of doing this as Small Things, too – though, then, they went to watch Pa do the Experiment, back when he was hopeful the world might change from his actions.

They leant forward into the wind, breathing heavier when they got to the steeper part. Adder yipped how she did when Aster was nearby, though Moss could not see the horse in the trees. But maybe the horse was watching them and maybe she'd find a way to tell Pa what they'd done. They stopped to rest at the top, leaning against the cliff and facing the ocean. Tide was almost full-in. Far out, the sea was seal-grey, waves frothing.

'White horses,' Moss said, pointing them out for Cal. 'Racing there. See?'

This was habit, pointing out the silver water at the tips of the waves, the place where the water broke. Moss always watched for real horses too, galloping towards the sand. Looked for another Aster. If it could happen once . . .

She looked for the land too.

'Can you see it?' she asked.

Cal's eyes watered as he looked. 'Not yet.'

Winds were coming stronger, though; Moss felt them grasping at her hair. They pushed back Adder's forehead, making her slit-eyed, sending her ears inside out. The stormflowers on the rocks were unfurling.

Moss bent to one flower, smelt its sweetness. She whisper-sang to it and invited its healing magic inside. She pulled off one petal and tasted it. Unlike the dried-out petals under Pa's pillow, this flower seemed strong: good. She rubbed another petal against her neck, felt the warm buzz it left on her skin. She wanted another but felt Cal's eyes on her also.

'Pa used to eat many before he'd start the Experiment,' she explained, picking another petal and pressing it to Cal's hands. 'You must eat some too, if you're going to help.'

He did it reluctant-slow, scrunching his face.

'Still not sweet for you?'

'Not 'specially.'

She darted to pick more orange-gold petals and shoved them into her pockets.

'I've been wondering if that's why Pa's been sickening. The flowers are changing. Maybe they're not so strong any more, not working?'

Cal shrugged. 'Maybe.'

They pulled the heavy cloth away from the cave entrance and went inside. Even in the gloom of the cave, Moss saw the vase on top of Pa's experimenting table wobble from the wind, heard pages rustle. She took wood from the pile and laid a fire in the hollowed-out hearth. Rubbing stormflower petals together, she threw them to the sticks. A spark came. She pulled a flaming twig out, and gave another to Cal, and they lit the torches around the cave. As she did, she looked at the spines of the books, then over to the swirls and drawings Pa had made on the walls.

Perhaps this was what life would be like if Pa never healed – just her, and Cal, and all the stories Pa kept. She breathed in the smell of old pages, that pleasant musk-damp. She brushed a couple of spines with her fingertips. Was everything ever to know inside those pages? Or were there more stories to learn, somewhere?

She stepped across to a book, its belly pressed against the cave floor, its pages folded back like broken limbs. She picked it up and pushed it back on the shelf. Once, Pa would never have left a book like that. She felt such an urge to fix all this – to heal not only the rest of the world but their own island too. If Pa were well again, if he did not hate Cal so . . . It had seemed so perfect here. Once.

'Come try the Pa's Experiment,' Cal said.

She let him lead her to the table. Gentle-soft, she touched the glass vase that had come on their boat all those years ago; then took the fresh-picked petals from her pockets. She tore them and dropped them into the vase, just as she had seen Pa do. The air went sweet-heady. She uncorked and poured a little of Pa's palm wine inside the vase, too, then found a scallop shell of sand from their cove and sprinkled that in.

'We need something of us,' she said, remembering how Pa always put something of himself inside.

Cal reached across and plucked one of her head hairs, then one of his own. He laid them next to each other on the table. Hers curled up instant-quick, sure-tight as a lugworm; his stayed wavy and darker beside. They went into the vase.

'Enough?'

'Don't know.' She spat into the vase like she'd seen Pa do, and motioned for Cal to do the same. Still, she squinted at the mixture.

'Blood?' she said.

She took Pa's birthday knife from her skirt-waist and, first, she cut Cal's finger with a tiny, quick movement. Drip-drop-drip over the vase, she held it. He sucked it after. Then she cut her own. Unlike Cal, she didn't even flinch. She found a branch and stirred it all together.

'Pa would kill us if he knew,' she said.

But what else could they do but try? It was better than just brooding by a fire. Already the mixture was swirling fierce, bubbling and fizzing like she remembered.

'Like fireflies pressed tight,' she said.

'Like fire.'

Soon, she heard the high-pitched singing noise.

'Show us land,' she whispered to the orange mixture. 'Make the flooding go down so we can see the other island. Make change.'

Inside the vase, the mixture came full-fiery. Cal pressed his nose close, watching careful, pulling her down to see too. Close up, the substance did not look like fireflies. Instead, the swirling inside the vase was fresh new wind. Whirring gold. Had she done it? She held the mixture towards Cal so he could smell it. He reeled back, rubbing his nose with the back of his hand.

'Alchemy,' Moss said. 'When one thing changes to another thing. Remember?'

'*Al-kuh-me.*' Cal rolled the word in his mouth like it was a song.

'We change petals to air. Now that air will turn water to land. Maybe it will.'

If she tilted the mixture in just the right way, it looked almost the same colour as the gold-glinting flecks in Cal's eyes. Moss sniffed the mixture and tried to hold the sweetness in her chest. It fizzed there, waiting. She gave Cal more stormflowers, and took some too.

'Eat! Pa uses the energy to bring the winds in.' Moss drew closer to the vase, cradling it. 'He also said if these flowers were in the rest of the world, things would always be beautiful there.'

'I remember those tellings.'

She led Cal to the cave entrance, the vase held close to her belly. Perhaps, if she held it close enough, the paining would ease inside her. Before they pulled the cloth back, she took more stormflowers from her pocket.

'Last bit of fuel.'

She ate, then spat out the fibrous remains and gave them to Adder.

The wind rifled through their coverings. Cal took her hand and pulled her forward, until they stood shoulder to shoulder on the ledge, his eyes serious-searching the horizon. The stormflowers on the rocks turned their yellow yolks towards the wind; pollen flew from their centres, making the air thick. Moss raised her hand like she remembered Pa doing, curled her fingers to beckon the building storm close. She prodded Cal to do it too.

'Concentrate on the stormflowers inside you.' She twisted her fingers. 'On the buzz, the energy they give – think about a wind coming near. *Imagine* it coming. They'll hear you.'

Cal rolled his eyes, unbelieving.

She prodded him again. 'It's never going to work if you're like that!'

Moss watched the grey sea swirling, and there – in the distance – a storm formed. Had she done it?

'Pa used to talk about the floods when he did this,' she said. 'He'd talk about rushing water, animals going under, drowning . . . things we escaped from. Do you remember?'

She raked her fingers through the air. A buzz built inside her as a small storm of its own. She thought about what might be out beyond that line – about exploring it with Cal. Tingling was all through her.

Still, she saw no land.

Moss opened the vase and let the flower-air go. They watched it sparkle.

'Go out to that storm wind,' she told it. 'Make the land appear.'

But the flower-air was hesitant. It hovered before them, swirling into a ball. A part of Moss wanted to reach out and take it back. She felt it quaking, shivering away from the bigger wind. She gripped Cal's hand. The storm's pressure was hurting her skull.

'It doesn't want to go,' Cal said. 'Does not want to be forced.'

The stormflowers were screaming now, not singing. Cal backed off. But they had to keep pushing if they were going to see the land.

'A little more,' she whispered.

She willed that tender wind out, watched the purple clouds swallow it. But something wrenched inside her. Then Cal dropped his arms. Her shoulders slumped as she did too.

And the storm swept low and whined around the cliffs, away.

'Couldn't do it any more,' he said.

'Or me.'

They waited for land.

'See it?' Moss said.

'Not yet.'

'See it now?'

103

'No.'

'Did the flowers . . . work?'

'Maybe they never do.'

Moss looked at him: he was trembling, like how he did in deep water. Like how the flowers had felt inside her. The Experiment hadn't worked, not how she remembered it. It had felt . . . wrong. Was that because Pa wasn't there?

'Maybe it takes time,' she murmured. 'Maybe we have to do it again, every day, like Pa used to. Maybe we haven't eaten enough petals!'

Cal shook his head. 'Maybe was wrong to try.'

Then he was gone, walking fast away. When she caught up with him, he wiped a hand rough across his eyes.

'They screamed!' he said. 'Did you not hear?'

She nodded. 'I felt it.'

She looked back at the water beyond the reef. No land. No change. No nothing but waves. And all those petals disappeared!

Cal moved away, watching remaining petals spin above his head. He raised his hands as if to catch and shelter them. Moss called after him. But he would not turn.

Still clutching the vase, she crumpled against the rock, watching him go. Her muscles still buzzed from the flowers inside. She felt as used up as fire ash.

And there was no land. Maybe whatever she had thought she'd seen with Cal was wrong. Maybe he was wrong.

Her chest heaved as it settled to deeper breathing. Moss opened her hand, felt petals settle there. She closed her fingers around them. No wonder Pa had stopped doing the Experiment. It *took* something from him. Took flowers from them all.

She shut her eyes, her body swaying. Maybe she could sleep and sleep and not care what she woke to . . . could sink down deep like Pa did. Maybe it would not be long before flooding came for them too; till they were drowned-gone like the rest of the world. Perhaps the island could no longer protect them.

But when she went back inside the cave to return the vase, there – at the very corner of her – was something else. She turned her head. Nothing – *nothing seen*. But she caught a smell of something spicy and warm, cooked tasty-good. Like honeyed plantain, but different too. She looked about the cave for something roasting, but 'course there was nothing but fire embers. Nothing else burning. She shut her eyes and smelt it stronger. Spices. A hint of sour. Somehow familiar. What was it? Where had it come from?

She opened her eyes, looked around the cave again. Pa was not here, Cal had not come back. She turned to see the whole cave. And the smell went, quick as it came.

But something else came instead. Something else . . . flickered.

She sat down fast as she saw it, stumbling into the cave wall. For a second – there, at the edge of her vision . . .

She blinked.

There!

She grasped at the rock behind her.

A man. Standing over her. *Curled* over her. Dark hair. Shouting. There for a moment, then gone. He was angry.

She crouched away, pressed back into the wall. Sudden-fast her ear throbbed painful.

Because . . . she remembered him. 'Course she did.

The man from the bottom of the ocean. But why again now?

She skittered across the floor for the entrance. Eel-fast. Adder

105

whined as Moss reached out for her.

'A vision,' Moss murmured. 'Like how Pa gets sometimes.'

It must be.

From eating the flowers.

A waking dream.

But, still, there. At the corner of her eyes, flickering.

Like how Cal's land flickered too.

It was making her spin.

She got to the cave opening, tumbling out. She shook her head hard. Then, cautious-slow, she breathed. The image of the angry man was fading now. He wasn't out here. She gasped in the cold, good air, and pressed her face into her dog's fur. First, stomach-paining; now visions too? Another sign she was getting sick like Pa?

Maybe the land Cal thought he'd seen had been a vision too. Maybe they were all getting sick.

ACT THREE. SCENE EIGHT.

Moss bent to give more tea to Pa.

'Cal's still not back?' he said.

She shook her head. 'Not even to bring fish.'

Moss lit one of their precious candles. Evening again now, and Cal not returned.

'Can't face he's been tricking us, maybe,' Pa said. 'About the land.' Pa broke into another coughing fit.

'Reckon you can get up yet?' she said when he'd done. 'You've been in bed four days.'

'A couple more. Leave me a stash of petals when you go out. Perhaps a strong burst will do the trick for this old soul.'

He tried to smile. She watched his face – greyer now and drawn down. Like Cal, he was disappearing too. She brought out a handful of fiery gold petals.

'Went collecting on the volcano.'

'Good girl. One strong-sweet burst to knock this sickness full-gone.' He reached up to brush her cheek. 'If you're so worried about Cal, we'll go searching in a day or two. Once I'm better. We'll take Aster.' He tapped her nose gentle-soft. 'Wonder why he's been gone so long?'

She bit her lip. She hadn't told Pa of the Experiment they'd tried, had thought better of it when he was so weak . . . when she remembered him hurting Cal. She arranged the stash of the potent stormflowers on the blanket.

'Don't eat them all at once,' she warned, avoiding the further questions in his eyes.

Leaving the hut, she saw the sea was only a little calmer than the night before. Used to be, once the Experiment was over, the winds Pa summoned went away. Now, since their attempt yesterday, Moss still felt those winds, getting under her coverings, cold-cold-colder than she'd ever remembered. This storm wasn't finished with them yet.

But still, no flickering land.

Moss drew her coverings tighter and grabbed a cooking pot. She tipped out deluge from earlier rain. She hadn't forgotten Cal's words about elvers under full moon. As she started to walk, the pain in her belly came again. Like the storm, that hadn't gone either. She wished she could gallop Aster on the hard shore, race this slow thinking and deep paining gone. Moss moved from the grass path to the pebblestones at the top of the dark beach, stepping careful. She smelt the flowers, still open; felt them, pulling.

Swirl with us. Run. Play.

They beat her blood fast. As the wind picked up and taunted her too, she clambered over rock pools to get to the tideline. Somewhere beyond the horizon, there might be buildings and trains and people and dancing and so many dogs. There might be answers for every question she'd ever had. Or there might be nothing but water. Maybe she'd never know which.

She remembered one day at these rock pools, moons and years ago, when Pa had scrunched her curls and touched the tip of her nose, smiling wicked-fun. He'd shown her anemones and sand crabs and fish that looked like gems.

'There are a thousand more things in these pools that we can't see,' he'd said. 'Secret things! Just because you can't see a thing doesn't mean it's not there.'

She had parrot-laughed, and Pa had laughed too.

Now Moss breathed out slow. It had been so long since Pa had been so simple-happy. She stared out past the reef. Maybe they could build a proper boat, one that couldn't capsize. If they were all together, maybe it wouldn't matter if they forgot their island.

She scanned the shoreline for treasure from last night's storm. Seaweed. Two dead crabs. Mussel shells. The seaweed, in places, looked like dark hair spread out. That made her think of the angry man from the cave and the sea – his dark-tangled hair. She imagined him washed up here, bloated and pale, imagined looking into his dead, dark eyes. She kicked an empty mussel shell, imagining she was kicking him away instead.

Adder darted ahead, then back again, and then circled around Moss so close as to make her stumble.

'Daft creature,' Moss told her. 'You are mad with a mood.'

Adder growled, mock fierce, wanting to play, full up with energy from the storm. Moss flicked her fingers at the air in the way Pa had taught her to send unwanted spirits away. Any more of anything inside Adder right now and she would be all wild dog. Moss brushed off some stormflower petals that had settled on Adder's tail, then grasped the cooking pot tight against the wind and aimed for the far end of the cove. She heard the waves as she walked.

Go . . . oo . . .

Stay . . .

Go . . . oo . . .

Stay . . .

'Make up your mind,' she told the water.

Island's full of voices. Pa had said that many times. And when she stopped to listen, she heard them right enough.

'Pity they never give me any answers, though!'

But maybe . . . maybe if she asked . . .

She picked up stones from the shore and aimed one far to reach the deeper water. Adder went mad behind her, whining and skidding, wanting to fetch but not enough to get cold.

'Go on, then,' Moss told the sea. 'Tell me what you hide. What's out beyond the reef?'

She curled her wrist, ready to send another stone flying. She skimmed it hard, and Adder barked and spun and chased her tail in frustration. The sea roared back, but if it was an answer, Moss could not understand it. Adder leapt at a bat and Moss pulled her down again.

Stroking her dog's velvet ears, Moss remembered Pa's words on the day she'd met Adder: *Six weeks old and already a killer. Eaten all her littermates and left only herself.* Moss ran her finger down the dip of Adder's snout. The dog's tongue lolled, eyes shining.

'Come on, then, killer,' Moss whispered. 'My wild, bad girl. Elvers time.'

Adder followed Moss's heels, then raced ahead to where the stream became salt water, followed it up the beach with nose down to where the grass grew and the water was fresh enough to drink. She guzzled loud. Moss bent to drink too, using the cooking pot as

110

a cup, her eyes already scanning for elvers.

That was when the cramp came. So much harder than before.

She cried out, clutched herself. The pain dug like a flint knife. She held her breath, crouched over. Let the pot fall to the edge of the stream. Once she could draw breath, she gathered her skirt, left the pot behind, and stumbled towards the trees. Adder was beside her already, wet nose against her fingers.

Moss did not have time to get to the outhouse. She squatted where she was, pulling down her smalls at the side of a thick-trunked pine that she held on to for balance. She was leaking. There was something dark. Blood! It was everywhere. Between her legs. Soaking her smalls. On her hands now, too. She shoved Adder away as her dog caught the scent of it. In places, it had clotted dark.

Was this sickness too?

She had asked the sea for answers, and this was what it had returned.

Sickness . . . more sickness . . .

Quick-fast, she checked the rest of her body. But there was no more blood, anywhere. It was only coming from that one spot in her. The female spot. It smelt like deep earth. Did not smell like sickness.

Moss took one shaky breath, pushed Adder away again. She pressed her hand to her stomach when the cramps came back. She tried to breathe deeper. The pain did not get worse. Maybe this would not kill her; not right away, anyway. She took off her smalls and bundled them in her hands. Then she wiped herself best she could, using her smalls and some thick succulent leaves. No more blood came. Wherever it was coming from inside her, it was not coming fast. Maybe she needed stormflowers to heal it proper. She took one more shuddering deep breath, then stood.

That was when she saw Cal.

He was on the beach, at where the stream turned to salt water, near where she had been crouching for water and elvers only a little while before.

He was watching her.

ACT THREE. SCENE NINE.

S tumbling, Moss backed up against the tree. A rushing feeling was inside her, pressing at her cramps.

'What are you doing?' She reached to feel tree bark, solid behind her. 'Were you spying? Following me?'

Cal eyes went flash-flashing, like darting fish. And when the cramp came again, she remembered his knife through fish guts, silver-sharp.

'Not following,' he said. 'Waiting.'

'For what?'

He watched her like she should know. She wanted to crouch against the tree again, sit back down in the dirt. Wanted Cal's hands on her cheeks like they had been the other night. He was closer now. Had he seen her bloodied smalls, still balled in her hand? Did he know what'd caused them?

Cal sucked in air, rolled it around his mouth. He tilted his head like the dogs did. 'Blood?'

His breath was between them. Even in the dark, she saw the gold in his eyes, the worry in his face.

She nodded slow. 'Think it's sickness like Pa's got?'

He tilted his head again, thinking. Then he leant towards her. She thought of the tip of his tongue against her skin, his lips on hers. *Winter storms*, she reminded herself, *stirring everything up. Things will settle come spring.* Gentle-soft, his arms came round.

'Maybe we're all sick,' she said, pressing her forehead to his. 'Pa's not woken proper, and I've got blood. You and me both saw visions.'

'Visions?'

When Cal frowned, she jumped in fast. 'The land you saw.'

Cal chewed his lip, considering. 'That's not vision.'

Another cramp came. She breathed out slow, took a step back from Cal to find the tree again. But Cal was looking at the blood on her hands, at the dirtied smalls she was tucking into her skirt. She saw the tip of his tongue on the edge of his lip, tasting the air. Investigating. Closer up he came, until she saw how his scale-skin shimmered in moonlight, silver-black, and till she felt his heartbeat – two thuds, two more. He threaded her bloodied fingers through his.

'You must come with,' he said. 'We must go now. I must show you.'

Cal pulled her hand, leading her from the pine trees, pointing out a path. Moss dug her heels in.

'What are you doing, Cal?'

Sudden-fast, Cal placed his palm across her mouth. 'He will hear.' Cal looked back to the hut, sweat on his lip, his fingers tight-painful on her cheeks.

He will take you. In a storm. He will take you from me.

Pa's words in her head . . . in the flowers' song. His warning about Cal.

114

And now Cal's hand firm across her mouth. His other hand firm around hers. She raised eyebrows at him.

'Pa has secrets,' he hissed. 'I have the look-see to prove. You must come, must trust.'

He glanced over his shoulder again, still holding her tight. But Moss bit his fingers. He took his hand away fast, and she glared.

'Stop it, Cal! You're getting crazy-whirred as him! I'm not just going because you say!'

That made him step back, made his eyes dart. She tasted his salt-skin on her lips.

Then, very faint, the ground trembled. It was so soft-soft at first, Moss did not full feel it. Though it built steady till its shake made her look up.

No smoke, though. Not like there was sometimes when the volcano rumbled proper. But there was trembling there, still – in the ground, in their skin. Again it came. And again. Like the island had shivers.

Cal stepped from her further. 'Another sign you come with?'

From camp, she heard Aster whinnying. She turned to see, and Cal spat on the ground beside her.

Pa staggered out from the hut, sure roused by the shudder too.

'If you do not come now,' Cal whispered, 'the Pa will stop you.'

Still, she pulled back. 'Stop forcing me!'

It was too late for leaving, anyway. Pa had seen them. What was Cal even thinking? As Pa stumbled towards them – unsteady as a newborn pup – she saw how wide his eyes were, his pupils like pebblestones. He must have taken all the flowers she had left on the bed.

'Come,' Cal said again, quieter.

115

But, like this, she could not leave Pa. And Cal knew it right sure.

When Pa arrived, he took her wrists. His eyes went wider when he saw the bloodied smalls in the waistband of her skirt. His eyes darted to Cal.

'What did you do?' Pa's voice was dangerous-low, his eyes narrowing.

'Cal did nothing!' Anger swirled in her chest. Why did he always think Cal was to blame?

Wind picked up around them, stirring and gathering where she stood. It whooshed towards Pa, clawing his hair. Again, she felt flower-buzz inside her, a little like how it'd felt when she'd pulled the storm across the sea.

Pa stepped towards Cal. 'You were always trouble. Ever since you arrived!'

Even in the dark, Moss saw the gold-glinting anger in Cal's eyes, the unspoken hiss on his lips.

'No, Pa,' Moss said. 'Cal didn't do this. I think I'm sick like you.'

Pa hesitated. The real Pa was there – Moss saw him – inside this sick-fevered man. There was a battle going on to listen to him, though.

'Sickness?' Pa shook his head. He drew a line in the sand in front of Moss, separating her from Cal. 'You do not take her,' he said to him. 'You do not hurt her.'

Pa was frowning deep, trembling. Sickening and maddening.

'Come with,' Cal said again, urging Moss with fire-eyes.

Cal looked so strong now and angry. Like this, Cal could hurt Pa – hit him back. Did he want to?

Again, the ground shivered. But when Pa stumbled, it was Cal who caught him.

116

'I know what you hide,' Cal said.

Pa turned, pulling away, shaking as if the storm were full inside him. 'You know nothing. You never have!'

Part of her hated Pa now, how he'd changed and sickened and had made them all go splinter-weak. But she still felt the clamp of Cal's hand over her mouth, too.

Cal looked at her steady, eyes glinting in moonlight. *Come with, come with.* So clear what those eyes were meaning.

But instead, when he opened his mouth, he said soft:

'I know a way off the island.'

ACT THREE. SCENE TEN.

Lightning started, glowing the trees. Moss strained to see Cal's figure hunching away. When the sky flashed, she saw him weaving and dodging the storm. What had he meant ... *a way off the island*?

That land out there? Another vision?

Pa grabbed her wrists, splayed open her bloodied hands. He pulled her down towards him. 'Cal hurt you, it is true, Moss?'

When Moss looked down at her hands, she saw that blood had dried dark in the crevices of her fingernails. But it wasn't Cal who had done this! She shook her head. Though when she looked back at Pa's glaze-fevered eyes, it didn't feel like she had his sickness either. She snatched her hands back.

Blood.

Like how Adder had sometimes.

Jess too.

And now – stupid-slow – she understood. She clenched her fingers to fists, growling. 'Course it hadn't been sickness like Pa's!

'What I've got's natural, Pa,' she said, sighing. *Realizing.*

He blinked at her, waiting.

118

In the books in the cave, she'd read about females bleeding. She'd seen it happen with the dogs growing up. Blood meant she was growing too, could be mating. This blood was not to be worried about. Why hadn't she realized it before? And why had it come now, besides? Why not earlier?

'No, Moss.' Pa shook his head. 'That wasn't meant to happen; you weren't meant to bleed like this, not now . . .'

She pushed herself across the sand, up on to her feet again. He knew what she was talking about! But then, why . . .? She stepped away from him.

Pa been wrong.

Pa got secrets.

Was this one of them?

But Cal had secrets too.

Or maybe neither of them had anything. Just visions. Just sickness. But *this*, her blood, that was real.

Again, Pa shook his head. 'You weren't meant to get sick, Moss. Not ever.'

'It's not sickness, Pa!'

'No.' He bowed his head slow-weary. 'But I asked the flowers so you wouldn't get bleeding. You weren't meant to grow, not so quick, not yet.'

She paused. Her working out of it was right – this were her natural bleeding – she knew it. But Pa was talking parrot-sense! She bent over him – wondering – her words coming through her teeth.

'Did you stop what was natural in me with flower-magic?'

He did not answer.

She felt in his pockets, found fresh-picked stormflowers, and tossed them to the wind. When he went to stop her, she said, 'No more, Pa!'

'They make me well!'

'I don't think they do any more. I don't think they make any of us well!'

Moss could see stormflowers in how he stared at her, in how he looked slight to the sides of her face rather than direct in her eyes. She remembered how the Experiment had made her skull-storm sick, too; had given visions. She remembered the angry man in the cave and in the ocean.

The wind got firmer. Soon, thunder joined it. Somewhere, a branch fell. The island sounded like it was breaking. Once, Pa would have gone up to his cave and made a mixture to calm this weather. And once, he had asked the flowers to stop her bleeding. To keep her as a Small Thing. She could've slapped his face!

Moss turned and walked. She did not go back, even when Pa coughed so hard it was like he'd lose all breath. Leaves rained down, and creatures screamed. Maybe she should find Cal, find the truth in what he said. But now what she wanted true-most was space from them both.

Moss pulled her coverings tight-close and walked the narrow cliff path, taking the way that ran next to, though lower than, the path that led to Pa's cave. She watched the moon make writhing monsters from the waves, not horse-shaped this time. She thought of the creatures trying to shelter under that thrashing water, hiding deep in the reef. Wondered about floodwaters coming for them all.

She climbed down to the smaller path that led to the warm pools. Here, she had a view direct to the ocean. The tide was racing in, clawing at rocks. If Pa didn't move off the beach soon . . . She squinted to find him: too dark. Sure-certain he'd get back to his bed without her help?

She didn't care!

She swallowed the guilt, bending to stroke Adder, who was skidding and skittering on wet rocks close behind. She held her arm out for Adder to lean against as she climbed down a sure slippery bit.

'You be safe,' Moss warned.

Adder licked her hand. The dog would not fall.

'Promise me?'

Adder gave another lick.

'Daft thing.'

This movement felt good, this stretching of muscles. She thought of the blood, still leaking from her, maybe staining the skin at the top of her thighs. Adder was shivering. The warm pools would be good for them both. In the water, she could think. She could make a plan.

Secrets . . . secrets . . .

That word on the wind again. That glimpse of more in Cal's eyes.

On the smooth ledge below, Moss dropped to all fours, crawled spiderlike across wet stone. Ahead, she saw that most of the rock around the pools was covered in seawater from the storm.

'Stick close, Adder.'

It would only take one big swell and they could both be pulled from rocks this slick. She reached out to grab her dog by the scruff. When a stone bounce-bounced along the rock ledge and over the edge and Adder barked, Moss grabbed her tighter. Her dog would not follow, not without Moss coming too. With her free hand,

Moss pinched hard the base of her dog's tail to remind her of where they were.

'Do not lose your mind.'

They skidded together across the rock platform until blood was scraped from Moss's knees and palms. Quick-fast, she checked the caves. Cal could've come here – it was somewhere they used to come as Small Things, after all. But there was no sign. She sheltered, crouched at the entrance to the biggest cave. The winds howled back. So where was Cal hiding? Where was this secret way off?

She watched the pool, smoking with heat. They'd wait out the storm; watch the waves settle and the thunder rumble away. Moss had watched many storms from that pool. And she needed to swim, be submerged. That the water was churning dark and angry fit even better.

She stripped in a small hollow where the cliff overhung the pool and rock ledge, placing her coverings where it was driest. The waves crashed so hard against the rocks beneath her that spray even hit her bare body. Final-sure, like Adder, she began to shiver. Quick-fast, Adder pushed past Moss to barrel in, splashing and yelping. The dog looked back, expectant.

'All right, I'm hurrying.'

Moss jumped. She knew from experience that the pool was deepest on the side nearest her: deep enough to gasp for air when she came up from touching the bottom. But the water was cooler than usual – the storm deluge spoiling it. She paddled like Adder did. Soon, she felt a bubbling rumble: more movement from the volcano.

She pointed her toes, moved her legs in circles to spin. She was a fish now, and her dog spun beside her. Two fish together. Moss flipped to her back. There was rain on her cheeks, shocking-cold on her pool-warmed skin. She watched the storming sky, how the lightning jags made it look purple, then copper-gold. The colours of Cal's bruised eye. And even though she felt mad-angry with him, she wished he could feel this warm water too. If he were here, she'd make him stop talking in riddles. Make him curl around her.

She swam.

With the cramps stretched out, her belly didn't hurt. Was she bleeding into the water, making food for the fish? Perhaps new stormflowers already sprouted on the earth where she'd bled before.

Following Adder, she put her head under the surface, opened her eyes. She heard tiny snaps from the sparkle-fish, hiding from the storm, saw them swimming in Adder's wake. Down here, Moss couldn't hear the crash of water hitting rock. Instead was a soft, still darkness. She dived deeper, keeping her eyes on the sparkle-fish. She'd never been able to catch them, and she and Cal had tried for days one sunny season. They were too quick, too bright, too impossible to see clear. Even Pa couldn't explain them.

'Phosphorescence, maybe,' he'd said.

But when Moss had looked up *phosphorescence* in Pa's Oxford Dictionary and had seen that it was another word for light, she knew that was wrong. These things were alive, fish and light in one. Adder swam in circles, and the sparkle-fish followed behind, giving the dog a golden glow.

Moss came up to the surface, breathed. She swished her arms through the water and the sparkle-fish followed. Adder tried biting at the golden cape they made, swallowed water instead. Moss spun again, so caught up in the sparkle-fish, she forgot about the storm. Forgot about her bleeding. Even about Cal or Pa.

Then a huge crack of lightning jolted her back, and the fish disappeared. Moss saw the island lit up. The beach glowed bone-white. For a moment, she could see right out across the ocean: all the way to the horizon.

And there was something out there. For a flash there was.

She frowned. Something dark and big. Out on the waves. Lit up by lightning and then gone. Flickering.

Cal's land? Or smaller than that? A raft? Something else? It had looked like it was moving. *Maybe.*

She kept hold of Adder and waited for lightning to flash again. But, quick as a tail flick, a cold sea fog was rolling in, smothering the storm and what view she still had. Moss swam for the side, her dog trailing behind. Soon, the island would be blind – at least until the fog rolled away.

Moss crawled out of the pool, every part of her straining for sounds. She went fast to the edge of the rock, as far as she dared with the fog.

'Stay,' Moss commanded Adder.

Moss looked out to the dark, gripping tight to the rock. *Splish-splash* . . . very faint. Like the sound of someone swimming? She shook her head. She was hearing things now!

But, still, could it be Pa out there, riled up from the flowers and swimming in storms? Or what if Cal had seen that shadow-shape and tried to raft to it? It could be his land, after all. She crawled forward until her legs were dangling over the edge. One tiny tip and she'd be the one in the waves.

What was it, out there?

'Cal?' she shouted. 'Pa?'

But only her own small voice came back.

* INTERVAL *

ACT FOUR
WINTER

The Scene: An Island

Several Days Previous

ACT FOUR. SCENE ONE.

Finn pushed hair from his eyes, tried to see. Stumbling as the boat spun, he lurched to the side. There were cracks and smashes in the dark. Things breaking. Stuff coming loose. Quickly, he moved up on deck and rain lashed at him immediately, pounding his face.

Where was Tommy? What the hell was going on?

Winches were undoing; he heard the whirring of lines as they escaped. A life jacket skidded past him.

'Tommy!'

Wind roared back. It tried to pull him, screeching like an animal. But he had to keep hold, couldn't let go. Rain was driving at him sideways now. And he was so wet. Freezing! Slipping!

He wedged his foot against the mast as everything tipped. Heavy, wet sails thudded against him. Now the cold sea was close, just below his shoulder. Roaring and black. Taking their stuff, swallowing it. Almost taking him.

Had it taken Tommy already?

He clung on tight. Spun.

Hell was here.

ACT FOUR. SCENE TWO.

Dawn was coming; light snuck above the horizon. Soon Moss would see what had been out there last night. She set water to boil. When they were Small Things, Cal and her had stored cooking pots and coverings in these caves and played homes with them; she was glad of that now. A brew of stormflowers may soothe her paining. But when she went to add the petals she'd just picked, she paused, hand hovering.

I don't think they make any of us well. She'd said that last night, hadn't she? And here she was, still trying them.

Instead, Moss hitched up her skirt. Less blood today. She lay one of the downy gull feathers she'd been searching for earlier on top of her smalls. She felt better already, more in control. Waiting outside the cave, she watched the sea turn from black to silver-grey.

Still no land.

She'd imagined it, then, last night – that shape, or whatever, out there. Another vision, just a trick of the sea fog. Now, in this delicate sunlight, that storm seemed impossible. Maybe she'd dreamt up Cal leaving, too. And Pa's Blackness? Maybe everything was just as it used to be.

130

Soon the sunlight pierced her in a thousand different places. She took the plain water – over-boiling now – from the fire and sipped it, sticking her burnt tongue out into the breeze after. This sunlight was praise-soft. Moss clicked to her dog, who was soaking in the heat outside the cave, white tummy pointing up. She looked like how the stormflowers soaked in rain, spreading her haunches wide. One of her eyes slit open.

'Come on,' Moss told her. 'We're going to see what's what.' Just because she couldn't see anything out there didn't mean nothing had storm-washed in! 'There'll be treasure,' she tempted.

Moss would *just know* – wouldn't she? – if Cal or Pa had been out on the waves? If anything had happened . . .

Clicking for Adder again, she climbed down the narrow cliff path and turned for the cove. It was hotter, so sunny, the island's weather on its best behaviour after its tantrum the night before. Following a big storm, it always felt like the island was holding its breath, waiting to see how much trouble it was in. On another morning, Moss might've laughed at this weather, might've let the breeze take her skirt as she ran. But Cal was gone. Pa was full-strange and getting sicker. And something had been in the waves.

Down from the cliff, she saw just how much the wild tide had washed in. Over near the rocks at the edge of the cove, where she'd been sitting with Cal those nights earlier, the sand was littered thick with seaweed and treasure. And the air was strong with the stench of dead things.

ACT FOUR. SCENE THREE.

Finn didn't open his eyes, not yet. He'd sleep a little longer.

He listened for Mum to start clunking things around downstairs, making breakfast. Toast and eggs. He'd smell that soon. Coffee!

He rolled over, reaching for Sebastian. But his dog wasn't there.

Grit, though. Heat. *That* was. But no blankets, nothing around him at all. And sweetness in his mouth. Like honey? Or like the ganja Tommy brought to parties? Was he passed out on some random couch? He heard water too. A shower running?

He licked his lips. The grit was sand.

Sand?

Slowly, he opened his eyes.

This wasn't a party.

He wasn't at home.

Everything was bright, too white. He still smelt that ganja smell. But it wasn't a couch he was lying on. And there was no shower running.

He turned his head and saw it: ocean! He was on a beach? It was gorgeous, one that could advertise honeymoons. There were even tiny, bright flowers, all over the sand and blowing in a light breeze. They were dancing, swishing their petals just for him. Like a million colourful hula dancers right before his eyes!

He'd never been to a beach like this, not even in an entire year of sailing. Those flowers, for one thing . . . that smell . . .

Slowly, he dug his fingers into the sand and pushed himself up. His head pounded and his throat ached. He needed fresh water.

A small cove. He saw that. Curved like a mouth, with teeth-like rocks at its edge. It had swallowed him.

And there was a horse here too. A few feet away. Watching him. *Seriously?*

He squinted at it. From where he lay, it looked huge and very white. Too white. Shining.

He was dreaming this! Had to be. When he blinked again, the horse blurred out of focus . . . came back. It made a soft whickering noise like it was laughing at him.

He slumped back down. Shut his eyes and felt his body sway. Again, he heard the flap of sails against the wind. The creak of the mast. His boat.

You'll never make it through the Pacific. Not with just the two of you.

Dad's voice. Was he here too?

He had a crazy image of his dad swaying like a hula girl, brightly coloured like the flowers in the sand.

Where was Tommy?

Again, he tried to drag himself up. Tried to see. But his head pounded, pushed him down. And the sand was so deep and soft. It welcomed him back. Wrapped him up. He couldn't . . . quite . . .

And he was swaying, swaying, swaying . . .

. . . going deeper. Following tiny lights. Diving to where it was quiet. No cracking or smashing.

To where it was cooler.

Green.

There, on the bottom of the ocean, Tommy was making a fire, waiting for Finn to join. Finn just had to swim down deep enough to find him.

ACT FOUR. SCENE FOUR.

Moss found Pa out front, crouched before the fire. He didn't look up, just kept poking at whatever he'd just burnt.

'Pa!' Moss said. 'I was worried you'd gone swimming in the storm!'

Pa looked at her, glassy-eyed, still not out of Blackness. Jess came over, whining for food and Adder licked her snout. Moss put tea on to brew for Pa, found scraps for Jess. But not stormflowers, not for any of them.

'Did you see anything out there last night?' she said.

'Floods,' he murmured. 'They're what's coming now. Only floods.'

Moss stared at him. 'But I saw something.'

Pa's eyes narrowed. 'Nothing out there, Moss.'

Then Moss realized what he'd been poking in the flames. There were words. Printed words. She read: *City. Lost. Drowned hopes.* The book she'd tidied up the other night in the cave, the 'classic'.

'You're burning your storybooks now?'

'The island needs them more . . .'

Moss frowned. Sudden-fast, she did not want to be anywhere near Pa. Not when he was like this. He made salt-tears prick her eyes, scared her.

She turned for the cove, Adder at her heels. Needing to see the treasure proper. Needing to get away.

On the wet sand were storm-blown crabs and bloated gillyfish. So many smashed-up shells. There was seaweed in armfuls, enough to keep their hut thatched for many moons. Each new object she saw was, for a moment, her fishboy.

'*Callan?*'

She whispered his name to the sea. Asked it.

Where was he? Where had he gone last night?

She saw his body bobbing in the waves, saw him shore-washed. But when she looked a second time, it was only a gull bobbing, or a wasted puffer fish on the sand. She walked further along the tideline. A jellyfish still pulsated with poison.

No Cal.

Moss breathed out. This cove was where things washed up first. If Cal wasn't here, that meant he was all right, didn't it? Wouldn't she feel it, bone-deep, if he weren't?

But what had it been last night in the waves? *Who?*

In seaweed further along was something buried. She hurried to get there, then bent to dig it out. Not Cal, but . . . a piece of wood, almost as long as her forearm. Red as lobsters. Storm treasure from the rest of the world! There were markings on one side of it. Letters? She traced them with her fingertips:

I M

She turned the wood. Or should they be *W I*?

She brought it to her nose to smell, even held it to her ear to hear

136

if it had stories. Who had touched this last, where had it been?

Half running now, she went further along the beach. There she found another piece, smaller but also lobster red. She took that piece, too, carried them both to a patch of seaweed and piled them there. This was good treasure to come back for. She ran along the tideline, searching for more, then shielded her eyes to look up towards the stream.

That's when she saw him. Farther up and flat-out on the sand.

Cal?

No. Not the same coverings. Not the same shape.

She backed up, turning for the hut. Then made herself stop and stand. She would not keep running back to Pa, not any more! Whatever – *who*ever – this storm treasure was, it was hers. Adder barked – one high, sharp, warning call – and the figure did not even move. Was it dead? Another vision?

She thought of how Cal and Aster had arrived – after a storm, after Pa had done the Experiment and she'd been desperate for something to change. Was it possible – she could hardly think it – possible she'd done this? Had the Experiment the other day even worked? Maybe the flowers hadn't got rid of flood water but brought in another spirit instead, just like Pa had done that day long past. She walked closer, Adder coming too.

Crusty yellow hair fell across his closed eyes. Scratches were all over his pale, pinkish skin, and his coverings were stiff-hard from salt. A bloodied deep gash was in his leg. He smelt sort of . . . stale. As if he had been turned over many times in salt water and had been crisping in the sun ever since. He did not smell like Cal, did not look like Cal, either. He was more like Pa. If it weren't that Adder's eyes were also locked on him, Moss might have thought she'd imagined this strange new creature.

This . . . spirit?

This . . . man?

This storm-woke gift.

But was he dead? He looked both drowned and sun-dried at once.

Moss leant closer. Drawing a quick breath, she prodded him hard in the stomach.

ACT FOUR. SCENE FIVE.

Someone was staring down at him. Not Tommy. Not a horse this time. A girl.

A real, live one.

Where had she come from?

Finn closed and opened his eyes. But she didn't fade away. He tried to focus on her dark, wild hair and green, green eyes. Eyes like a rainforest. He could drink those eyes. She was saying something, but his ears felt thick – too thick – and he couldn't understand.

Blinking, he waited for her to stop spinning. Her hair sprang around her face like a black halo, and there were tiny braids in parts of it, unwinding as he looked. There were petals in those braids. Like gemstones. Like the flowers in the sand.

This was a dream. Girls who looked like this weren't real. Here was an angel. He'd died . . . drowned! One of the dancing flowers had come to life!

That storm . . .

Those waves . . .

His eyes closed. When he opened them again, she was still there. She bent closer, studying him like he was a bug. She smelt sweet, like the ganja smell he'd had earlier. And there was a . . . dog . . . too. Nothing like his Sebastian. This one was feral-looking, all teeth and slobber and with a big, square head.

That, at least, didn't seem like a dream.

'How did you get here?' the girl said.

This time he heard the words and understood them. He wanted to ask the same of her. Wanted to ask where *here* was. But his head was pounding him, splitting him.

'Perhaps you can't speak?' she said.

He tried to open his mouth, form sentences, but it seemed like he was only made of salt and snot, and nothing came out. She was watching his face so intently he worried she might prod an inquiring finger right into it, straight into one of his eyes. Instead, she leant even closer and pulled his shirt collar from his neck. When he flinched away, she held him firm.

'Stay,' she growled, almost like she were talking to her dog.

Up close, she smelt even sweeter. Again, he blinked and tried to focus. Maybe he was hallucinating. Maybe this was really Tommy leaning over him.

'Water,' he said, blinking hard. 'Tommy, man, don't be an ass, water . . .'

He tried to say that, anyway. He wasn't sure how it came out. A bundle of strange sounds. Like an animal. And Tommy didn't come into focus. It was just . . . her. Finn tried to move backwards, tried to see. He needed to work this out – where Tommy was, who she was. But the girl held him tightly.

'Shhhhh,' she murmured. 'Shhhhh.'

She brushed her fingertips – so lightly – over his skin. Then she leant over him again, until her nose was almost touching his neck, and she . . . smelt him. Finn was so surprised he didn't even back off. He watched her from the corners of his eyes. Slowly, she breathed him in, starting at his ear and moving to his shoulder. The dog even joined in with a sniff of its own. When Finn jerked away then, the dog licked his forehead.

'You don't smell like fish,' she said. 'Not much of the sea about you. Not like Cal.'

He blinked. Her dog's slobber smelt like fish, that was for sure. Again, he tried to speak. Again, he made a *murrr-murrr* sound.

'Shhhhhhh,' she said again. 'Words will come. And I'm good at teaching stray creatures,' she sat back on her heels, still observing, 'if that is what you are. When did you come out from the sea?'

Come out? Surely there were more important questions right now . . . such as, where was he? Why? Where was Tommy and his boat? Again, he tried to ask.

She leant forward and touched his cheek, her fingers so light and gentle. 'Shhhhhh, shhhhhh,' she went, and she sounded like calm waves on sand. 'Don't try.'

His eyelids were so heavy, and that hot, sweet air was everywhere, filling his nostrils, making him dizzy.

When he shut his eyes, he saw Tommy again. Grasping the mast. Spinning the rudder.

We've hit a reef!

But there's nothing on the charts! Nothing's meant to be here!

I'm telling you, we've hit a reef! There's land!

Finn's breath caught and he coughed. Hard. He winced, curling towards the sand. Kept coughing. Couldn't get any air! His chest tightened until darkness swam before his eyes. Clawing at him. Wanting him. He fought its hold.

Why hadn't Tommy washed up too?

He coughed and coughed. No air! Gasping loud, he gripped at the sand.

He heard the girl somewhere, talking to him, soothing. Then he heard her voice go further away. He coughed. Now he was falling, sinking back into those waves . . . into that deep, dark cold.

Then her fingers returned, sticking something under his nose, telling him to sniff. An intense sweetness shot into his brain, like the sweetness from before but with added strength. He could breathe!

'Only sniff once,' she said. 'That's enough.'

Then her hand was gone. He was breathing fine. But his nose was tickling like he'd inhaled a whole pine forest and he was buzzing like she'd given him drugs.

ACT FOUR. SCENE SIX.

'Strange,' Moss murmured.

The flowers had worked that time, exactly as they always used to . . . full-strong. She'd seen it right enough, the way this boy had been fading and losing breath, and how he'd snapped back with a sniff.

She gave him the shellful of water she'd fetched, too. He drank greedy like the dogs did, not even pausing for breath. She snatched it away before he could have too much.

'You need to get out of the sun,' she told him. 'I'll help.'

He shook his head, still struggling, still looking for the water. But she tipped the rest to the sand. When he widened his bluebird eyes at how the sand drank it up, she added, 'You'll be salt-starved if you have too much of that . . . you don't want that as well as storm-woke!'

Grabbing his elbow, she supported him. He wasn't so heavy as Cal, but had more substance than Pa. His fingers grasping around her shoulder were starfish-cold and thin, red from the sun. There were flies swarming around the gash in his leg. She waited till his breath went regular and he was proper secure before she stepped away and left him wobble-tall. He gurgled more sounds, and she shushed him.

So, what was he . . . spirit or human? If he were spirit, made by stormflowers, she'd be the first person he'd seen, just like she'd been for her fishboy, Cal.

Could she even dare to believe he was . . . human?

'You will burn berry-red if you stay here,' she told him, prodding him to walk.

He kept looking around at the cove, squinting and stumbling. He wasn't webbed or scale-shone like Cal, and he was so much paler. He looked like the men in Pa's storybooks, like the Princes from the fairy tales. Again, he coughed hard, and Moss smacked him on the back. His eyes widened once more. They were strange, bright-coloured eyes – bluer than Pa's, bluer than the reef water in sunshine.

'I'm Moss,' she said slow, pointing to herself. As Pa had once taught her to do, she drew her own four letters into the sand. 'M-O-S-S. *Moss*. Can you walk?'

He didn't answer. She remembered how long it had taken her to teach Cal his words – how many seasons it had been before he had spoken like them.

He took a step, wincing when his gashed-up leg took some of his weight. She balanced him when he wobbled like a fresh-hatched chick. She remembered Cal on this beach that first day, how he had been shivering too.

What would Cal think of this new creature?

'*Here*,' she whispered on the winds to him. '*Come see. Come see this treasure.*'

Only the sea whispered back.

'Go slow like this and you'll be parched-out before we get anywhere,' she told the spirit-boy. 'You'll be salted sandfish by midday.'

She heard him dry-swallow. Before he took another step, his eyes roamed over her, as if he were reading her in the same way Pa read the storybooks. Full-curious. There was intelligence in him, right enough. Could she dare to think what that meant? She pointed to the rocks at the edge of the cove, where the path went up towards their hut.

'Rest there.'

Slow-careful, they moved across the sand. After he'd rested, she'd take him to the hut. There, if Pa were well enough, he'd heal his bleeding leg. Maybe this spirit-boy's arrival could be enough to snap Pa from Blackness. Maybe then Pa would make sense of him.

When Moss heard the spirit-boy's breathing go gasping again, she explained. 'The island air is thick from flowers . . . makes it hard to breathe deep.'

She remembered explaining this to Cal. She thought she could even remember Pa explaining it to her, once. Back then, in those early times, parts of the island had remained fuzzy for a good long while, colours blurring into each other before they'd crystallized. Her hearing had been stranger then, too: noises had swum in and out of her head, startling her.

She looked again at the spirit-boy. Could he hear the buzz from the opened flowers? Could he see clear the island colours? He was frowning hard as if to try, and his head was turning, searching, turning . . .

'Breathing gets easier,' she said. She watched his blue-bright eyes as they flickered and focused.

Limping the final few steps, he stumbled against a rock. While he rested, she touched the gash on his leg; perhaps she should stem it now with raw stormflowers. But he needed deep sleep. And besides, Pa was always better at healing.

She felt a light tapping on her shoulder, the spirit-man's fingers brushing against her. When she looked up, his eyes were more alert, watching her. Soft-slow, he raised his fingers to his chest and pushed his thumb into it.

'Finn,' he said, quiet and concentrating. 'My name is Finn.'

Moss stumbled back so fast that she tripped over Adder. She stared at him. His voice was soft and round, thick with salt and fatigue. But it had made words, clear enough. Though it was nothing at all like Cal's voice. More like Pa's. *Hers.*

'How can you do that?' she said.

'Do . . . what?'

'Do *talking*. Who taught you?'

He frowned, swallowing.

'Everyone knows talking,' he said, soft. The crusted corner of one side of his mouth curled up. 'You can do it too.'

Was he trying to make a joke, teasing her?

'But you're a spirit . . . aren't you?' She didn't look at him as she spoke, didn't dare to hope.

'And you're a loon.'

A loon? Now she frowned. There was no reason to call her a bawdy seabird.

His mouth twitched. It seemed like he might want to smile but was too tired to make it stick. He wiped a hand over his face, pushing his yellow hair away. Moss saw bruises on his neck and salt in the cracks around his eyes. There was a dried bloody scratch under

146

his left ear. He stared at a patch of orange stormflowers.

'I'm still on Earth, right?' he asked.

'Where else would you be?'

He shrugged. 'A dream? This place, it's . . .' He glanced back out to the sea and the reef.

'It's real enough.' She put her hand out so he could feel it. 'I'm real.'

But looking at his expression, she wasn't sure he believed it. Everything inside Moss screamed a million questions – she wanted to make him speak and speak until he had no breath left.

Are you human?

Have you come from the rest of the world?

How bad are the floods?

How did you get here?

But she was struck shy too. She wanted all his answers, sure, but she also just wanted to tend the gash in his leg and let him speak in his own time. She wanted Pa, or Cal, to see him so she would know that he was really there. *Real.* Not another vision.

He looked back at her like he was wondering the same thing.

There was that flicker of a smile again, before the spirit-man lurched forward to fondle Adder's ears, and Moss stiffened because he did not ask first. But Adder thudded her tail, happy enough. The spirit-man found the dip between Adder's forehead and snout and, just as Moss liked to, stroked her there. Adder wagged harder, her mouth wide and tongue lolling.

'Not as fierce as he looks,' he said.

'*She*,' Moss corrected him. '*She* is called Adder. And she is fierce.'

She thought of the hundred times that her dog had bitten heads and tails from lizards, had fought brutal with the wild dogs . . . had eaten her littermates. Her dog was the fiercest thing she knew. When she looked back, the spirit-man's mouth was curling sideways.

''Course she is.' He coughed again – hard – then went gasping.

'We should get you to camp.'

But when she went to take his shoulder to pull him up again, he stopped her, shaking his head.

'Not leaving until I've found him.'

'Found who?'

'Tommy.' He sucked at air till he could speak again. 'He's washed up too, I hope he is. He was with me . . .'

She stared at him. 'There are more of you?'

Finn nodded. 'Tommy.'

Moss squinted, shielding her eyes to look across the cove. 'Where?'

Finn tried to stand, tried to move back the way they'd come. 'I think our boat wrecked. It's . . . hard to remember.' He went zigzagging and stumbling, like Pa in storm-fever. The gash on his leg was turning black with flies.

'Your name is really Finn?' she said, chasing after him. 'Like the side of a fish?'

But if he really were a spirit, she should be the one asking – no, *giving* him – his name. Like they had for Aster and Cal.

'Short for Finnegan,' he said, looking towards the pine trees. 'Nothing to do with fish. Might sound weird coming from a sailor, but I actually hate fish.'

Sailor?

She watched him sure-careful. ''Tis more like a song – *Fin-ne-gan*.' She gave the word three notes, as if she were singing it to open the

148

stormflowers. She turned to watch them too, to see if any opened wider, to see if any closed tight.

'Not a song, not a fish, just a name.' He shrugged. 'My mother is old-fashioned and nerdy.'

Mother?

Finn squinted as he looked out to sea. 'How did we get *here*?'

She stepped closer to him. 'Last night,' she said, hesitant. 'In the storm. I thought I . . .' She moved her head, indicating out beyond the reef. 'Was that you?' She swallowed, steadied her breath. 'Do you have a . . . boat?'

Finn closed the distance between them fast, gripping her shoulder with sudden strength. 'What happened to it? And Tommy, did you see him too?'

Panic was in the wideness of his eyes, in his sharp-furtive movements. She remembered the pieces of lobster-red wood. Of course! She led him to where she'd piled them.

'Found these before I found you,' she said, showing him.

Finn sank into the sand, cradling the wood in his lap. '*Swift*,' he murmured. 'My boat.'

'What I saw last night?'

He nodded, hands shaking. He looked across the sand to the sea.

She watched him careful, trying to work him out. Was it possible he was what they'd been waiting for? A sign from the rest of the world? One Pa couldn't argue with? Was it possible he had a boat too, and there were more just like him?

Soon, she couldn't help a smile. She watched the apple in Finn's throat bob down, so fragile. So *human*. Sort of beautiful.

'Not a spirit,' she whispered. 'Really real . . . Come to us from across the horizon line?'

Finn blinked at her, did not answer. But Moss didn't mind. The answer he might give was almost too wondrous for words, too strange . . . too impossible. After all these years . . . all those flowers Pa had sent out on the winds! Even just the thought of Finn being something other than spirit made her buzz inside, made her crawl up close to inspect him more careful. Made her smell him again and press firm his skin. Made her pluck his yellow hair and twirl it 'tween her fingers.

'A real, live human boy,' she whispered. 'And I found you. Perhaps you will be the one who brings Pa back from sickness. Who brings us all back.'

ACT FOUR. SCENE SEVEN.

C al went careful down from the rocks where he'd slept, listening for the hiss-hiss-scrape of them lizards and sniffing for their stenchings. They were close – there was stench enough. Would do no good to meet one. Them lizards were tricksy with only hands and feet to fight them; Cal had claw scratchings as proof. Them lizards would not forget the catching he'd done of their brothers and sisters, the eating of them, too. If Moss's Birthday Surprise were not so down-deep in these rocks, he would not put himself so close.

His feet grasped the rocks quiet-quiet. On toe-tips, he passed burrows where those reptiles curled. He smelt them stronger then. Their stench tanged his nose like air round the volcano did: sharp-thick. He licked his lips and brought the smell into his mouth. This close up and it was all rotten meat and salt. He hissed to get rid of it. Careful-careful, he picked hands and feet down.

Almost.

There.

Almost...

He moved 'cross grey rocks, thinking of the surprise deep in their belly – Moss should be seeing that. But Moss did not right-trust him. Had not followed. He pressed his toes hard against rock, growled quiet-quiet. Without Moss, he was deep-hollow too.

Cal spider-climbed down and down. Here, on this side of the island, he saw the land again. There – flickering – at the sides of his eyes. Maybe here Moss could see it too.

Western Beach was full of storm treasure; Cal would be treasure-rich before sundown. Pa and Moss were stupid never to search here. And all 'cause of a few reptiles in rock?

No!

Was not reptiles that kept the Pa away.

Cal stretched full-tall. Felt freedom in his spine. He held his hands out, made fists. He would've hurt the Pa last night – wanted to. He shook his head from the memory and loped to the middle of the beach. There, he sifted quick-fast through strange new things that glinted when sun came through clouds. There was rope, and he tied strands of it around his waist. There was so much wood. He dragged some of it to the dunes, piled it there.

The sun hurt his brain, sent painings from the sides of his eyes and down his spine, bone by bone. He heard them bones creaking and hissing, whining. Them bones would still like to be sleeping. All of himself would like to be that. But, the treasure! Think of that. Think of the surprise in the grey rock and what he might need for it.

He dropped on all fours to the still-damp sand, smelling. Treasure had all sorts of stench. The smell he got first was the damp reek of wood, then something slippery-stale and clogged with salt water. That was . . . what? He sniffed hard, made sure. Yes! Something still living. A fish. Big one. Maybe a whale. He'd hurry for it before lizards got its wind. Cal could save a whale if it were not too gone – he and Moss saved dolphins before – he'd send it back out swimming. P'raps if he whispered soft enough, it'd carry him out to the land.

Though if it were a shark instead . . .

He might eat shark. Might give some to Moss. She'd cook it up spicy-good, crisp its skin like drying leaves. If she were here and trusting . . . if she had chose Cal's thinking 'stead of Pa's. But Cal would not even give blubber meat to Pa. Not even a grubworm! Was not fair, what he said. Not fair he said Cal hurt Moss. He'd never!

It was Pa doing the hurting! And not just 'gainst Moss, neither.

He got closer to the stench – to the thing that was living but not by much. He sniffed his way ahead, seeing how it was not the right shape for a whale or shark, not even big enough for a dolphin. It did not smell of any fishy he knew, and it were tangled in coverings.

He had a bad picture in his brain then – right-bad. He saw Moss there, underneath – her face bloated and dried firm with salt. P'raps she had followed him last night. P'raps he'd not waited to see. P'raps that storm – or even the Pa – had sent her to the waves. He hissed quiet. Again, he shook his head. He would not think it. Moss was safe. He would feel it in his bones if she were not.

His fingers now with trembles, he took the edge of the coverings and lifted. Slow, slow, until . . .

'Eeeeeeeeeeeeeee!'

The noise came through his mouth before he could stop it. He dropped the coverings again quick-fast.

This were no fish.

ACT FOUR. SCENE EIGHT.

'**Y**ou can touch me, you know,' Finn said, watching the girl. 'I'm not going to disappear.'

From the other side of the fire, Moss stared back like she didn't believe him. When she didn't say anything, Finn crawled a little closer, first dislodging the dog. He winced at the pain in his leg.

'I'm really not, I promise. I'm not a ghost. Or a . . . spirit? Isn't that what you called me before?' He smiled, waited for her to return it, but she just kept looking at him really intensely.

It was so strange, the way this girl was being with him. It reminded Finn of a documentary they'd been made to watch at school, something about first contact with tribes in Papua New Guinea. A handheld camera had documented tribe members running in fear from the filmmakers, some covering their eyes. He remembered, too, how others had only stood and stared in amazement.

It'd been like this with the other one, too – that 'Pa'. He'd stood and stared at Finn almost like he'd never seen another person in his life! He'd even dropped the book he carried and ran back into the hut.

'A spirit, Moss – that's what it is!'

'He's a boy, Pa.' That's what she'd replied. 'A real, live human boy! He's come from the Old World.'

And then the man – that Pa – had cried. *Really* cried. Finn had heard it through the rough-cut walls of the hut – a grating, desperate wail.

What did it all mean?

Finn shifted uncomfortably as he tried to get his head together. Who were these people? They seemed sort of nuts. But they had helped him too. His leg no longer throbbed so bad, at least.

When he reached over to stroke her dog, Moss's eyes were back on his, still so curious. Back home, girls never looked at him like that. If Tommy were there, he would have laughed about it.

Tommy!

Finn tried remembering how he'd got here from that gorgeous beach – if he'd noticed any sign of Tommy along the way. The only clue was just more of the *Swift*, pieces of wood splintered across the sand. Perhaps wherever the rest of his boat had washed up was where Tommy was, too. Perhaps they were both all right. Battered, but . . .

Maybe.

When his head stopped spinning, he'd ask Moss how big this island was, where the places were to shelter. He'd make her help.

'How's your leg?' Moss said, jolting him back.

She looked at him for approval before her cool fingers were peeling back the dressing of the colourful flowers, checking the wound. Remarkably, it had stopped bleeding, was hardly hurting at all. But if he tried to stand on it again, the pain would come as a sharp stab. He'd tried it once already, when they'd first arrived at this strange camp. He'd been trying to leave while she'd been trying to make him stay.

'I need to find my friend!' he'd said.

'You need to be still!'

She'd made him some sort of herbal tea, and the Pa man had come back out of the hut to help. He had dressed the wound, whispering and murmuring, almost as if he were speaking spells over it. Then that Pa man had plastered more flowers on top. He was like some kind of tribal medicine man, a witch doctor, maybe.

After this, Finn had slept, his mind strange. He didn't know for how long. He wondered now . . . had they drugged him? Again, he shifted uncomfortably. His head felt heavy enough to drop right off his shoulders. Like this, could he even get to Tommy? Where would he start?

Moss made a kind of clicking noise behind her teeth as she prodded and pushed at the wound. She peeled away the flower petals slowly and cast them aside. She didn't look like someone who would drug anyone. Actually, if anyone looked drugged, it was that Pa character. Maybe Finn had somehow stumbled across some New Age hippie commune – he'd heard about those things happening on the islands around Thailand and Laos; he'd seen *The Beach* and all those *Survivor* shows. But Moss was clear-eyed and serious.

'You'll be able to walk proper again come morning,' she said.

He moved from her fingers. 'But I need to search for my friend now.'

'Wait till morning.'

'I need to know if he's alive.'

'Morning, I said!'

They glared at each other.

156

How could she, this stranger, tell him what was most important? Tommy could be suffering. He could be wounded, needing his help. Finn ran a hand over his eyes. Or maybe . . . maybe Tommy was already out searching for Finn? It'd be just like Tommy to be back on his feet, sorting out the mess they'd got themselves into. Though Finn also knew Tommy could just as easily be kicking back at a bar, ordering up the local booze – if there was even anything like a bar in this place. Somehow, Finn was beginning to doubt it. He tried to imagine Tommy drinking a tequila cocktail here, a coloured paper umbrella sticking out of his glass: couldn't.

When he looked back, Moss was still watching him. 'This island is different at night. Believe it.' She said the words softly enough, but there was iron firmness to them.

Finn remembered those thousands of colourful flowers, and the big white horse that had watched him on the beach. This island seemed different enough by day. This girl in front of him, and the raving man in the hut . . . they seemed different enough too.

'Listen,' she said. 'If your friend is sensible, if he has shelter and a little warmth, the island will be kind. There'll be no more storms tonight, and tomorrow will be calmer still. We can look for him then.'

'I want to search *now*.' He tried to stand and, again, felt that stabbing twinge.

'You've set healing back!' She tutted as she reached for the flower petals, his wound bleeding again. Finn sighed. Like this, he wouldn't even get back to the beach he'd washed up on, let alone anywhere else.

'You go looking for me, then,' he said to Moss. 'Please? He could be dying!'

'In morning I'll go. I have things to search for too.'

There was no convincing her.

Finn looked away, back towards the ocean, which was calmer than a swimming pool now. There was still enough light to get a good search in.

Why couldn't that useless Pa go look for Tommy? He wasn't doing anything, far as Finn could see, except for lying about in that hut and crying like a child.

'Will be dark soon,' she added. 'Will be cold. Trust. We'll set a poultice on this tonight, and you'll be good come morning.'

After she'd rewrapped his leg, she turned away to where the fire had gone low. Now that she'd said it, Finn could feel the cooler, late-afternoon air, getting under his shirt and wrapping around his stomach. Could feel it plucking the hairs on his neck.

And Finn could feel another coldness inside him now, too, growing darkly. That feeling got colder when he looked back at that water. When he saw the sharp, rocky points jutting out of it. When he thought about the last time he'd seen Tommy.

Tommy on the mast, taming the sails. Tommy with a wave the size of a building behind him. How could Tommy have survived it?

How had Finn?

Finn, at least, was a strong swimmer. But Tommy? For all his bravado as a sailor, he could hardly manage a doggy paddle. What were the chances of him even being alive?

Again, Finn tried his leg. And again, Moss growled at him. He was mad at himself, for sleeping so long, mad at his stupid bloody leg, mad for being so confused. A part of him knew he couldn't help having a concussion, and a part of him knew he'd never forgive himself for it. Not in ever bloody ever!

He jumped when he felt Moss's fingers on his arm.

'We'll look in the morning,' she said again. 'First light. Promise. And I'll look for Cal besides.'

The tightness in his throat wouldn't let him speak back, not even to ask about who Cal was. She'd mentioned him a few times now.

When he looked back at the sea, he was shocked at how the sky had changed: where it had been blue before, it was now turning orange as a traffic cone. Like many of the islands they'd been to this past year, sunsets happened fast here. So, where was he?

Finn shook his head, wiped his eyes. He wouldn't let himself crumple. Not in front of this girl. Not when he didn't know anything for certain. Tommy was resourceful, if not exactly sensible, usually much more so than Finn. Maybe he was kicking back with his own pretty island girl, flirting shamelessly.

Moss poked at the fire, then got on to hands and knees and blew hard at its base. Light flickered brightly. Finn watched sparks fly into the darkness, dance around them. He winced. Those sparks reminded him of the house lights on the opposite hills of his home-town – of all the times he'd sat on the bench outside his house and looked across the valley, watching those hundreds of lights blink on and wondering who they belonged to. He'd been younger then, and stupider – he'd wanted to find a place where no house lights existed at all. As he looked now at the burning orange sky above that dark ocean, he guessed he finally had.

Tommy had sat on that bench with him, plenty of times, looking at those lights.

'I can take the *Swift*, and we both know how to sail,' Finn had said. 'What's the rush in going to university straight away anyway?'

Finn had convinced him. 'A life-changing adventure,' he'd said. 'A coming-of-age tale. Our very own story!' Like he'd been quoting some novel. Like he was some sort of pompous, well-read fool! But all that seemed a long time ago and very far away.

Wood popped in the fire, made him flinch. Moss swore something filthy-sounding under her breath, and poked at the fire until more sparks flew up. The dog came over and rested its wide-boned head on Finn's knee.

There had been sparks of light, too, down under the ocean, like tiny bright fish. Finn had followed them. Had Tommy seen them as well, followed them to safety? Moss took a piece of flint from the edge of the fire and started scraping it against an ancient-looking fork to make another spark. Her dog barked and snapped at the light, but Moss found flames quickly.

'You're good at that,' Finn said.

She shrugged. She came back to sit on one of the big stones beside the fire, near him. 'Not as good as Cal.'

Finn wondered if this Cal dude was anything as crazy as the Pa man, and whether he'd be coming back anytime soon. Perhaps Cal could help him look for Tommy. He was about to ask when he saw how deeply Moss was frowning at him, like he'd just committed some horrible social faux pas. But before he could ask what he'd done, she said, 'You're different from how I thought.'

'You're different from everyone,' he replied immediately.

It was true. She was sort of gorgeous, but strange and wild-looking too. She said things that made him wonder what her life was really like. One day he'd tell stories in pubs about this girl. That was, if he ever got home to any pubs to tell them in. If he ever lived past this island. If he ever found his friend. He felt the tightness start in his throat again and looked back to the darkening sea.

'Did you mean what you said before,' he said fast, 'about never seeing a boy?'

It'd sounded like a throwaway line, back when she'd been explaining why that man Pa's reaction to him had been so strange. Perhaps he hadn't remembered her words right, not with how he'd felt so hazy. When he looked back at her now, he was expecting a laugh, but she didn't even smile.

'Not a boy I remember,' she said. 'Only Cal. Only boys in story-books. In dreams.'

He smiled. 'Weird.'

He didn't know what else to say. If Tommy were here, no doubt he'd make some joke about this – about being the boy of this girl's dreams.

'I've always wanted to be a dream boy,' he murmured, trying to picture Tommy beside the fire, slurping back that herbal-tasting tea and enjoying himself like he always did in strange situations.

Moss was still frowning at him. He didn't blame her. He ran a hand through his hair. It was this place, making him act like a moron. It was not knowing where he was or what was happening. Not knowing what had happened to Tommy.

'Pa's a boy, I s'pose,' she added. 'Was once.'

Finn waited for her to finally explain who Pa was, but instead Moss leant forward and placed her hand against his arm. Her fingers were warm as she twirled one of his arm hairs.

'Gold,' she said. 'You're all golden.'

He stared at her. 'And you're seriously strange. Do you even know how strange you are?'

But he smiled. Because in this moment, she was the one who

161

looked golden, whose skin in the setting sun glinted like shined chestnuts.

Her hand moved down his arm, investigating his fingers, making him tingle. 'You don't shuck many oysters, do you?'

Again, he wished Tommy were there. *I would*, he could imagine his friend saying, complete with his best charming smile, *I would for you.*

'Not much call for oysters in my house,' Finn said instead, moving his arm away when his skin felt too ticklish. 'Takeout pizza's more our thing. Indian, on a good night. My parents work too much to cook.'

Finally, if only to stop her frowning at him, Finn asked about Cal. She smiled a little then, and Finn wondered if Cal was her boyfriend.

'He's like the black sea bass,' she said, 'but he is a shining thing. A boy like you, but with stars for eyes.'

Finn listened to how the fire cracked. Should he feel jealous of a boy with stars for eyes but who also looked like a fish?

She pressed his arm, more urgency in her stare. 'He wasn't in the water, was he? Not last night, in the waves?' She explained how Cal should be with them now, how she was worried. 'He's not come back, not proper, for days.'

Finn shook his head. 'Never seen anyone like that,' he said truthfully. He wanted to add, *How have you?*

She slumped. 'Cal must be settled in the island, then, hidden deep.'

She spoke so strangely – almost old-fashioned – her words were like something Finn might read in a book. He wanted to pluck her arm hairs so he'd feel she was real too. He watched her roll grass between her fingers, easily weaving it into a small rope.

'I think you must tell me a many-lot of things,' she said, soft, 'many truths.'

'Me tell you?' He'd thought it'd be the other way around. 'About what, exactly? What do you want to know?'

'Everything.' She looked at him in quick glances, like how a bird might look at a worm it wanted to eat. 'You need to tell me . . . umm . . . about where you are from and how you got here. About what happened in the sea and to your boat. Tell me right now while Pa is sleeping.'

And, slowly, he did. With the night setting in and his leg still hurting, there was nothing else he could do, anyway. Besides, he also wanted to know about her, and this place . . . that Pa and Cal. Maybe she'd talk if he got her confidence up first. He told her about the many months he and Tommy had sailed around the world, and about some of the things they'd seen.

'Sharks big as houses round the coast of South Africa . . . cheap drinks in Cuba . . . and the Cayman Islands are gorgeous . . .'

He explained how they hadn't been expecting land for days, not proper land, anyway.

'Maybe a rock outcrop or two,' he said. 'Not an entire island like this!'

More hesitantly, he told her of the storm that had arrived from nowhere.

'It took my boat,' he said. 'My father's boat, actually. We . . . wrecked. Is there a reef or something, hidden rocks? It was all so . . . weird!'

'You're not the first boat to wreck here.' She looked away as she spoke, dropped the wound grass rope and found a stick instead,

163

poking it in the fire.

'Why, who else has come?'

Perhaps there were other people on this island; perhaps Tommy had found them!

'Just us.' She shrugged. 'Just us for as long as I can remember.'

'Just you? Seriously, you and the Pa guy? The only ones?'

She shrugged, turning away. 'Pa's better to tell that story,' she said, 'how we got here. I don't really remember.'

'Wait.' He leant forward. 'This island isn't your home?'

She shrugged. 'We came on our boat, before the floods hit proper.' Abruptly, she turned back to him. 'But what about where *you* live? What's that like?'

'Well, OK . . .' He sighed as he watched her, wanting more. But again he reasoned it – if he started speaking, maybe she might too. 'It's just an average town, I guess, where I live. It's old, it's got a big, smelly river and a weird, ugly church and lots of other buildings . . . it's down in the southwest of England. Nothing special. Like most of the towns there, really. Couple of pubs, cafes, even a small cinema . . .'

He watched her mouthing some of his words, repeating them for herself. It was so odd, the way she reacted to him; it made him shut up entirely.

'Pa said everyone died,' she whispered. 'Or nearly everyone. He said all the towns were gone.' Her voice was so soft, as if she were talking only to the fire. 'He said the waters swallowed them,' she added. 'Said only the flowers would bring them back.' Finn had to look closely to see her serious expression and make sure he'd really heard her words correctly.

'Flowers? What do you mean?' he said. 'And who's everyone?

Died . . . *how?*'

Again, Finn wondered about that Pa in the hut. Perhaps he should shake the strange man awake right now and get his take. But he also wasn't sure he wanted to spend the night so close to someone who could be truly crazy.

'Pa said the floods got almost everyone,' Moss said. 'Dark floods swept the rest of the world away.'

'What . . . floods?'

She looked at him, eyes big. 'The ones that rose when we left our home, of course. We got away, were lucky. Perhaps you were too?'

Finn reached into his memory, into everything he could recall learning about the world in geography and history class. 'How long ago was this?'

She frowned. 'Ten years. Maybe. That's what Pa said once, anyway. That's the date in his scrapbook. Don't really know. The thick air here . . .' She shrugged. 'It's hard to remember . . . You've felt how the flowers are, the air . . . you know . . .'

But he didn't know, not at all. Big floods? Everyone dying? What was she talking about?

'Where, exactly, was this flooding?'

'Everywhere!'

Finn looked at her light brown skin, at the frizzy corkscrew curls of her dark brown hair, trying to work her out. She could have come from any number of places he and Tommy had passed through. Hell, she could be from anywhere at all! Australia had bad floods once, didn't it? He vaguely remembered a news report about floods that'd swept crocodiles into houses and left people stranded on roofs. But she didn't sound Australian. She didn't sound . . . anything. Only like herself. Only unique. Though that Pa had an

English accent, didn't he? But there'd been no floods like she talked of in England!

'The water flooded everything!' she added. 'Everywhere! Buildings, trains, cities . . . all swept away.' Her voice shook, and she did not look at him now. 'This is what Pa told me. It's in Pa's book.'

She turned the stick sideways, using it as a hook to retrieve a charred feather from the coals. Was she certifiable too? Perhaps this island had made her and the Pa man mad? Her fingers trembled against the stick. Maybe he should feel sorry for her. Because . . . what, exactly, had she been told? Was it possible that someone could be so entirely sheltered on this strange island so as not to know anything? To think the whole world apart from here had . . . disappeared?

She pulled a small package wrapped in leaves through the coals towards her and left it to cool away from the flames. Perhaps it was drugs – maybe this was why she was speaking all this weird shit to him.

'You're from the rest of the world, aren't you?' she said slowly, almost as if she were talking to a three-year-old instead of him.

Finn chewed his lip. 'Not sure.'

'Well . . . you know things like trains and governments and libraries and schools?'

He stared at her. 'Sure.'

'But you don't remember the storms? The floods?'

He shook his head. 'Not any like you say.'

She raised her eyebrows. 'Tides swelling, temperatures rising, ice melting, global warming and the selfish people who used too much . . .?'

When he didn't say anything, she sighed again. 'Perhaps the

166

floods didn't get everywhere?' Cautiously, she added, 'Or perhaps Pa's Experiment even . . . worked? Maybe the waters went down true-fast and none of it actually . . .'

Before she could go any further with her crazy questions, he reached across, took her shaking hands from the stick and held them in his.

'I don't know of any floods like that,' he said. 'Anywhere. Maybe you had some floods once, a long time ago, and that's why you sailed here, but the rest of the world didn't get them. I didn't even hear about them!'

She looked away. Gently, he warmed her hands, rubbing his palms over hers.

'I don't know what you've been told,' he added, 'but the rest of the world is fine. I've just come from it; I've *seen* most of it this past year. No apocalypse! A few bad people doing a few bad things, sure, but nothing like you say.'

She wrenched her fingers back to the stick, which she used to deftly remove the leaves from the cooling package. Spices steamed out underneath.

'The world is not fine,' she whispered. 'It . . . can't be.'

Finn forced his hazy mind to think. 'Well . . . some day something like what you're talking about might well happen. I mean, with global warming and floods. But, Moss,' he said gently, 'right now, the rest of the world does *exist*.'

'I know it exists,' she said crossly, 'but it doesn't exist like you say.'

She went back to unwrapping whatever food was in that package. Finn's stomach growled to get at it.

'Why would I lie?' He rolled his eyes in frustration – why should he have to defend himself to a stranger! Why even talk about this nonsense when Tommy was still out there, maybe needing him?

'How many humans are there, then?' she asked.

'You mean . . . in the world?'

'Of course *in the world*!'

She dug out a shell from the package of leaves and bounced it on her palm to cool it. A snail? He'd eaten snails before, liked them. Especially with garlic butter.

'About seven billion,' he said. 'Though I doubt they counted you in the last census, so perhaps there are more.'

'Billion?' She crawled back from him fast, dropping the shell. 'No, not *billion*!'

'Geography was my best subject!' He raised his palms in protest. 'Least I thought it was. Until I ended up on an island that doesn't exist!' He grabbed the shell, unable to resist any more. 'This for me?'

He dug his finger into the snail shell, but its fleshy inside burnt him and he dropped it again. Moss grabbed it and dug out the flesh in one easy movement of her thumb. She held it out on her palm, challenge in her eyes.

'Sea snail,' she said. 'Don't they have them where you come from? Don't any of those seven billion eat sea snails like us? Or is that too strange for you?'

He looked around – at the orange sky, at the thousands of tiny flowers that were still out even though it was getting dark and there was no sun to warm them any more. He thought of the raving Englishman who believed the world had flooded and had told this girl that, too. He thought of that spooky white horse on the beach. This was easily the strangest place he'd ever been. He bounced the snail, considering.

'I've eaten sea snails,' he said, though less confident than he meant as he studied it closer.

She waited. He swallowed it.

The taste was pure salt; the texture, sand in a jelly pot. He tried not to cough when it got stuck in his throat.

'Mmm,' he said, eyes watering.

She surprised him by grinning. Then she crawled towards him, opened up one of his hands, and placed another hot, fleshy snail on his palm. 'But that one wasn't done yet!'

Finn smiled cautiously back. 'Believe me, you're far stranger than where I come from. *This place* is far stranger.'

She pressed at his palm. 'This is a really good one,' she said. 'Salty and fresh. Trust.'

So, with her smile so pretty and with his stomach now rumbling, he ate another.

ACT FOUR. SCENE NINE.

Cal dragged the fish-that-were-no-fish across Lizard Rocks – it were too heavy for a right fishy, not slimy-cold enough, it had hairs vivid-bright as stormflowers, and a million sunspots. It was bloating-sick. Not full there.

Cal stopped to get breath back, placed it to the rock – they couldn't stay here, not with the sun about to drop. He lifted its coverings and prodded it . . . this *human*-fish. It did not whisper back. But Cal did not think it'd given up its living yet. Maybe it were just deep-dreaming sick. Like how the Pa got.

He put his ear to it – this human-fish had breathing yet. Had hope. Cal lifted and hung it 'cross his back, leant forward to balance. He would make it safe and warm. He'd been washed on to this island too once, after all.

He picked web-toes careful over sharp rocks and past lizard dens – still sleeping and snore-shuffling – towards tunnels deep. He paused to shift heaviness, waited to hear its breathings again. So fragile. Could Cal push his own breath into it, make its chest rise up? Not yet, not here. Here were night breezes, things scuttling-loud, flowers opening and singing.

He could ask flowers for healing for the human-fish? Already flowers were turning, pointing their egg-yolk centres to Cal like eyes. He put the human-fish down to see them right. One was calling loud!

He bent to that flower, easing fingers into still-warm soil. He finger-dipped down till he found flower roots. There, he held them like he would like to hold Moss's fingers, and those roots tingled and tangled. He could pull the flower slow-careful from the ground and hold her in palms. Could bring his head close and touch tongue to her. *Taste*. She might be sweet-good. He could also take her purple petals and smoke them. Like that, this flower might wake human-fish. Might heal. Might put thoughts into human-fish's mind.

He bent closer.

'*Dreamings.*'

Cal thought he heard.

'*Water.*'

And . . . softer . . . maybe . . .

'*Stories.*'

This flower might turn the human-fish into something like Pa, too. Put those thoughts in.

Cal let go. Her roots twisted like tiny octopus legs to find earth again. He brushed dirt to cover her. He would not use flowers for healing. Not this time. But he would give something back.

Careful-quick, Cal was on four limbs; this time he went down, down, down, to the slapping ocean. All the way till he leant from rock to water. There, he scooped sea, holding palms together, using webbings to cup cool saltiness. He carried it back.

A slithering of tail into rock – he saw! Quick as an eye-blink. He

171

paused to sniff, but night air was too fierce for strong reptile scent. He waited, squinting in the dark. Nothing else came.

As he sprinkled water on the flower, her head bobbed. He felt her song around him.

'*Salty-fresh! Taste-y!*'

She was watching him, yolk-bright. Did she want him to taste her too? Or did she want to be inside the human-fish instead?

'What is it you're wanting?' he murmured.

Again, he looked to find the Flicker-land. Saw it – there for one flicker-moment! *Real.*

But as he turned, he saw the lizard was back too, on the rock behind him. It was watching, air-licking, not letting Cal pass. Cal waited, Pa's tales about fierce lizards strong in his brain. Least it were not full-grown. Cal could fight it, sure, though he would do better if Adder were here. He drew his lips back over his teeth and hissed. Lizard hissed back. Cal thought it were sniffing for the human-fish. But its hard, small eyes turned to the flower instead. It were wondering, thinking, wondering . . .

'I don't take,' Cal said. 'I leave be.'

Lizard hissed again. Did it want Cal to take the flower after all? Eat it?

Cal did what Moss would do – he thought to the creature, wonderful-kindnesses right inside of its brain. And it turned its fat, solid head to the side, considering, wondering.

The purple flower sang louder; Cal tasted the sweetness of her song, felt its sway. Darting its tongue out, the lizard tasted it too, bobbed its head in rhythm. After one more look to Cal, it went to the flower. Cal felt the reptile's tongue dart against his leg, spike-sharp as it passed. It settled with eyes closing next to the flower. No fierceness to this lizard now, not like how the Pa had warned of in fire-tales.

Still, quick-fast, Cal lifted the human-fish, shifting it 'cross his shoulders. He moved away into the wide, dark passage inside Lizard Rocks.

He knew the way easy, had practice – earlier, he'd wound seaweed and tied it to rock sides to guide him through twistings and turnings. He went by feel, knowing the rock beneath would be dry, then wet again, before he was there.

Soon, he was in the cave. Where he'd already laid fire.

Cal smelt it – Moss's Birthday Surprise, that secret – even if it were so far below. It were like rust and salt, like deep-down-deep.

'Soon,' he whispered.

He thought of Moss's face as she'd see. Would she smile?

Soon . . . soon . . .

Cal lowered the human-fish next to the fire. With coverings he'd taken from Western Beach, he folded the human-fish in tight, like how otters fold their Small Things in kelp. Secure-like. Safe. He lit the fire.

In firelight, Cal saw that the human-fish's skin was grey, saw how his breath came faster and lighter than flutterby wings. How he faded deep. Cal muttered to keep the fire steady and strong. P'raps the human-fish would not last if Cal went to fetch Moss. P'raps all he could do was make it warm. Stay close. Wait.

Gentle-soft, Cal dabbed water to the human-fish's forehead. 'Not be scared,' he whispered. Because that were what Moss had said to him, back in early days. Because her words had made him warm.

He tried to make the human-fish take water. He did, a little.

When he coughed, Cal rubbed the smooth skin across his chest. Then the human-fish's eyes flickered open. Cal saw them go wide when he saw Cal staring down.

'Do not worry,' Cal said. 'I'll get you strong.'

And the human-fish – this whole new boy lying below! – nodded. A smile went breeze-swift 'cross his lips.

'Dreaming,' he said, looking at Cal. '. . . so beautiful.'

And Cal did not know if this were a sort of thank-you, or a word about him.

ACT FOUR. SCENE TEN.

Moss woke. The fire was gone and it was shock-cold, even though Adder was tight at her side. Quick-fast, Moss looked across the firepit. Finn was still there.

Real.

She hadn't dreamt him.

He was curled like a seedpod, perfect-like. She went across and touched his face gentle-soft. This boy. *Finnegan.* Proof that the rest of the world was there and safe. Not flooded. That Pa and his scrapbook were wrong.

She hovered her finger over his nose and cheeks, noticing his pale freckles for the first time. She could trace them and make a picture, draw islands in a sea. She looked over his neck and sinew-strong shoulders, over his long, thin arms. He looked . . . like Pa. She stared harder. With his fair skin and hair, Finn could have been Pa's child.

'What's it really like?' she whispered.

Last night Finn said he'd sailed his boat around the rest of the world – said he'd been to at least sixty countries. She tried to imagine it, piecing together bits from the storybooks with the stuff

Finn had told her.

Seven billion people. Dry land. So many different animals and plants. So many stories!

She brushed fingertips over Finn's yellow hair, then checked the poultice on his leg. Still he didn't stir, not even when she removed the flowers to let his healing skin breathe. Those flowers had made him sleepy as a puppy. Unable to wait any longer, she pulled her coverings tight and clicked to Adder.

She felt Aster watching before she saw her. Ghost-quiet in the trees, the horse's gaze moved between Moss and the sea. Moss saw dents in the earth from where she'd pawed her hooves. 'What is it that you really want?' she murmured to her. When Aster lowered her head, Moss placed her hand against her soft coat. 'Can you see the other land out there? Have you known about it all this time?'

The horse whickered, and her ears twitched towards a noise only she could hear. A yes, then. Maybe it was. Or maybe she was just listening to the flowers.

With Adder chasing her heels, Moss went to the cove. The new morning was still starlit. Only a slit of pink, low in the sky, the glittering sea ahead. Behind her, pine trees murmured and sent smells of growing. Even the stormflowers were quieter. It only added to her feeling about what she was about to see. She stood at water's edge with toes in, looking with the corners of her eyes. Exact same as Cal had shown her. And . . . yes . . . it was there! Like she'd known it would be.

Cal's land.

It seemed right to see it again, now that Finn had arrived.

She squinted at its far shadow – it didn't look so big after all. It was low to the sea, shaped like a skimming stone. But she'd seen it!

She ran fast to tell Finn and Pa.

But before she got to the hut, she heard singing.

Pa?

It skidded her short.

'Our packet is the Island Lass,
Lowlands, lowlands, lowlands, low . . .
There's a laddie howlin' at the main topmast,
Lowlands, lowlands, lowlands, low . . .'

One of the songs he used to sing, back when he was happy most time. Was he healed, flipped out from Blackness? Washed better by the storm? Or, maybe, made happy by Finn's arrival? She heard Pa's two-note bird trill next, calling to open the stormflowers. Then she heard flower-song – those high notes on the wind.

She walked closer. Pa was dancing, flinging his arms before him in the lanky heron-bird way that always used to make her laugh . . . back when they'd dance any time they wanted, night or day or in rain or sun. But this time, he wasn't dancing for her. Instead, Finn was sitting up, watching . . . smiling! Moss frowned. Yesterday, Finn had seemed almost scared of Pa.

Moss squinted at something in Finn's hand. A scallop shell? Pa had given him stormflower-water? But Finn's leg was healed; he did not need any more flowers! Unless . . . Pa was telling his stories? That was why he was up and cheerful! Already, she smelt flower scent. But why had Pa made today a story day? Why for Finn?

She strained over the flower-song to hear his words and, yes, she caught tales.

'. . . the island's been here for all time,' Pa was saying, 'but it only ever has true-magic when there are dreamers here too. Then the flowers open!'

When Pa saw her, he threw his arms wide.

'Moss-bird! Will you come and hear stories? I could get my book?'

His smile was so wide and his mood so high that a part of her would've been happy to sit beside the fire and hear tale after tale, to cuddle in against Pa's chest as she used to and slip to dreaming.

'Our new spirit likes my stories!'

That stopped her tracks. She looked across at Finn, who waved and raised half his mouth to a smile.

'Not a spirit, Pa,' she said. 'Remember what he told us? He didn't come like Aster or Cal – not from the sea or from flowers.'

Pa bird-laughed. 'Well, if I didn't call this spirit in, you must have! You've been doing the Experiment without my knowing, little Moss?' He winked at her, like he knew it already.

Pa was so different this morning. Full-joyous, filled up on the buzz of the island. This was the Pa Moss liked most. But today she stayed wary.

'I've been thinking,' he said. 'Maybe flower-magic is leaving me and coming to you instead . . . maybe soon you'll control the magic of this place, stop the floods and heal the world of its dark. Would you like that?'

'There are no floods, Pa,' she said, looking to Finn to confirm it. 'Not so much darkness as you think.'

But now Finn was grinning at the stormflowers Pa had opened, reaching to touch their petals and then laughing at how they shied away. When he looked up at the trees, he gasped at flowers opening there, too. Pa threw stormflowers on the fire and the air went heavier with their smoking scent; she saw Finn's eyelids go heavy.

'What are you doing, Pa?'

'Breakfast?' Pa wiggled his eyebrows like they were furry cater-pillars, like he used to do to make her laugh. When he pointed to a pot of mussels boiling in flower-water, she shook her head.

'Don't worry, Moss,' he said. 'We've a new spirit, is all – it's what all these recent storms have been leading to, all this recent strangeness.'

She looked across to the 'new spirit'. He certainly seemed happy enough. Now he was laughing at how sunlight danced between his fingers as if playing a game.

'He's not a spirit,' she said again.

'He came from the sea, didn't he?'

'In coverings and shoes! In a boat!'

'And where is that now?' Pa shrugged. But Moss saw doubt – there, for a moment, flashing across his face. It confirmed her own thinking.

'He's a human boy,' Moss said. 'He told you and me yesterday. He had a shipwreck, like we did. The flowers didn't form him from ocean.' She came towards him, stomp-angry. Why was Pa not listening to anything she'd said? He never listened! 'The rest of the world is fine,' she repeated. 'Not gone!'

Now her words came bitter and throat-pinching. And – yes! – there was true-sad now on Pa's face as she spoke them. Perhaps it had finally landed – the knowing that they'd been waiting on this island for nothing!

'And Cal's land is there again,' she added. 'I saw it.'

She spoke softer, not meeting Pa's eyes. She couldn't. She felt strange-guilty, like she was the one in the wrong. Ruining Pa's stories.

179

Nothing as it seems . . . secrets, secrets . . .

Pa sighed deep. 'Show me, then, Moss. If Cal's true, I'll believe him. You know it.'

She turned back to the sea, urging him to stand. She pointed. 'You have to squint and look from the sides of your eyes.'

But she couldn't see it now either – nothing at all. She moved a little from the fire – but still, nothing. Where had it gone? She turned side-on and tried to see like that. No! She could kick-kick the fire over in frustration! How had it gone again?

She pressed at Finn's shoulder. 'Can you see land there?'

Finn frowned as if remembering something. 'There's not meant to be land . . .'

She gripped him. 'True? You neither?'

But she knew it already: Finn was drowsing-dreamy, smiling like he might be half sleeping already. Stupid flowers!

'Maybe if we go closer,' she said. 'Before, I didn't see it until I was almost at tide's edge.'

But when she led them down to the sand, there was still no land. Just water. Just as before.

'Nothing there, Moss,' Pa said. 'But I understand how you'd want to believe Cal, 'course you would!' Pa put his arm around her to lead her back.

She gritted her teeth. She had seen it; this time she'd been sure!

'Maybe sometimes what we want to believe seems more true than what's there,' Pa suggested.

She looked away. He hugged her, tried to. She smelt the smoke and sweetness in his beard, was not settled by it.

What was going on? How could something keep going in and out of sight? And what did that mean about there not being any floods?

Back at camp, Pa led her to the fire and sat her next to Finn. When he took her hand and placed it inside Finn's, she let him: Finn's hands were warmer than hers, anyway. She felt strange-warmer still when Finn smiled.

'This place is crazy,' he whispered, plucking a petal from her hair. 'You, him – *crazy!*' Though he was laughing-sweet as he said it.

Perhaps he was right. He didn't seem too worried about finding his friend any more, either. Had he even remembered? Like Pa, he'd been flower-struck. It made the unease in Moss's stomach grow.

From beneath his coverings, Pa pulled out one of the few plastic bottles they had. Inside was gold-green and sparkling: flower-water. Pa's eyes were storm-drunk, too.

'Moss, all those flowers I ate were not for nothing,' he said. 'Can't you see? Another spirit has arrived – one just for you this time!' She frowned as Pa sat close to her other side. 'Just listen, Moss,' he continued. 'I've a theory – I've been thinking it makes sense why your bleeding came now, too . . .'

'Pa—'

'Just listen! This spirit – this *Finn* – maybe he's meant to be your mate: the companion you'll stay with when I am gone! Maybe you called him in, just like I called in Aster . . . It's your time, Moss, your dreams taking over . . .'

She looked at how Finn was grinning-goofy at Pa. Though his expression changed a little as Pa's words sank in – not so keen about being her dream, then.

'You said once it was Cal I called in, Pa.' She hardened her words. 'Which is it?'

Pa shook his head, impatient. 'Cal was just an accident. He was never meant to come like Aster. But Finn . . .'

Pa cupped her cheeks, his fingers hot as volcano stones. 'Moss – we'll bring spirits to us. Instead of leaving, we'll create a new world here, like we thought would happen after Aster came.' He looked at Finn. 'Only we'll create it together this time. With all the different kinds of spirits you would like!'

She heard hope in his words, heard the flowers sing louder. She saw petals open up like sunshine-stars around them. But these were old words, from a time that was finishing.

Pa pressed the bottle of flower liquid towards Finn. 'This'll help you, spirit-boy; it helps us all.'

Moss watched Finn turn the bottle, the colours inside changing with the movement.

'Drugs?' he asked.

Pa shook his head. 'Flowers. Completely natural. They healed me. My mind was hurting before I got here; they changed it. Made me sing!'

Finn took one sip, then another. He gasped as he looked down. Moss saw it too. The remaining gash on his leg was sinking back into his skin, first becoming a silvery scar and then, after a few eye-blinks, nothing at all. Soon it was as if Finn had never even had a mark there.

'Not even a scar,' Finn whispered.

He held up the glinting bottle, frowning.

It was the kind of healing Pa used to do, the kind of magic Moss once adored. When she saw it, could she doubt the strength of those flowers to bring in a spirit from the sea? Doubt them to do anything?

She shook her head from the flower fug. Still, something wasn't right. She felt it deep.

'We need to go,' she said to Finn. 'Before the sun is too hot. We need to find our friends.'

She needed more answers. Different ones.

'Just share one drink,' Pa said. 'One with your old Pa before adventuring. See, Finn likes it.'

And, even if full-desperate for Finn to leave right then, she could not shift him. He was mesmerized by the bottle of flower-water, even took another sip.

Maybe, if she drank what was in that bottle too, she'd see the land proper. Pa always said the flowers showed you what you most wanted. What if what she most wanted was that land?

The green-gold liquid was buzzing-mad when Finn drank again. His head jerked back, eyes wide.

'Not too much too soon,' Pa said, taking the bottle back. 'Moderation, that's the key!'

But Pa wasn't moderate, not cautious at all!

Pa tipped the bottle towards Finn in a kind of greeting before having his own swig. He held it out for Moss. She took it from him, slow-careful. Once, she wouldn't have hesitated to drink. Now she looked inside to see pieces of petal, swirling pollen. Cal didn't like how the pollen felt inside him, said it buzzed his thinking to a different shape. Moss thought about how Pa's moods were getting worse, how he slipped to dreaming, and darkness, more often.

The bottle warmed to her touch. She saw flowers buzz and sway. She remembered how, once, the whole island seemed more full with colour than it ever was now – more alive and happy. What had happened to change it?

Then she true wondered it – what exactly did the flowers do? Draw down floods and heal people? Show islands? Or did they just make Pa more black?

She stepped towards the fire, the bottle grasped tight.

'There wasn't a flood.' As she said the words again, they felt more true.

The flower-water buzzed harder, making the bottle near-burn her skin. What did they want? To soar with the smoke, fly on the airs towards the volcano? Or did they want her to drink by the fire and dream more of Pa's stories? She watched how petals crawled up the bottle's sides as she held it out to the flames.

'Something's not true, Pa. Something you're saying's not right . . .'

Pa's mouth opened. Maybe this was the core of it, what Cal had been thinking too, what he'd warned her about. Pa's stories and secrets. *Not as they seem.*

She turned on him, throat tight. The air was syrup-sweet, but it wasn't that not letting her breathe – it was this not knowing.

Secrets . . . secrets . . .

There on the wind.

Pa shook his head, mouth gaping. There was more behind his eyes – she saw hesitation . . . again, doubt.

'There *were* floods,' he said. 'Heavy rains! That dark! Everyone said there would be more . . . and I was so sick, Moss, I had nothing. *We* had nothing. We had to leave.'

Moss heard the stormflowers, crying now. She wanted to cry with them. Because she did not remember the floods, had never remembered them. But she did remember wanting to get away . . . remembered pain in her ear . . . fear.

She reached for more, but there was nothing. *Always nothing!* The memories stopped! It was this flower-water, making her forget, making it worse.

She opened the bottle and tipped the mixture to the fire.

There! No more flowers for any of them!

Pa stumbled back. And then her vision was swirling, swirling, swirling, like the flowers above the flames. The world was tipping, *she* was tipping. Finn stood, stepped closer, placed a hand against her back.

Truth, she felt like screaming at the flowers. *Show me truth!*

She saw petals dance on the smoke. Would images come from the flames, like they had once in Pa's stories? But the petals moved away, swirling towards the trees and then forging a rainbow path towards the volcano.

Again, she could breathe.

When she turned, Pa was staring at her. The doubt she'd glimpsed before was in his eyes, with new darkness underneath.

'You think it's for nothing?' he said. 'Coming here, all this time on the island? You believe this boy over me? He doesn't even believe it himself! Look!'

Moss's breath caught. Had Pa just said *boy*, not *spirit*? Pa looked away. His fingers were like leaves in a storm, shiver-trembling as he pointed at the ocean. 'There's nothing out there,' he said again.

She risked what she'd been thinking. 'So let's go beyond the line and see.'

'*I saw*,' he whispered. 'Floods and darkness. A bad world. You don't want to be there. Trust me, Moss.'

But right now, she didn't trust him at all.

Pa bent over, shaking his head. The way he crouched reminded her of Cal's arrival on the beach so long ago. *An accident*, Pa'd called Cal. *Never meant to be here.*

But right now, Cal seemed the most true-constant. And

she wanted to see him.

Down deep, he'd said. *Hidden.*

And, quick-fast, she realized where Cal had gone! Of course Cal would go to the most dark-dangerous place, to where there could be treasure . . . where Pa wouldn't go looking.

Now when Pa left, stumbling up the path towards his cave, she didn't follow him. Now she had another place to go.

ACT FOUR. SCENE ELEVEN.

Aster snorted, but lowered her head all the same. Moss motioned for Finn to come closer.

'I can't ride a horse, if that's what you're thinking,' he said. Moss frowned. 'But you just sit there. She does the rest.' She vaulted on to Aster's back, quick as a grasshopper. Grabbing a chunk of silver mane, she leant down towards Finn. 'Take my hand. Jump!'

After a moment, he did, though he almost pulled her back off Aster into the dirt below. Moss gripped hard to steady herself as Aster danced and skittered.

'No saddle or bridle?' Finn asked, his hands clasping tight around Moss's stomach.

'What do you need anything like that for?'

'This place is so weird,' he said, a smile playing about his lips.

Was he still feeling the flower-water inside him?

Maybe, as he rode, he might feel like he was flying.

'Awesome,' he murmured, staring at the petals in the pine trees.

Again, Moss wondered it – just how different this island was from the rest of the world, how different she might be from all the other people Finn had met there. She wiggled; Finn's fingers felt too tight around her waist. If Cal had been behind her instead, he'd have gripped hard to the horse with his own legs rather than relying on her.

'Anyway, you're the strange one,' she said. 'Not knowing how to sit on a horse. There are plenty of horses in your world – I've read about them.'

'It's your world too. I didn't cross through some magical wardrobe or train platform to get here.'

A whole real, *dry* world beyond the reef? Maybe she'd have to learn to read it, like she'd learnt to read the books in the cave. But why wouldn't Pa believe in it?

'Where are we searching for Tommy first?' Finn said.

'Western Beach. If something's not washed up in our cove, then it's always there.'

It'd be where Cal was, too.

Moss whistled, and her dog bounded up the side of the horse into Moss's arms. She perched between Moss and Aster's neck, clinging with claws, making Aster's ears flick in annoyance. Moss urged Aster on. They picked their way across the cove towards the pine forest. Beyond the trees were the dunes; it'd be late morning by the time they got there. She tried to push down the worry she felt about leaving Pa alone. What would he do in his cave for so long, brooding?

When Finn's fingers lost their grip around her waist, she leant back to let Aster know to go slower. Finn lurched sideways anyway; seemed he was right about not being able to sit on a horse. She reached behind to grab him.

'How does she know what you want?' he said.

'She's not just a horse.'

Moss explained that Aster was a spirit; come from the ocean and forged from flower-magic. 'Pa wished for a companion and sent flowers to the winds,' she said. 'Aster came.'

Cal did also.

'That's what he thinks happened with you,' she added. 'That he called you in. Or I did.'

'I'm a spirit?' Finn laughed. 'Made from flowers? That makes absolutely no sense!'

She felt his breath, hot on her neck. Cal hadn't thought he was a spirit, either. She slowed Aster further.

'Aster just knows,' Moss said when Finn asked again. 'You think what you want her to do and she feels your energy.'

'Like what Pa said about the flowers? That they respond to . . . what was it . . . *desire*? That's how they got rid of the floods?'

Moss swallowed. 'You said there were no floods, remember?'

'Oh, yeah. 'Course not.' In the silence, she almost heard him thinking. 'It's a nice idea, though – magical flowers responding to people's energy. Someone could write about that – some novel, some play!'

She shrugged. Not everything on this island had only been a 'nice idea'. The flowers *did* heal; Finn's own wound, clean and closed now, was proof of that.

But why also Cal's island, coming and going? And why hadn't Pa seen it? There were as many mysteries as answers here – *more!*

After they'd been in the pine forest long enough for her eyes to see, Moss noticed the rough bark on trunks, tiny crushed pieces of shell in the sandy soil, the lazy out-of-season bumble zigzagging ahead. She listened for cracks from branches. Maybe Cal, or

Tommy, were here instead?

She spoke to keep Finn awake and fighting the heavy air and so she didn't have to think about Pa feasting alone on stormflowers.

'It takes almost two days to walk round the island,' she said. 'Less if you ride. But if you go through the middle, it's quicker. Even with the volcano.'

'Volcano?' Finn looked up. 'Is it active?'

'It smokes and rumbles sometimes. Especially when it's storming.' She remembered the other night when she'd felt the island tremble: the last time she'd seen Cal, the night that Finn came.

Finn rested his cheek against her back. 'Well, I hope it doesn't rumble while I'm here.'

'Already has.'

She swallowed. Again, she remembered the dreams and stories Pa had written in his book: about the one safe piece of land left in the world . . . an island with flowers that could heal anything, an island made of fire.

'Flower Island,' she murmured. 'What Pa calls it.'

Finn moved to prop his chin on her shoulder, where it bobbed with Aster's every step. 'Somewhere called Flower Island was definitely not on my map.'

'Pa said this place isn't on maps, though,' she said. 'Instead we had to feel it out, trust it was here.'

Moss peered at a tangle of currant bushes, saw stormflowers growing even there. Finn shook his head, and his hair tickled her skin.

'So, who is this Pa anyway?' he said.

Moss wound her fingers tighter in Aster's mane. 'What do you mean, *Who is he*?'

'Well, is he just another dude who was shipwrecked?'

'He was shipwrecked . . . with me.'

'So, he wasn't here when you came, then . . . kind of like, hiding out?'

'No,' she said. 'He came with me. Or I came with him.'

'Hmm.' Finn looked up again. 'It's just, I kind of had this idea that maybe he was a fugitive?'

'Fugitive?'

'You know, escaping something, on the run . . . a criminal!'

Moss looked at the currant bushes, the trees. 'He's Pa,' she said. 'My pa.'

Again, she could almost hear Finn thinking.

'*Your* pa?' he said eventually. 'As in, your dad? You serious?'

'Of course.'

'But . . . he looks nothing like you.'

'So?'

Finn sat up straight now; she felt his fingers shift from around her waist and settle on her shoulders. 'But you guys don't have the same skin colour. Not the same eyes, or nose . . . you don't even *act* the same. Are you adopted? And how old is he, anyway?'

She could answer that one. 'Thirty-seven years on his last birthday.'

'Seriously? Island life's not been kind to him, then. He looks way older.'

'He's sick.'

Moss watched a forest owl flap ahead of them. She thought of how dark Cal was, and how light Pa was, and how she was something in between. It wasn't the first time she had realized this, but here – in Finn's words – it was the first time it had seemed full-strange.

191

'Maybe my mum was darker.'

'You don't know?'

'I don't remember,' she said. 'Hardly anything about where we were from. Just that we came on the boat. And . . .'

She shrugged. And . . . what?

Something spicy-good.

Hiding in a dark, small place.

An angry man.

Those images from Pa's cave. Could they be memories too?

Finn sighed. 'Do those flowers make you forget?'

She shrugged. 'Sometimes.'

She didn't like this conversation, or the way it left her feeling perched and uncertain as a new-hatched kittiwake: if she took one step too far too soon, she'd fall. There'd be sharp cliffs to catch her. She peered again at currant bushes, looked again at pine trees. No fishboy hisses, no shadow-slip of a body moving through branches.

'The flowers do good things too,' Moss said, quiet. 'They made Aster come.'

'And they're pretty! So brightly coloured! If they were back home, everyone would have them. Could charge a fortune for a bouquet of them!'

As Aster weaved through the forest track, Moss told Finn how Pa'd once made the flowers glow wonder-bright just from thinking about them. 'They swayed when he passed by.' She paused, remembering how the flowers used to glow even more so, how they lit up pathways on the sand. 'It's only recent he's been going to Blackness again. Cal thinks it's the flowers changing him. I'm not sure.'

Finn was silent for a good long while. When they ducked under branches, he laid his forehead against her.

'You know,' he started, 'I can see why someone wouldn't want to leave this island. With those flowers and how pretty everything is – with how no one would know you were here. It doesn't actually matter what the rest of the world is doing when you're in a place like this. It's the perfect place to hide. If you'd done something wrong, I mean. If someone was not entirely right in the head . . .'

And again there was that swirling feeling inside her, tying her stomach up – there was something in what Finn said that she didn't want to think about. Moss pressed her legs against Aster and urged her faster. The quicker they were from the dark pines, the better. The quicker they got to the wide stretch of beach . . . found Finn's friend and boat . . . found Cal. They'd make a plan then, the four of them. Work out what to do about Pa. Decide how to get to the Flicker-land.

'Western Beach is the biggest beach,' she said chipper-quick, as much to change her own whirring thoughts as to tell Finn. 'When you were in your boat, do you remember seeing a stretch of big sand? A long point going into the sea?'

Finn shook his head.

'Any lizards?'

'*Lizards?*'

'Sometimes they swim in the water.'

'How big are these things if they're swimming?'

'Big as Pa's tall. Some of them.'

She felt Finn glancing from side to side. 'Would they hurt Tommy?'

'Not if he's smart.'

'What if he's unconscious?'

Moss kept quiet, gave Adder's ears a scratch, checked the sky:

greyer now, sure, but the wind wasn't up. Surely Pa couldn't – *wouldn't* – bring in another storm? Why should he after so long? But why eat all those stormflowers earlier either?

When they were almost out of the forest, she nudged Aster into a trot before remembering Finn couldn't cling on.

'Warn me when you're going to do that!' he huffed, gripping hard to her waist.

The trees thinned as the ground changed to dunes. Moss felt Aster's muscles strain as she started on the uphill. When was the last time Pa had taken her here? When Moss was a Small Thing, she and Pa would gallop Aster till her sides heaved and she went calmer. Moss touched her withers now, gave gentle thoughts.

Finn scooched closer behind, until Moss felt his warm chest pressed full against her back. It made her remember the way she'd slept against Cal.

At the top of the dunes, Finn looked over her shoulders, straining to see. Like Aster, his body was tense with excitement. Moss felt herself grow tense too. Perhaps they would find Finn's boat, and maybe Cal and the new human would be mending it already! Then it would only be a short while until she saw the world from the storybooks . . . the *unflooded* world. Where would they go first? Once there, would she remember this island at all?

'You'll love where I live,' Finn said, almost as if he were reading her thoughts. 'You know, you could stay with us until you got yourself sorted. Mum wouldn't mind. Just until I went to uni, at least . . . Maybe then you could even come with me. And Tommy's just down the road; you'll like him too.'

He was speaking so fast, babbling like a songbird. Strange words from a strange world.

Uni . . . come with . . . got yourself sorted . . .

A real, live mum.

Finn reached forward and grasped hold of one of her hands. Adder snuffled at his fingertips. 'I'll help you fit in with the rest of us,' he said. 'Promise I will.'

And that felt nice, his warm, soft hand on hers.

'What else would we do?' she said, daring herself to imagine it. 'Go to a library? A supermarket? I want to see dancing! Shopping!' And all the other things she had read about in books!

Finn laughed. 'All of that.'

The wind was playing with her hair and coverings, teasing them closer to the sea.

'We could go searching for your home,' he added softer. 'For your mum, even! Find out what really happened to you. If you wanted to.'

That made her feel swirling again. She heard Finn swallow.

'There must be places we could go to find out, I mean,' Finn continued. 'Maybe you were in the news. A disappearing child doesn't just, well, disappear. There must be a story.'

'I wasn't *disappearing*.'

The swirling and swirling. Her own story. A story that might be different from the one she'd always been told. What, exactly, did Finn think had happened to her? Who did he think Pa really was? And, anyway, did he not think Pa would come with them on the boat too? What else would he do?

When they were on top of the last dune and looking down on Western Beach proper, she heard Finn's breath catch.

'Now I'll believe there are unicorns,' Finn said, his head turning as if to take it all in.

It sounded like a line from a storybook, something she'd read. But after the dark forest, she supposed the beach did look like something shining. Flowers sprouted purple on this side of the island, patch-covering the beach, sending honey-violet scent their way. She could see aster-flowers too, growing among them in a slightly different purple shade. Again, she looked for the land on the horizon. Again, saw nothing.

She scanned the sand. The wide beach was torn open by the storm, and she saw quick-fast there was no boat ready to sail. There were other things, though, brought in on the waves – lumps of wood and twists of material. Perhaps that's where Finn's friend was, tangled up and needing help. Perhaps this was where Cal was too.

'We should get closer,' she said.

'Good idea.'

She was looking to pick their path down when Finn leant over Moss's shoulder and kicked Aster in the side.

'No, don't—' Moss started to say, leaning back and grabbing the horse's mane.

But it was too late. Aster took off, headstrong and lightning-fast down the dune, throwing them both forwards. Finn's fingers gripped harder around Moss's stomach, Adder scrabbling to stay steady also. Moss clung to her dog, wrapping her other hand tight in Aster's mane. She tried to send calm thoughts to make Aster slow. But Aster was wound up as a whirling-wind, pointed at the water. Moss willed the horse's twig-snap legs not to find a rabbit hole.

Quick-fast, they were down the dune and going to the ocean. When her hooves found the sea-smacked sand, Aster's speed went full-quicker. Almost too fast to breathe. But still she hadn't lost

Finn, or even Adder, off the side: Moss felt claws and fingers digging sharp into her as proof of that. Maybe they should all jump off? They might have to if Aster entered the sea. Moss heard the roar of the waves, calling them close. She tightened her legs around the horse, trying to lean back and calm her that way.

'No,' Moss whispered. 'Not time for you to be in there, Aster. Not for any of us.'

And, whether because of her thoughts or her strong embrace, the horse slowed. A little. Adder leapt off to run alongside. She tried to get in front of the horse to cut her off and round her back. She barked and barked.

'Aster-spirit, easy, soothe yourself.' Moss murmured the words over and over. She leant forward over the horse's neck and whispered in her ears. 'Stay with us. Walk now. Easy. Not yet to the sea . . .'

Aster slowed a little more.

Finn gasped, his breath back in a rush. Moss felt the tension in Aster stretch out further. Moss couldn't turn her from the ocean yet, but she would. She just had to keep the horse calm and listening.

Slower now, the horse went, till she was cantering again, then trotting, then in a walk. Moss unwound her grip from the mane, breathed deep. She turned to face Finn, glaring.

'Why did she take off like that?' Finn said between breaths.

'You kicked her, that's why.' Moss might have hit him if she were not still thinking calm thoughts to Aster.

Finn was looking at the ocean, at where there were rock-teeth surfacing in the waves. 'I didn't think she'd want to go in *there*!'

'I told you, she's *not* just a horse! Got her own desires too!'

And maybe, this time, a part of Finn believed it.

When Moss did turn Aster from the sea, they walked on wet sand, avoiding flowers and storm treasure, in the direction of Lizard Rocks, to where more rock-teeth waited. And, maybe, two more boys. The horse's ears flicked from the sound of the waves, to Moss's soothings, to something only she could hear. Soon, there was a large shape up ahead: storm treasure they'd seen from a way back.

'It's the sails!' Finn slid fast from Aster, started digging through. 'But they're all twisted!'

Moss laid her hand against Aster, skittering now at Finn's voice. The flight had gone from the horse, sure, but her skin still twitched at every noise; her ears still flicked to a sound too faint for Moss to hear. Flowers singing?

'There's nothing but the bloody sails!' Finn kicked the salt-stiff material. 'And they're so busted!'

Moss came to where Finn was searching. No Tommy. No Cal. But she could see, scattered throughout, shards of red painted wood, bits of metal, and stretches of rope. More of Finn's boat.

'All splintered,' she whispered. 'You can't fix it, can you?'

ACT FOUR. SCENE TWELVE.

Finn kept quiet. But she knew the answer – 'course he couldn't fix the boat. Finn could no more do that than she could fix Pa. They were stuck here. At least until they could build a new boat – and not one like the shaky raft Cal and her had built when they were Small Things, either. A proper boat, one ready to sail a long way. But even with Finn's knowledge, how easy would that be?

Finn found a glinting thing, tangled up. 'Compass,' he said, tossing it on his palm. 'My dad's. Weird that this survived when everything else . . .'

They watched its needle, spinning and twisting everywhere, never quite coming to rest. Finn shook and tapped it.

'Another thing I've broken.'

He put it in the pocket of his shirt, in front of his heart, and stared across the beach. Moss sat beside him. After a moment, he put his arm around her shoulders. She leant into him and stared at the ocean too, looking for Cal's land. She felt Finn's sadness, heavy, as if it were a blanket they shared. She added her own.

'Sorry,' she said.

'What for?'

'That your boat is broken . . .'

That this place is breaking too.

Finn shrugged. 'It's just how it is. Can't exactly go back in time, can we?'

Finn rested his head down against hers. It felt nice, like they were sharing thoughts. She shut her eyes. Maybe if she concentrated, she would hear his thoughts – he'd be worrying about Tommy, maybe, that they were stuck here for ever. She imagined going back with him to his town on the hill, wondered again what his home looked like. She was surprised to realize that she wasn't as excited as he'd clearly wanted her to be.

'That boat was my dad's,' Finn said, making her eyes open again. 'Like the compass. He always said what me and Tommy were doing was stupid. "Why d'you want to go sailing around the world, anyway? You'll just end up worrying your mother" – those were his words. Guess he was right. Guess I've worried a lot more people than just her now.'

Moss pressed her temple to Finn's shoulder. 'We'll get you back to your home. Somehow we will.'

Though she didn't know how. Moss thought about the raft she and Cal had made – how they hadn't even gone far beyond the reef with it. How the weather, the storms, or something, had dragged them back. Near drowned them. She remembered, too, the watery man in the deeps, and hard-shivered. Finn squeezed her shoulders.

'We'll find your Tommy, and then we'll make a plan,' she said firm.

They'd find Cal, too.

Adder was racing in circles across the sand, and Moss was glad to see her wild movement. She smiled when Adder brought them a piece of boat in her jaws, head held high and tail wagging.

'At least *she's* happy it smashed,' Finn said.

When Adder circled round a second time, Finn drew the dog into his chest, hugging her close. He buried his head into her fur. After a while, he looked up at Moss, studying her.

'Guess it wouldn't be so bad being stuck here,' he said. 'It's pretty, at least. An adventure!' Half his mouth curled up into a sort of smile. 'Maybe I could drop out like Pa, get those flowers to numb the pain. I could write about it some day. My memoir about the place that didn't exist . . . that no one would ever find to read . . .'

He made a noise halfway between a laugh and a sob. Adder looked over her shoulder, her tongue lolling sideways and her tail thudding against Finn's legs.

'Daft dog,' Moss said. To Finn, she pointed out the route they'd take through the Lizard Rocks. 'That's where we need to search next.'

Although parts of the rocks seemed to slither and shift, like scales glinting in the late-morning sun. Adder growled, noticing too. But it was too early in the day for the lizards to be waking. Unless the recent stormy-strange weather had set them off, changing their patterns.

'Come on,' she said. 'Let's go before it gets any later.'

She pushed at Finn, who'd gone flower-dopey again. She saw the heaviness, sure, in his eyelids. But she also saw the determination in his face as he stood up and stumbled towards the rocks. Moss took one last look at the ocean.

Could she see it again, out of the corner of her eye – flickering? She squinted. Maybe there was something, far, far out. So far it almost looked like a storm cloud. She couldn't be sure.

She prodded Finn. 'Can you see any land there now?'

He frowned. 'Maybe . . .'

She straightened. 'True?'

He frowned harder, then looked around at the rest of the ocean. 'I think it's just a cloud or something.' But there was doubt in his face.

As there'd been doubt in Pa's.

But quick-fast he shook his head and pulled her on.

'It keeps appearing, Finn,' she said, holding back from leaving. 'I'm telling truth.'

He looked at her like she was the strangest creature he'd ever seen. 'Land doesn't just appear, Moss,' he said soft. 'It's either there or it's not. Geography's not like that.' He brushed the backs of his fingers against her arm. 'No matter how much you . . . or anyone else . . . might want it to.' He waited, watching for her reaction. When she didn't give him one, he sighed. 'Look, I'll tell you something. When floods happen, do you know they actually flood islands first? This place would never have been left dry with the kind of floods you talked about.'

She shook her head, impatient. 'It's different here, we have stormflowers, remember? They make things change – they protect this place. The last safe—'

He reached forward and took her shoulders, turning her to him and stopping her words. 'How can one island have different rules from the rest?' He looked hard into her eyes. 'Water doesn't just disappear – it can't, it has to go somewhere. Islands don't just pop out of the sea. Water doesn't just go down. The world doesn't work like that.'

'This world does.' Moss looked away. 'And things have come out of the sea before,' she said. 'Cal. Aster . . .'

Finn squeezed her fingers. 'You don't think this Cal could just be a washed-up boy like me? You don't think Aster could just be a horse?'

She shook her head. Because Aster was not *just* anything. And Cal had gold dust in his eyes. And the longer she and Finn stayed there talking, the longer she wasn't finding him.

ACT FOUR. SCENE THIRTEEN.

Cal rested on his heels. The human's skin was moist-warm as a reef anemone, almost so red as one, too. Fever-y. Was Cal cooking him? But what else could he do but keep him warm and with water, but try to slip juicy-soft clams down his throat? He could go back for stormflowers – that's what – could smoke them and heal the human like that. Maybe then Cal could use petal-smoke to put new dreams inside him. Like Cal'd been thinking the Pa had done with them. Cal could make flower-smoke wind like vine inside the human's mouth and into his thinking. P'raps, like that, Cal could get the human to want to hurt Pa – make them all free that way.

Kill the Pa and they all go walking.

He shook his head quick-fast. This thinking were dark as seabeds. But it were brewing still, biting as a weaselmouse. Cal had memory of flower-smoke – of how Pa brewed it strong. Of how Pa told stories when he did. Made pictures come.

Of how spirits came from ocean.

Of how Pa made them come.

Of how Pa made him come from a fish in the sea.

Cal did not believe.

'Pa keep us trapped,' he whispered to the human. 'Moss and Aster and Cal. Keep us trapped on island. Will keep you trapped too. Smoke you with flowers.'

Cal blinked, head heavy, wanting his own sleepings. He dabbed the human's forehead, putting cooling mint leaves he'd gone for specially against his temples. Again, the human's eyes flickered open. They were clear on Cal, not like how eyes go when they're flower-smoked.

'Finn?' the human whispered.

Cal frowned. 'What you say there?'

But, quick-fast, the human were sleeping again. Deep-good. Healing-like.

And there were dreamings – deep-thick – just waiting for Cal also. He'd been healing the human so long, he didn't know when his sleep came last.

When his eyes closed again, he could fight no more.

Down he went . . .

. . . down next to the human . . . till there were his own dreamings . . .

. . . soft and floating . . .

. . . and he were gripping round a sharp stick and placing it to water. He were spearing! And there were another, darker, hand on top of his – with no webbings on it – and that bigger hand were guiding him towards a fishy, helping him to spear.

He blinked awake.

He should not go to full-slumber, not when the human was so sick. He pressed his nails hard into his arm to wake himself, then ran his fingers 'cross the chest of the human, let them rise tiny with each new breathing. Cal saw dreamings spark 'cross the human's eyelids. Saw salt in his eyelashes.

Human would live.

Cal turned to where the hidden thing rested. Deep-down-deep, below the rocks, with all its hidden things inside . . . the hidden thing that were meant to be Birthday Surprise. If only Moss had come.

'Kill the Pa,' Cal said, whispering the words, trying them out. 'Kill the Pa and we all go free.'

It were dark thinking. He could not do it. Could not make the human do it, neither. But if he could . . .

Cal thought of the dreaming – of his hand, just now, on the pointy stick. He thought of what the Pa might have taken. Taken from him.

Not the Flicker-land, though. That had come back.

The human's eyes shot open again. Settled on his. Cal waited till he were certain the human were seeing him before trying a smile.

'Hello,' Cal said.

'Hello,' the human said, more clear-eyed still.

'*Cal*,' Cal said, pointing at himself.

'*Tommy*,' the human said.

'Hello, Tommy,' Cal repeated, pointing at the human.

'Hello, Cal.'

The human – the *Tommy* – slight-smiled back. When Cal pressed mint to his forehead again, Tommy reached up and caught Cal's hand. Cal waited for Tommy to see the webbings and scale-sheen skin, ready for him to shrink back as Pa and Moss had done first time they saw. But Tommy put Cal's hand back down, not even seeming to care.

'Thank you,' Tommy said, squeezing Cal's hand, webbings and all.

P'raps it were his sickness, making him hazy, not making him see Cal proper.

'I'm not dying, am I?' Tommy said next. He looked around the cave, at the fire.

Cal watched, wondering. 'Want to test?'

Tommy coughed, then winced after. 'Why not,' he murmured.

'Can you get up?'

Tommy nodded. 'Need to piss, anyway.'

Cal put his arm under Tommy's shoulder and helped him upward. 'Just to tunnel opening . . . just a look-see . . . just a test.'

'Test and a pee.' Tommy looked at Cal true-serious. 'You're not going to kill me, are you?'

Cal smiled to ease him, and that made Tommy smile too.

'You're right,' Tommy said. 'Your face is too pretty for killing.'

Tommy was light as dried thatching weed. They walked slow, Tommy leaning and gasping air. At tunnel opening, Cal felt Tommy sway sudden, wind-blown.

'Where the . . .?' he said, looking out to sea. 'What is this? Where am I?'

But Cal were looking to horizon line, unanswering. His Flicker-land were there. Come back! He'd had feelings it would. He'd had feelings this Tommy would see it too. Because Tommy had not had stormflowers – not one – Cal had made sure.

Quick-fast, he was moving Tommy's head, just as he'd moved Moss's those nights past. 'Can you see it? The land?'

And – yes – Tommy looked, and – yes – Tommy saw. Cal saw it true in the way his eyes squinted, then widened. He shook his head

207

free from Cal's grip.

'You mean that scrap of rock?' Tommy said. 'That land?'

'Rock?'

Tommy nodded. 'The one with all the bird shite on it?'

Cal tried to see what Tommy could. Couldn't . . . quite. Just shadows. Just something not clear. Flickering. Coming. Going. But a land . . . sure.

'That's just rock for a colony of seabirds, mate,' Tommy said. 'Not really sure it's real land.'

Then Tommy coughed hard, went gasping. He stumbled back against the cliff and steadied himself.

'Seabirds,' Cal whispered. '*Shite?*'

So it were not land with humans like him on it? What, then, was it?

Behind him, he heard Tommy pissing long, pee splashing from stone.

'But it's there though?' Cal called back, not looking with his words. 'You *saw*?'

'I saw the same bit of rock I think our boat crashed into! It's there.'

Tommy sighed out with the last of his piss, then stumble-fell against the rock. Cal turned from the Flicker-shite-land, and caught him.

ACT FOUR. SCENE FOURTEEN.

Moss pulled her coverings tighter and reached down to ruffle Adder's ears. She indicated to Finn the path ahead through the Lizard Rocks. She remembered doing this with Cal as Small Things, back when they'd been shaking-scared about the reptiles Pa'd warned them about. Up close now, she saw no movement in the rocks, no lizards yet. There were only black-backed gulls, muttonbirds and razorbills, and none of them were screeching any warnings.

She looked to the ocean – Cal's land was still there. If she squinted and looked proper hard, maybe she could make out rocks on it, rising up. Back down on the beach, she saw the silver-white of Aster, calm and waiting.

They climbed further towards the point. If Moss remembered right, the openings to the tunnels were not far along. Passing dark crevices where lizards could be slumbering, Moss heard no slithers. Only the whir of birds' wings, the crash and roar of the sea. She heard no sign of Cal or Tommy, either. They reached the ridge, and that was empty too, wind-beaten. Now there was only the pinnacle ahead, the pointed finger of rock with its caves within – where Cal would go. Hidden-deep. The one place where Pa had proper warned them from.

'It's different here again,' Finn said. 'Empty and spiky, not so many of those flowers.'

'Pa always told us to stay away, says it's the darker side of the island.'

But Moss realized she now felt safer here – in these rocks she was always warned off – than she felt back with Pa. Even with lizards lurking. Even with sea slapping hard against the cliff drop below. Now this island seemed topsy-turvy. Danger had become safe, and safe had become skitter-stones.

She grabbed Finn's hand and pulled him on. 'The tunnel to the caves,' she said, pointing it out ahead.

His eyes widened. 'How would Tommy have ever got up here?'

'Cal helped.' She was getting sure of this now.

Moss scrambled on. The skin on her palm gashed open as she tried, too quick, to get a grip. She cursed low. But her fresh blood smell was on the air now, on top of whatever scent still clung to her smalls. She saw by Adder's nose-twitch that she, at least, could smell it. Moss moved quicker. She was halfway towards the tunnel opening when she heard it: claws against granite and scales against stone. Adder growled.

'Hush,' Moss whispered. ''Tis only lizards stirring in sleep.'

Adder's scruff had risen at the noise, making her neck mean-thick.

'Come on,' Moss said to her. 'Don't lose your mind.'

She gripped tighter on Finn's hand, too. 'Don't you lose your mind, either.'

To one side was steep, vertical rock, with the sea below. To the other were burrows and small caves: easy-big enough for reptiles. A hiss came closer, making Adder sudden-skid.

Quick-fast, Moss let go of Finn's hand, put herself between her dog and the drop. They were only a few hut-widths from the tunnel. They couldn't turn back now. She could smell smoke, too. Was there a fire burning somewhere inside? Cal's doing?

Then she saw it following – a lizard, about the size of her leg, algae-green and open-mouthed. Not far behind. It was sudden-woke and disgruntled, hissing low. Moss looked ahead to the tunnel, pushing Adder.

'Go there,' she told her dog. 'Go find Cal!'

Adder barked in Moss's face: a warning. She would not leave. Moss climbed faster then, grabbing Adder's scruff and trying to pull her along. Adder growled, fight-ready. Moss hoped Finn was following close. Still trying to yank her dog on, Moss smelt the lizard's foul breath. When she turned, she saw its dark, long claws and the glisten of its lips. The pink of its tongue. It skittered towards them and Moss seized Adder, launching across the rock to the opening.

But the lizard was quicker. It bit at them, its jaws grazing Moss's leg. She felt the pain instant as a sharp, salty cut. When the lizard snapped again, Moss almost fell. Adder's stocky legs flailed out, above the dagger rocks and frothing, angry sea.

'Stop struggling,' Moss hissed to her dog. 'Be still so I can grip you better.'

Moss kicked out, found the lizard's head with her boots. She skidded backwards, Adder howling and twisting in her arms. They were sliding, almost falling, down the steep side of the rocks towards the sea; she jabbed her fingertips into the granite. The lizard hissed loud. She heard Finn, too, shouting at it.

When the lizard darted forward, its teeth grazing her skin a second time, she was ready to kick again. But Finn got there first and punched it. With the way Finn's mind had seemed so fuzzy just before, Moss was surprised he had it in him. By the look on Finn's face, perhaps he was too. Now he pushed her forward. She clutched Adder tighter, and went. And the lizard backed off, hissing foul air, not putting up the kind of fight she'd expected. Moss pulled Finn with them into the darkness of the tunnel.

Then there were other arms, grabbing her, pulling her inside. Adder leapt away from Moss to run on into the black. And those arms were pull-pulling her, away from the lizard. Into the dark.

Cal.

She smelt the saltiness of him.

'Course it was.

She breathed out in a rush. Hugged him deep, then gripped his fingers to stop him pulling her so quick.

'There's Finn too,' she said. She reached back, felt Finn stumbling behind. 'Keep up,' she said to him. 'Try.'

She didn't want that lizard coming in after. Though it had backed off, she didn't quite trust it to keep away. Not after all the warnings from Pa.

There was light up ahead, leading them. A fire! So this was where Cal had made camp. As she ran, she shouted to Cal, explaining what had happened.

'I've brought a boy! A real boy! I'm serious, Cal. He washed up. As you did!'

'I believe.'

'All has changed!'

'I know it.'

Then they were tumbling into the cave where the fire was, and Moss was grabbing Cal and hugging him true-proper. She was smelling his damp-salt smell. It was so good to see him, like when the sun returns after a storm. She threaded her fingers through his. Did not want to let go.

Then Cal was speaking close in her ear, looking at Finn. 'And there is other one, too. The one I saved.'

He turned her gentle-slow. On the ground, snug in coverings, was another boy. A second human. Just like Finn had promised.

'Tommy,' she said.

Cal had wrapped him so tight, Moss could only see his face amid the coverings, but it was pale – so much paler even than Finn's. Sick-looking.

'He's been awake,' Cal said fast. 'Not dead. Only recent he gone back to sleeping.'

She looked back to Finn, who was blinking in the sudden light from the fire, full-confused by where he'd just got to. When he noticed his friend, he lunged across the cave towards him, though fear flashed across Finn's face when Tommy did not respond to his shouts.

'What's wrong with him?' Finn said, turning to Moss.

Moss swallowed. 'Storm-woke sick, maybe. Flower-heavy? I don't know.'

His eyes were so wide. They widened further as he, then, saw Cal proper.

'Cal,' he said, realizing.

Cal smiled, all white teeth in the gloom.

Finn frowned. 'But the Pa man said you were a fish! A . . . fish-spirit!'

Cal went eye-rolling. 'The Pa been lying.'

'You're just like us!'

Cal spat at the flames, making them hiss. 'I know it.' Moss squeezed his hand, and his eyes flicked to her. 'I been healing the human with no flowers,' he told her. 'He's been getting better. Swear it.'

Moss crouched beside Finn, looking down at Tommy. Close up, Moss saw that his face was wider than Finn's, his hair orange-red and almost so vivid in colour as stormflowers. He looked sure-sick, but not so bad as Pa looked in Blackness. Her hands hovered above the dark crevices below his eyes, above the sweat on his forehead.

Cal came close. 'This Tommy can see the Flicker-land, too. When he was woke, I showed and he saw. Is not just me who see it proper now.'

'And I saw it again.' She looked at him. 'And Finn. For an eye-blink, at least.'

She felt for the beat in Tommy's neck, found it steady. His skin was hot, but not storm-fevered. Cal checked it after her.

Then he held out one of his hands in front of him, turning it . . . frowning.

'What are you doing, Ca—'

But Moss saw it – *there!* – just for a moment: His scale-sheen skin changed, the pattern of him faded. Flickered! Just like how, at first, she had seen the island. How she had seen the angry man in Pa's cave and, before, under the sea. Like how Finn's scar had gone, too.

Flicker-gone!

Only, Cal's pattern came back again, quick-fast. Like it had never gone at all. She blinked.

'Whoa!' Finn was crawling away from Cal, watching wide-eyed also. 'What just happened to you?'

'Do not right-know.' Quick-fast, Cal smiled. 'But you saw it too? No scales! For one moment, no nothing!'

Moss leant forward to touch Cal's skin. It was soft, but scale-shined again now. 'Which is right?'

Then Tommy coughed – awake! Moss bent back over him. Now Tommy's eyes were open, and he was gasping like a storm-drowned fish. Finn turned him to the side and thumped him on the back till Tommy went gasping more. Cal came with water, scooped in a shell, which Tommy drank greedy.

'Can you see me, mate?' Finn said loud, waving his hands before his face. 'We've crashed on an island. And the *Swift*'s gone. Smashed! Can you hear me?'

Tommy stared at him. 'Stop bloody shouting.'

Finn laughed. 'Mate!' He reached down to hug him. 'Do you remember the storm? Anything?'

Tommy nodded. Least, it looked a little bit like a nod from where Moss was crouching.

'Do you remember trying to get the sails down? And I was spinning the rudder. And the boat was . . . ?'

'Sinking,' Tommy finished. 'I remember. A . . . reef. A bloody big rock. We crashed. Don't know where the hell you went after that though . . . don't know where anything went.'

Tommy grasped Finn's shirt, and Finn helped him sit up. Tommy was frowning as he stared first at Cal, then Moss, then Adder too. Moss wondered if he was even seeing them clear; perhaps he thought he was still on the boat.

'You're in a cave,' Finn said, maybe thinking that too. 'You're

OK. Everything's going to be OK. These people are . . .'

'I know.' Tommy's fingers dug into Finn's arm. 'This nice man rescued me.'

Cal smiled proud, rolled his shoulders back. Finn frowned, then leant closer as Tommy spoke again.

'Something pulled us, in the ocean . . .'

'A storm,' Finn said, giving him more water. 'A big, bloody storm!'

As Tommy drank, Finn explained how Moss had found him, how he'd ridden a horse with her across the island to get here.

Tommy frowned. 'Horse? I saw a horse.'

Finn paused with the shell half raised to Tommy's lips. 'But you're in a cave, Tom.'

Tommy shook his head. 'Not here. In the water. A white horse. Big thing!'

'White?' Finn looked at Moss.

'Aster doesn't go into the water,' she said, though she was thinking about their dash across the beach just before. 'Least, she didn't used to. Not that I ever saw . . .'

But she'd just seen the pattern of Cal's scale-sheen skin flicker. And she'd seen human boys, two of them now. Nothing was like it used to be. Change was threaded through them all.

Soft-gentle, Cal pressed fingers to her arm, staring ahead to the dark drop at the other end of the cave. 'Your Birthday Surprise is here also, Moss,' he said. He crouched over, turning away, moving closer to the darkness. 'Come,' he beckoned her. 'Follow. The island has more secrets still.'

Quicker than a wink, he crawled over the edge.

ACT FOUR. SCENE FIFTEEN.

Moss watched Cal slip into the dark. She went to where he'd disappeared. There was a rocky edge, and beyond that a drop. A hole. Was there another cave somewhere below? The sea? It was so dark, she couldn't be sure . . . but she could feel damp in the air, like it was coming from salt water.

'Follow.' Cal's voice came up through the black.

She remembered Cal's words: *A way off the island*. Was this it?

When she looked over at Finn, he was still talking soft to Tommy, explaining and reassuring.

'I'll come back,' she said. 'Won't forget you.'

She waited till her eyes had adjusted enough to see Cal, then she began to make her way, slow-sure, so Adder could follow. There was a kind of path, but very narrow. In places, she had to hug and hold the rock wall.

'What's down here?'

'You will see.'

'How did you find this?'

'Been searching long.'

Secrets, secrets . . . she heard the word on the air. Was it the flow-

217

ers whispering, or Cal, or voices in her mind?

Down into the deep, Moss followed the hunch of Cal's back, the path descending sudden-steep. Rock water dripped on to her neck, shivering her. She turned to Adder, worried that her clumsy paws might stumble, but Adder was secure and tongue-lolling. This cavern was far bigger than any of the caves they had explored as Small Things.

'Are there lizards down here?' she called forward.

'Not seen any.'

'How deep is it?' She skidded as the path got steeper still.

'All way to the sea.'

The saltwater smell got stronger. She squinted into the dark and – *there!* – Moss could see now: a huge, shadowy shape below. Was this what Cal meant? Her Birthday Surprise?

She edged a little closer. When Cal reached behind to grasp her arm, she felt the tension between his fingers and her skin as a warm buzz. It reminded her of bumble-wings, beating swift.

'Almost there,' he said, keeping her hand in his.

From what she could make out, the shape below was moving, gentle-slight up and down. Was it a vision this time, or real?

They climbed down into the cavern, with only the sound of Adder's paws on rock. Now there was more light, sun from outside. She heard the thick, rushing sound of the sea. Then they were in a huge rock room. Ahead was an archway, the sea beyond. It was all so sudden-bright.

'A belly in the rocks,' Cal said, spreading his arms wide. Then he pointed ahead at the shape. 'Belly been holding this.'

There, floating on this secret inlet of water, Moss saw it proper. But how had that got here?

'You found it?' She bumped into Cal's back in her rush to see it better. 'But it was all gone!' She climbed down the rest of the way quick-fast. 'Finn and me found pieces on Western Beach, and I found more before that in the cove! So, how's it whole?'

Then her breath caught. Because her thinking didn't make sense – 'course it didn't. Cal had found this Birthday Surprise long before she'd found Finn, or even the smashed-up pieces of his boat in the cove. And because it was not *Swift* – the name of Finn's boat – that was painted in black letters on the side of this one. It was another name.

Cal came close, lacing his fingers in hers again. 'This been here long time . . . this been waiting.'

'But who . . .?'

This boat did not look wrecked. It just seemed a little old and tired-looking, with its dark red paint faded. And, something else . . .

This was a boat she knew. *Remembered.*

'It can't be,' she whispered.

Cal nodded at her, like he was wanting her to say it out loud. She shook her head, but still . . .

'Pa's boat?

She was staring at its side, at the painted letters there. A name so similar to Finn's boat, but . . .

'The *Swallow*,' she said. 'Its name!'

Sudden-quick, there were a hundred thoughts, no . . . *memories*, inside her, arrived like bees in a swarm. Being in its cabin. How it had moved on the waves. Pa telling stories on its deck about the island they were sailing to . . .

Magic Isle . . . Flower Island . . . a place to cure pain . . .

She shut her eyes, swaying. Had these memories been inside her all along?

She ran her eyes over all of it. Then, careful-slow, she climbed down the final section of rock to touch the old, fraying rope that moored the *Swallow* to the cave. She could remember tying that rope in another place once, on a proper metal ring... throwing it to Pa in a harbour. *Harbour?* Was that what that place was called? With the wooden pathways and all those other boats bobbing?

What were all these new-sudden thoughts inside? Memories? Stories? She'd thought before they were dreams.

She realized now what Cal had meant. 'When you said there was a way off the island...'

He nodded. 'This.'

Still, though, she could not believe it. Pa's boat, here?

How?

Because Pa's boat had wrecked in a storm. On the rocks and the reef around the island. He must have told her and Cal a thousand times.

Cal watched her. 'Pa tells stories, Moss. He been doing it long time. Come-see.'

Quick-fast, he leapt from the rocky outcrop where they stood, and landed on the boat's deck. Moss followed Cal's path and leapt too. She held her arms open for Adder and caught her with an *oomph*. When she turned, Cal had already disappeared inside the boat's cabin, leaving the door open.

She ran a hand across the boat's side, touched the rudder, then grasped its edge. She had done this before. She could remember her hands – so much smaller then, but grasped tight around this very rudder. She remembered turning it and feeling the boat sway.

Rudder – even that word she had not remembered till now.

She followed Cal into the cabin, and this – *this!* – was familiar too. It was a dull familiarity, more like the half remembering of a dream. But there was the bed Pa had slept in – she could *remember* him sleeping in – only it was no longer made up with bedding. And there was the cupboard – where she had made her own bed once, curled quiet and dark. She frowned – why had she been sleeping in there? She blinked and pressed her fingers to wooden walls to steady herself, sudden-fast as light-winged as a flutterby. How small must she have been then?

Now the cupboard doors were open, with no clothes inside. She thought of Pa's shirts, all faded and holey in the hut beside the cove: they'd come from here. Near-everything in their hut had come from here, hadn't it? The bedding. All those books in Pa's cave! She walked around the cabin in a kind of fever daze. Apart from looking old and tired, the empty cabin was perfectly sound. Seaworthy. What, then, about Pa's tales? Of their shipwreck so many seasons ago? Why was this boat bobbing here?

Nothing left, my bird . . . Only what I could save in the storm.

'You remember?' Cal said. 'From when you were very small?'

She nodded. 'We came on this. I . . . I remember the journey, some of it.'

Even if she still didn't understand.

'He left other stuff,' Cal said. 'Look-see.'

From the floor under the bed, Cal tugged out a wooden box. He opened it with a creak and pulled out loose papers. Moss knelt.

'Look,' Cal said again. '*See.*'

The papers felt soft as skin, damp and cool. She recognized Pa's handwriting – the cursive. Here was another of his scrapbooks!

Though the words were mostly faded and smudged, she saw fragments of sentences.

...think I am coming closer to finding, to knowing...

One last mystery...last place for dreaming...

Hope for the world...for me...healing my brain, my illness... away from unkindness...where I can be...free...

Had he just forgotten to come back for all this? Forgotten his boat was here at all?

Like in the other scrapbook at camp, there were sketches too. A stormflower, so real-looking. The cliffs and Lizard Rocks. She flicked on. Soon the sketches were swirls and circles, with jagged lines through the middle, confused and unhappy somehow. Ahead a few more pages was a different sort of sketch again: a small girl, crouched in the corner of a boat. She had dark, frizzed-out hair and big green eyes. Moss swallowed.

'You,' Cal said, face close over her shoulder.

But she knew it already. She traced her fingers over the picture.

It was how Pa had seen her once. She should show this to Finn, make him see how close she'd always been with Pa, how she'd been with him all along. But there was a swirling in her stomach, and she knew she wouldn't say anything.

'Keep going,' Cal said.

She turned another soft page. Here was another sketch of her as a Very Small Thing, but this time with her arm around a patterned dog. Moss recognized her too.

'Jess,' she whispered. But she was so much younger and smaller, all legs.

The dog in the picture was a bit like how Moss first remembered Adder too. She stroked her finger along the sketch-dog's back.

Moss had lain curled with Jess on this very floor – she remembered that! – Jess had nuzzled her ear. Moss turned and pointed the sketch towards Adder.

'Can you recognize your mum?' she said. 'She was on this boat once, too.'

Adder stared goofy back, not even proper looking. She pointed her snout and whined at the cabin door.

'There is more,' Cal said, turning to the next page.

There, Moss breathed in sharp. Skidded backwards. He was back. The man from her dreams and visions.

Here!

The angry man.

'Again?'

Cal caught her, pressing palms to her spine. 'You know him?'

And now she was back in the ocean. Near-drowning! This man stood over her, pushed the water towards her. She gasped and shook her head. She was back in the cave where he'd shouted and pointed. She placed her hands over her ears. She didn't want his noise, or the throbbing it gave.

With feather-light touch, Cal pried her hands away. He held her fingers in his. 'The man from your dreamings? From the sea?'

She nodded. 'The visions.' She found Cal's fire-eyes instead of looking back at the page.

Pa had drawn him. In a long-ago sketchbook that he'd since forgotten. Why? Had he seen him too?

This picture made her want to run and hide, go somewhere dark. 'Turn it over,' she said. 'Please.'

She felt Cal's breath on her neck as he moved the pages. Moss thought she'd be glad to see the angry man gone, but he was still there, in her mind. She shut her eyes, but he was there too – shouting, hurting, pointing. How had Pa known?

Cal stopped on a page. 'Another thing.'

Cautious-careful, Moss looked. A loose piece of paper, folded many times and stuck inside the scrapbook. She breathed out, glad not to see another angry man, but then frowned as she unfolded it. On this page were two sketched blobs: one bigger, one smaller. It looked like a sort of map, shaky drawn . . . *ancient*.

Moss traced the bigger shape with her fingertips, over its scalloped coves and long, straight stretch of beach. She recognized, too, the shape of the rocks and how they pointed, as a finger, to the sea.

'Our island,' she said.

'Flower Island,' said Cal, pointing out words, written beneath in unfamiliar handwriting.

The other blob was another island drawn, too. Much smaller.

'Bird Island,' said Cal, again pointing out words not written by Pa.

Then Moss understood. 'The land on the horizon?'

'The Flicker-land.'

She nodded. The word *real* was written below it. There were numbers and letters there like she'd seen in Pa's atlas. *Co-ordinates?*

'Also called Bird Shite Island.' Cal smiled. 'But here's proof – Pa saw it first, he knew it was here!'

Moss wanted to catch the smile on Cal's face like she'd done on the rock in the sea. This map was why he'd wanted her to see this sketchbook, not because of the pictures of her as a Small Thing, or even because of the angry man. This map was proof that Cal's Flicker-land was true, that he'd really seen it.

'Pa been lying,' Cal said.

'Or forgetting, maybe.' Moss chewed her lip, thinking. 'Doesn't explain why we only see it sometimes, though. Why it flickers.'

Cal kept her gaze. 'Maybe that land is not the one that's flickering.'

Moss frowned, trying to understand.

Cal shrugged. 'Maybe we're all flickering? All of us here?'

He held up his hand to her again, and there, for a moment, his scale-sheen faded. Gone, then back again. He smiled like a fishtail spin. Silver-sharp.

Something made sense – Moss felt the wisp of knowing it. Finn had said their island was not on maps. Pa had called it a *dream island* . . . *Flower Island* . . . It seemed to bend and shift, like the magic of Cal did. She shook her head, could not grasp – quite – at what all this meant.

There was a rumble beneath them, making Moss sit back on her heels. The volcano had not given up, then.

'Our island's not happy, whatever else it is,' she said.

She looked up at a wooden ceiling she now remembered staring at before. Then across at the circular window that she remembered once thinking had looked like an eye. Why had Pa lied that all this had gone? No boat? No way to leave?

'Nothing what seem,' Cal said.

Not even Cal. Not Pa. Maybe not her? Her whole world flown up like ash from a fire.

'What is real, then?' she murmured.

Cal took her face between his fingers and she watched him so close, followed the way light glinted in his eyes. He was the most beautiful thing here, not the flowers, not the magic.

She leant forward quick and kissed his warm, soft lips.

Real.

So real.

She was sure.

But the *feeling* that came with this touch . . . that was more dream.

He grinned. Now she saw the scale-sheen in his cheeks flicker: the tattoo of scales fading, then coming back, then fading, then returning again. If she kissed every part of him, over and over, would it fade for ever? Maybe she should try.

As she was thinking it, he kissed her back, his tongue ting-tingling on hers. Spark-wild as the flowers! Was he checking she was real too?

She lay her head against him, considering. 'What if we leave and it's not real there, either? What if everything always flickers?'

Because Finn seemed full-strange as anything she'd known! What if where he came from was more dreaming still? She felt a tremble in the boat again, heard rumbling in the cliffs. Adder whined, snout pointing determined at the cabin door, when rough water rocked the boat harder.

Moss left the sketches, climbed up from the cabin and on to the deck. There were endings to be grasped still!

On deck, she saw tiny scratches in the wooden floor, and quick-fast remembered – again! – knife-scratching them when she'd been a Very Small Thing, counting days at sea. The lines were straight and even, not made in storms or rough tides: lines scratched on sunny, calm days.

'No flooding,' she whispered, tracing them. 'Just as Finn told it.'

'I got the plan,' Cal said. 'We take the boat. Them two boys sail.

We go to Flicker-land, or beyond. We go till we find.'

'And Pa?'

Cal's eyes hardened.

And now, watching him, something inside Moss was a resisting thing, a swirling-wild thing. She could not leave Pa, not just like this, even if he'd not told truth . . . 'course she could not. She needed to know why he had hidden things away. And, anyway, he was . . . Pa. The swirling feeling grew. Made her fingers tremble. She thought of Finn's words as they had ridden.

. . . maybe he's a fugitive . . . done something wrong . . . not right in the head . . .

Seawater smashed against the boat as the rocks shuddered harder. A part of her wanted to smash her fists hard against Pa too – make him talk, hit him like he had hit Cal on the beach those nights ago. She shook her head. Maybe there was truth appearing on the horizon like Cal said, but there was truth still to find here, too. She could not leave till she had it clasped tight.

She took off her boots and handed them to Cal. 'Keep safe for me. 'Tis not time to take the boat yet.' She walked to its edge. Saw sandfish hiding in the shadow of the hull – flipping and swirling – where Cal must have caught them those days before. 'I will bring Pa back,' she said, firm. 'Then we all leave together.'

She dived into the inky black water. And Adder followed.

ACT FOUR. SCENE SIXTEEN.

She swam further out of the cavern, heading towards the wide sea. The rocky archway was tall enough to sail a boat through. Was this what Pa had done, so long ago? Lied about their boat wrecking and put it here instead?

Away from the cave was true-choppy water, as tangled-churning as the mess in her mind. Thoughts were swirling, dangerous-fast. A rip tide. Tempest-brain.

Their boat was not wrecked. Pa knew about the Flicker-land. Pa had lied.

And the sketch of the angry man . . . how did Pa know about him?

She kicked her legs harder as she felt a shiver up her spine.

Adder kept up with Moss, despite how quick-fast she swam. Ghost-pale, huge stingers came and kept pace with her too. Moss hummed sounds to their twisting bodies so they wouldn't sting.

Moss swam from the rocks and into the light. The sea was rough-wild beyond the shelter of the cave, its current dragging her towards still deeper parts . . . towards the horizon and Cal's land and that possible point of forgetting. She bobbed her head up to see.

Cal's land was there. Firmer now. More real. Covered in birds like its name. It didn't look like a place they could sail to and live. Did Finn's homeland look more welcoming? Beside her, Adder strained to see too.

Maybe, with Adder being half wild dog, half islander, she wouldn't forget anything when they left. Then Moss wondered something else: maybe *forgetting* was another one of Pa's stories. Maybe she shouldn't feel worried about that at all.

But Moss was worried. If she forgot this island, who was she? And with so few memories of before, would she find her old home so easy? Did she even want to? As she stretched her arms out, slicing through water, Finn's words drummed in her mind.

Nothing like you.

Not the same.

So who was her Pa, really?

She would find out.

Soon, she was above the reef again, swimming faster and harder back to shore. She looked down, opening her eyes against the salt. The stingers were still there, not so far below. So, too, were the pinks and greens and oranges of the coral reef, the darts of purple fishes, the sashaying red of the anemones. There were starfish and sponges and seaweed, everything swaying in the pull of the tide. Moss and Adder glided over it all. The stingers followed, eyes swivel-fast to watch them, guiding them in.

As the water got shallower, the stingers drifted away, until it was only dog and girl swimming to the shore. Moss moved like a mermaid, legs together and swaying, the fabric of her skirts tail-swishing. Soon, it was shallow enough to stand. The waves, as they pawed the shore, had turned shining, shimmering blue. *Bioluminescence*, Pa had called it when she'd asked him once. It happened when there was so much oxygen in the air, so many stormflowers swirling. Perhaps, soon, that glowing blue would seep even further into the water, maybe even as far as the reef and beyond that to the horizon. Maybe, soon, all the water would be glowing.

As she stepped from the sea, again she felt a tremor in the sand. She looked up for volcano smoke, but saw nothing. But if it did blow, what then? Maybe they would never leave the island after all, even with a boat. Moss shivered as she turned towards the dunes. High up in the sands, horse-shaped and silvery, Aster was waiting. Moss smiled to the lowering sun in thanks.

She crawled on to the horse, Adder scrabbling up after. She crouched tight over Aster's withers, letting the horse's warm body help her own to dry. Aster danced from the feel of the sea salt, tossed her mane to coat it more. She leapt to a gallop in one stride.

And then they were riding hard. Back to Pa and the truths that had been hiding.

ACT FOUR. SCENE SEVENTEEN.

The storm came sudden, sharp-biting, rain starting before they reached the pines. Adder tucked in closer, pressing her damp doggy fur to Moss. Aster's mane rose with the wind.

Was Pa making this storm? Even now?

Moss shivered. The swirl feeling was fierce – had not left since she'd set eyes on the *Swallow*. She crouched in tighter. She'd never known it so cold on the island. And, still, the volcano rumbled. She felt its vibrations all the way from the ground through Aster.

Soon ... soon ... time ...

She half heard voices on the wind. Though when she turned her head to catch them full, they disappeared. She dug her fingers into Aster's mane, then rested her head there, smelling the salt-musk of Aster's skin ... that strange, heady, *horsey* smell.

'What are you, then?' she whispered. She thought of Cal's scale-shine pattern disappearing. Just like Cal's land had done. Like the angry man she'd seen. Flickering. Half real. Rising up. Going down. Moss stroked fingertips against Aster's neck. 'Not a spirit? Still a spirit?' Aster's ears flicked at Moss's voice. 'Just a horse?'

Aster felt real enough, beneath her, carrying her fast back to camp.

'And were you really in the sea?' Moss said. 'Or was Tommy just caught in fever dream?'

What did Aster do when they weren't watching? Did Pa even know?

Moss grit her teeth as wind pulled her fierce. She would make Pa tell truth. Make him remember. Then they would leave. Before the volcano rumbled harder. Before this storm made the sea too rough. Though there was the anxious swirl inside when she thought about leaving, too.

She urged Aster faster, pressing with her calves. Through the trees they raced, as if Aster were a bird and not a horse, her wings skimming. The winds got stronger, making trees spit their leaves. Flowers on the branches and ground were opening, turning to see them as they galloped close, their petals spreading wide, colours glowing. She watched Aster's ears flick to them as they passed, saw how she cat-leapt to avoid crushing them. Moss gripped tighter. She was angry with those flowers, too! Stormflowers – not floods – were the real reason they were on this island. They were the reason Pa had come here; the reason, too, that Pa had changed.

'Magical things,' he'd called them. 'Wonders.'

But maybe those flowers were not so wonderful at all.

The wind slapped hair to her cheeks. Again, Moss crouched down tighter to the horse, clinging as the wind whipped her dry. She would pull the memories from Pa, too. Make him remember. But the thought gnawed at her – why hide a boat that could be used?

Then they were out of the pines, Moss squinting in the late-afternoon light as she looked across their cove. Cal's land was still there, the sea twisting before it, grey as a seal's back. A storm buzzed inside her now, too, urging Aster faster.

But when at last she reached camp, it was quiet. Too empty. The fire embers had been kicked aside and the hut door left open, banging in the wind. Moss leapt down from Aster.

'Pa?' she called, her voice whipping away. 'Jess?'

The wild weather had come into their hut and left it messy and changed, as if a whirling-wind had blown through. As Moss stepped inside, Adder ran around it, whirling it further, skittering clothes and candle stubs. Then Adder stopped sudden and barked. She whined and scratched desperate at the dark space beneath their bed.

'What?' Moss said, bending down to see. 'Why go so mad?'

She looked under. Squinted at what she saw.

Beneath the bed was a small, soft shape. Not moving. The swirl grew in Moss's belly, down where the cramp had been. She knew this shape. Adder barked and barked, pushing Moss to go closer. Again, Moss called out for Pa. Again, he did not come. Adder bashed her big head against Moss's arm, full-urging.

'Calm, puppling,' Moss soothed.

Slow-careful, Moss reached through the dust and cobwebs. When she couldn't get close enough, she crawled full under. A small body of black-and-white fur lay still. Two old dog eyes stared back. They weren't glinting now, not bright like they'd once been.

'Jess,' she whispered.

She touched the old dog's ears. Adder crawled in with Moss and whined at her mother's side, licked her desperate as if she could lick her awake. Moss wound her other hand in Adder's so much warmer fur. Gentle-careful, she kissed Jess's snout.

'Dead?' she whispered. 'Gone?'

She did not understand it. Why now, when they were just about to leave? Why ever? She pressed fists to her eyes when the tears came.

Jess . . . Jess . . . The flowers sung beyond their hut, the note high in the wind.

She wanted to cry out too, wanted to cry her old dog back.

Soon Adder's whines went to whimpers also and she rested her chin on Jess's back, her eyes slits.

Moss remembered Jess that morning. She'd been no more sick, or old, than other days, had she? Moss wished she'd stroked her nice-good, given her a special limpet or periwinkle.

Soft-slow, Moss carried Jess from under the bed. She was almost pure bones, sagging skin. How had Moss not noticed? Adder whined again as Moss set Jess down on the fraying rug. Moss tickled beneath the old dog's chin where Jess liked best. She remembered Jess whirling and spinning on the sand. Remembered her barking and dancing for snacklings, balancing on her back legs. Remembered being with her as a Small Thing. Back on that boat. Back at . . .

Moss stroked Jess's snout, over and over, as she remembered. There was somewhere else she'd been with Jess.

The memory was dusty, tucked in the back of her mind. As she stroked Jess's fur, it came a little clearer.

Jess had sat in dirt with a mud-stained snout. Her tongue lolling. She was all legs, so much smaller.

Moss almost smiled to remember it. Was it the first day she'd ever seen the dog? She couldn't remember anything about her before it. Where was that?

Tail-wagging, Jess had sat beneath a wide, tall tree. It was hot. They were somewhere green, with trees. There was a house – a *real* house like the ones in the books, made from wooden planks and glass windows. Jess had licked Moss's ear.

Now Moss felt the sensation again. She reached up and touched where she remembered the dog's tongue from that day. Salty-rough. Warm. That tongue had licked all the way from the top of her ear and down to her throat.

She'd been paining, she remembered that too now. Jess had licked where it hurt.

Moss shut her eyes to remember, buried her face in the old dog's fur again. This wasn't a vision. It was *Before*, another memory. It was coming easier.

There was more.

Moss had followed Jess. Out of that garden and into a street like in the books too, one with colourful trees and cars. Pink blossoms. Moss had followed that black-and-white feathery tail to a place with boats. All waiting in bobbing lines. Wooden pathways in between. A . . . harbour. Jess had led her to a man with long, pale hair who was kind to them both. There'd been a storm coming that day, and she had told him so. He'd smiled at her as if she were the most important person in the world.

'Magic how you know that,' he'd said.

That was the first day. She remembered now. There were many more days.

She remembered . . . it all. She was beginning to.

She left Adder whining soft beside her mother and moved away to lean against the bed. She breathed one deep breath, then another. It was like she'd just arrived, gasping like this. She stumbled outside to find different air there.

At the firepit, she looked up to Pa's cave. Coloured mist was above it. The Experiment? Now? Again, she heard the volcano rumble.

Did Pa know about Jess? He deserved that at least. And she deserved knowings too.

She went back to fetch the old dog, wrapping her in the softest pelts she could find. Outside, Aster was pawing and dancing. Moss grabbed a tuft of mane and vaulted quick to her back, careful to keep Jess wrapped close-tight to her chest. After only a few strides, Moss heard Adder racing after them, claws scatter-digging at the dirt, whines high on the wind. Moss whistled for her to run with them. And they went, wind-fast.

Pa stood outside his cave like he'd been waiting. Aster skid-stopped before him, skittering on the ledge.

'My girls,' Pa whispered. 'Come back.'

Adder ran around him in a circle.

Moss held out her arms to show him Jess, tucked in the pelts, but Pa wouldn't look. And there were a thousand words inside Moss's head, and a thousand things she needed answers for, but all she could do was stare at him. Pa was bare-chested, even with the worsening weather. His skin sank inwards below his ribs and hung loose around his collarbone. Thin as his dog, he was. How had she not noticed that *oldness* of him, too? And there were colours smeared across him – oranges and yellows streaked his shoulders, gold swirled around his belly button. Crushed stormflower petals. Pa was not even shivering, despite the biting wind. Were the flowers still working, then, keeping him warm?

'Been trying to bring in more spirits,' Pa said, pointing to the building clouds above. He moved his hands through the air as if drawing swirls. 'Trying to create a new world.'

Moss coughed through scent-thick air. There was a smell behind that heavy scent that was different, too – like burning wood, but sour. Again, Moss held out Jess, but Pa acted like he couldn't see. Pa moved his hands through the air, making his swirls smaller. Spirals now, winding down. She was a little scared of this Pa, but she stayed, holding Jess, waiting.

'Found any more spirits on the sand?' he said. 'Has my Experiment worked once more?'

Aster danced beneath Moss as he came closer. It was like he was in another world, swirling and moving. Moss touched fingers to Aster's withers to soothe her. Careful-sure, Moss slid from her. She held out the coverings with Jess inside them, and looked at Pa straight.

'I found Jess where you said I would,' Moss said, 'in the dark space beneath the bed. Dead.'

ACT FOUR. SCENE EIGHTEEN.

Pa blinked hard in the light from the setting sun. Sudden-quick, he whirled away, backed up towards the cave. 'No,' he whispered. 'Not yet. No dying yet. Not the cycle for it!'

He tumbled through the covering across the entrance, getting tangled, still not looking at his dog. Moss followed, carrying Jess, heady from the air that got full-stronger when she came inside. She took a breath of sea air with her.

'Stay,' she told Adder, pointing to where Aster was outside.

She took a moment to see in the sudden dark. Mess was everywhere: books strewn about, pieces of the Experiment half done, a fire raging in the grate too big, and that strange sweet-sour smell. Stormflowers floated or were crushed in the vase on the table; they clung to the ceiling and bookshelves and walls. She felt another tremor beneath her feet.

'Jess,' Pa murmured. 'Jess, Jess . . .' He pulled books from the shelves and held them in his arms. 'I've been waiting for her to come; she's taking her time . . .'

Moss looked at him careful. Pa hadn't believed her? Didn't want to? Couldn't . . . see?

238

'Pa,' she said again. 'Jess has gone. She's dead.'

Throat-tight, she walked across the cave and gently placed the wrapped-up Jess at his feet. He glanced at his dog, then fast-sudden back to the fire as if he were burning that glance away. Adder whined from the entrance as Moss untucked the old dog for Pa. He made a tiny noise, like a dog's whimper itself.

'Not dead,' he said. 'Dreaming.'

Blink-quick, Moss got an image of Pa sleeping with Jess curled in his arms: tight-cosy together. Not an image from their hut, but from their boat, long ago. Thoughts and memories were getting easier now, coming fast.

Following Jess to the Swallow.

That first day.

Jess started this.

'Pa, you need to talk to me.'

No more forgetting. No more trying not to see.

Pa poked the fire with his ebony branch until glowing embers rose. He shook all over, as if he had winds racing through his veins. He was murmuring words so fast and low they were hard to catch and hear: whirring winds too. He opened a book and flicked through.

'The rain it rains without a stay,' he murmured, 'in the hills above us, in the hills . . .'

She recognized these words, had heard them before when Pa had read to her and Cal.

'. . . *the sea calm as a clock . . . And our little lives are rounded with a . . .*'

These, too, were story words: some of Pa's favourites. She came closer. When she grabbed his arms for him to look at her, he didn't see her either. His mind was where the words were: in the sleeping and sailing and flooding of these stories. He was gulping the flower-air, drawing more inside him.

'Have you heard what I've said at all?' she asked.

As Pa poked the fire again, she realized what the sour-strange smell was. In the embers were pages torn from books, burning in scrunched balls, then fluttering up to mingle with the flower petals. There were book covers, too: hard-spined books, burning whole. Moss gasped as she realized. He'd started this morning at camp, and now he was continuing: burning the books in the cave, murmuring their words. Sure enough, as she watched, he sent the book in his hands to the flames.

How could he? They were her stories too, her knowings of the rest of the world! Pa couldn't just get rid of them as if they meant nothing!

'Stop this,' she screamed.

He tore a new page and sent it, scrunched, to the fire. Words burnt and shrivelled, flew up on the heat. She ran at him. Grabbing his arm, she wrenched the next book from his hand, prying it from his fingers.

'The island needs them!' he shouted, clutching tight another armful of books off the shelf.

'Our stories, Pa!'

She saw words from the burning page caught in the air:

. . . a kind of light . . . ran together . . . ribs ached . . .

She remembered that story! It was start of the exciting part, where the characters worked out what they'd lost.

'The island needs them more than we do!' Pa said.

Moss rescued Jess from where the flames had risen, carried her further away. Pa chucked another book to the flames.

'We must save the island from flooding, Moss!' he cried. 'The last safe space in the world!'

She looked at him slow. 'But the rest of the world hasn't gone, Pa. There were no floods. No floods are coming here!'

Now she felt this more than ever. In the bones of her knowing, down-deep. Like how she felt there were more memory-thoughts lurking inside her too. But he whirled away, found another book from the shelf, and tore out pages.

'No!' Moss yelled, reaching for it.

Again, he turned from her. 'We give the stories back . . . we feed it! The island will stop rumbling hungry then.'

''Tis the volcano that rumbles, Pa!' she said. 'Burning books won't stop that!'

Or . . . would they? Moss felt as if she knew nothing any more. And Pa was full-flipped, not listening. But he was full-certain in what he did with these books.

How many flowers had he eaten already? Moss got sudden panic: if Pa was so deep into dreaming-fever, how could she get any answers from him? And if he got worse? Spiralled and spiralled until he was nothing more solid than a piece of kelp on the tide?

She didn't want that Pa.

But she needed to know.

'Pa, listen,' she said. 'You tell me what's true! You do it now!' She forced him to look at her. His pale blue eyes were red-rimmed and watery. 'Then you'll come with us to the Lizard Rocks, and we'll leave this island. It's time.'

'Leave?'

She nodded at the sharp flash of doubt in his eyes. 'Do you remember?' she whispered. 'Do you know what's in those rocks?'

The swirl inside her grew. It was running through her blood, around her insides. A tiny wind, whooshing: a kind of energy. Pa gripped so hard at the books, he made marks in their covers. And the wind from the sea blew in, taking her still-damp coverings and billowing them out, making the firelight dance higher.

'The *Swallow* isn't wrecked,' Moss said. 'Cal found it in the Lizard Rocks. But you know that already, don't you?'

Quick as a weaselmouse, Pa tore more pages and threw them to the fire. Moss stretched forward to pull them back, but already the flames licked at them, then swallowed, getting hotter as they chewed. Sucking on her burnt fingers, she watched the words turn to smoke.

. . . wish I had amnesia . . . showed me a place so different . . . sand and . . .

Pa shook all over. 'No boat, no more . . .'

Maybe this was where all his sicknesses had been leading. To this full-blown fever. Total Blackness. To the Pa she knew – or thought she did – disappearing full. As she tried to make him move from the flames, he grabbed her shoulder.

'Look-see, Moss,' he murmured. 'The words . . . transforming. Here is fuel. *This* is what it's time for. Not for dying. For creating!'

Petals swirled and gathered around them. And there, in the middle of the fire where it burnt blue-hot, she caught a different sort of flickering. Images! Tiny ones. She remembered when Pa had told stories for her with images like this in flames. But these images – now – were jerky and she saw right through them; they disappeared and returned. She squinted and saw . . .

The slick wet head of a seal bobbing.

A girl curled tight.

A man, wandering.

Were these images from the books he'd thrown? Or his thoughts? What was the story he wanted to tell now? Did he even know? Pa tore and threw. Tore and threw.

'Fuel so we can live!' Pa shouted. 'Stories! To keep us safe from the rest!'

She backed away from the fire, from where more images came. On the flames now she saw . . .

Huge storms.

People hiding, scared.

She saw dark water, spilling over. Covering it all.

A man with his head in his hands.

And there were images cycloning inside her, too, whirling-tangled.

Inside her, she saw . . .

Brown boots running.

Dust kicked up.

A man ahead.

She blinked them free.

As Pa tore more pages, he whirl-danced around the fire. No! Moss would not let him whirl so full from her!

'There is another scrapbook,' she said, making herself, as well as him, remember. 'On the *Swallow*.' She stood in front of him so that he could not whirl past; she grabbed his arms. 'You drew pictures in it that I'd never seen before.' She looked at him careful to see if he remembered, but he was staring at the fire over her shoulder, murmuring, murmuring . . .

'"I will send rain," he said. And the water increased and lifted up the ark, so that it rose above . . .'

'Pa, stop!'

But she knew this story too – a great flood sweeping the world away, a boat with two of every animal, starting a new life . . . He spoke its words like a spell.

'Just speak truth!' Moss yelled. 'Not stories all time!'

He blinked at her before adding, '. . . and the ark went on the face of the waters . . .'

She growled. 'I know you've seen the other land! We saw the map in the *Swallow*!'

'Map?'

That stopped him. The rocks rumbled again. Pa looked at her, frowning. For one moment – one tiny hair's breadth – he was lucid. Calm. His eyes were clear.

'You will kill this place, Moss,' he said, quiet. 'With this thinking. This talking. Do you want that? I only try to keep it alive.'

Not breathing as she watched him, she waited for his meaning. But, quick-fast, he broke from her grip and went back to whirling.

'. . . Then the flood came upon the Earth . . . and the water increased and lifted up the ark so that it rose above . . .'

She felt that wind-beat of new thoughts inside her, more like whooshing now. Like she had her own flood tide inside. Pushing . . . pushing . . .

Someone chasing her. Running so fast. Getting . . . away.

She placed her hand to her chest as if to contain the thoughts, but they surged against her.

'You knew the other land's there!' she insisted. 'The one Cal saw first. But you pretended it wasn't! Why?'

He paused again and Moss saw it – that glimpse of almost-remembering. Something had snagged on his mind: caught.

'Answer me, Pa. *Please* . . .'

And that word snagged his eyes back to hers, too.

'I've seen it myself, Pa! The shipwrecked boys have!'

'Not time, Moss. Not yet. Land can't come back until it's . . .'

She pulled him towards the entrance of the cave. On scuff-dragging feet, he came. Once outside, Adder nipped at his ankles, nudging him forward too.

'Look!' Moss shouted.

Because the land was there, shadowy but there in the sea as if it had always been. She saw its skimmer-stone shape better now. Saw the birds circling above it.

'Bird Island,' she whispered.

But Pa was shaking his head, wasn't looking . . . wasn't *seeing*.

'No land,' he said, turning back. 'Not there.'

'Look-see!'

She took his face between her hands. Held him jaw-strong. When he tried to shut his eyes, she pried his lids open.

'It's there!'

He frowned, concentrating. Was he willing himself not to see?

'True story is,' he began, 'there were floods, Moss. They covered the Earth. All the countries where bad things happened – smothered evil politics and unkindness, a tide of hate . . .'

She relaxed her grip on his eyes, watched his face as he spoke. How could he still keep saying this? After she'd seen the *Swallow*? After she'd told him so?

'You lie, Pa,' she whispered, stepping away. 'Like Cal said you did.'

He shook his head. 'I tell a story.'

And – *there!* – at the edge of her was another memory, one she couldn't quite see, couldn't quite grasp. Another story. *She* had another story. But . . . what was it full?

'Great floods have flown from simple sources . . .' Pa murmured, '. . . and great seas have dried when miracles have by the greatest been denied . . .'

More story words. More make-believe!

This time when she looked back to the land, it was gone. Once more, nothing but sea. A horizon line. Rain clouds. A sun that was nearly set. So where was it?

She squinted, hard. Why this flickering again? Behind her, she heard Pa still mumbling about his stories. Then, at last, she thought she might understand.

'Can *you* do that?' she said, still looking at where the land had been. 'Is that you making it go?'

A corner of his mouth turned up.

'*You* make the land go away? Somehow, with the flowers? With your words?'

She released her grip on him and he raised his hands towards the horizon as if about to call a storm. Stormflowers came circling, swirling. She heard their giggle-song. Now she remembered something else. The flowers had acted strange-different when she had tried the Experiment with Cal. Now they were laughing – they *wanted* to work for Pa in a way they hadn't for her.

She stepped back further from Pa, her head reeling. But Pa kept his smile. She had understood something, sure.

'Why, Pa?'

She thought further – the flowers had screamed, not giggled, when she and Cal had tried to send them out. Was this because . . . she'd wanted the opposite from Pa? To see the land, not hide it?

Could it be ... they hadn't wanted to show her? Was it possible Pa had sent flowers out not to end floods but to hide the other island ... somehow? Was it possible the flowers wanted that too? She shivered, it was too big ... too much to understand.

'They do that?' she asked. 'Hide things?'

Pa's smile grew.

The idea wriggled inside her. Was that what the Experiment had really been about? Hiding? Strange, rough magic? A lie? Keeping things in dream?

Her bleeding, Cal, that land out there ...

Lies ... lies ...

Again, she felt that whooshing inside her – that tiny new wind. But it was an angry wind now. A brewing tornado.

When the volcano rumbled next, she'd known it was coming. She stood firm when Pa stumbled; she turned him back to the sea.

'Is the reason we're here anything to do with floods?' she said.

She felt Pa tense. Again, Finn's words, like a tide in her brain:

Fugitive ... not right in the head ... perfect place to hide ...

'There's a world out there, isn't there?' she said. 'A whole flood-less world. And you've been keeping it from me all this time. Why, Pa?'

And – *there!* – on her next glance to the water, it returned. Cal's land. That rock with the birds. Flickering into life. She saw by Pa's face that he'd seen it too. Had *she* done that? Just by thinking it real? *Knowing* it was there?

Quick-fast, he turned her, pulled her away from the cliff and back into the cave.

'No, Moss!'

But now she was starting to understand ... *she* was making it

247

come. She could see the land because it was there – for her, at least. Because she wanted to see it!

Adder barked and spun as she bounded into the cave after them. When Pa raised his hands, the flames leapt higher and more images came – Moss saw them swirl from the fire.

Waterhorses, riding on waves.

Mermaids swimming.

And water, water, water, coming at them . . . flooding them. The huge floods Pa talked of.

Stories . . . dreamings . . .

Wind rushed in from outside then too, bringing petals, thousands of them. All the different flower colours. They spun and danced, buzz-singing. Two tones, one high and one low: a bird's trill call. Whole plants of stormflowers whooshed in next, their dirty roots waving. Towards the fire they moved, swirling. Some dived straight into the flames. High-pitched. Laughing. Singing. Screaming. Moss felt their desire. They wanted to make Pa's images come. She steadied herself against the cave wall as the volcano rumbled. Beside her, Adder nuzzled with her damp snout.

As the fire raged still bigger, the back of her neck went hot and she felt the tipsy spin of nausea. Too much smoke. Too much sweetness. For a moment she was floating, above the cave and the cliffs, looking down. Swirling in the airs. Swaying with those petals. Letting go. She felt the flowers inside her . . . ready to create mermaids and kelpies and spirits in the flames like they did for Pa. She felt the thrill of it. She breathed in a lungful of sweet smoke, wondering. Could she make images like Pa did? Or, maybe . . . could she make truth on the flames as easy as he made his stories? Just now, she'd made Bird Island appear . . . hadn't she? She'd made

248

something change . . .

She raised her arms and swirled her fingers to spirals. Her movement made Pa turn.

His eyes went paler, watering from the smoke. 'Moss,' he said, full-warning in his voice.

And that made her more curious still.

What could she do, really? She opened her hand and felt petals settle on her palm. She watched the flames, concentrating on that whooshing wind inside her. When she felt its energy like water spilling over, she sent it out to the petals. They left her palm and went to the fire.

'You'll kill this place,' Pa said, watching. 'You don't understand.'

The images in the fire changed. And she was making them. She could feel it.

'Truth,' she whispered, echoing the word that was pounding inside her. 'My real story.'

What she most wanted.

She stayed steady as the cave floor shuddered.

Then she was the tiny figure in the flames. Her as a Small Thing. She was with Cal, holding hands tight-close. They stood on the edge of their cove, staring to the ocean. And there was Jess, eyes bright. They were all looking out. Towards the horizon? The Flicker-land? When was this, how many seasons ago?

Her vision shivered. The cave was blurring now, fading back, and all she could see were those images in the flames. The fire burnt bigger as she focused on that tiny wind inside, sending it out. Her will. Her desire. She'd made those images. She'd done this! She could whir those flowers into a frenzy. *This* was how Pa did it: the stormflowers latched on to his will, and they made visible what he wanted. She *felt*, rather than understood, the sense of it.

In the fire, her and Cal. Small Things. On the rough raft they'd made, the day they'd almost drowned. They were bobbing out towards a skimmer-stone-shaped land. *Bird Island.*

She gasped. It had been there, even then? Had she seen it, just for a moment, before it went hidden? Before that huge wave had pushed them back?

From somewhere far away, she heard Pa take another book and throw it into the fire. Moss's images were sudden-gone. Instead, words flew up before her.

Fish . . . love you and respect you . . . will kill you dead . . .

An image of a whale came diving from the flames. Moss flinched before it evaporated into thick syrup air. She braced as there was another tremor. Could she make her images come again? It was a battle between Pa's stories and hers.

'Stop it, Moss,' Pa said. 'We must give the island our dreams, keep it alive!'

But she wanted truth. *Her* truth.

Dust fell as the rocks rumbled. Sent Pa stumbling. This time she caught him. This time when she turned him back to Jess, she knew he saw his dog. She *willed* him to. Kept him steady till he did. He couldn't stop the look, this time.

And finally, he bent to Jess, scooped her close in his arms. He had tears straight away – she saw them full. And he was seeing, seeing, accepting, seeing . . . His shoulders shaking like storms.

Had she made him? Made him come back to this moment, in this cave?

He looked back to Moss, eyes drowning. 'You destroy the island with your story.'

ACT FOUR. SCENE NINETEEN.

When the rumbling in the rocks came again, Finn put his hand under the back of Tommy's head to shield it from the stone floor. He swallowed the fear that was rising. Why hadn't Moss come back yet? Since she'd left, Tommy had returned to feverish sleeping. Now Finn needed to get help for him – proper help – before he got any worse. He shivered as he looked across at the hole Moss had disappeared down and Cal had come back up from alone. Cal had said there was a boat down there. Sailing a boat from a rock cavern, without Tommy to help, was not on the top of his to-do list. But staying on an island where a volcano was erupting and his friend was getting sicker didn't present many options.

Finn stared at Cal across the fire. Finn didn't think this dark-eyed boy liked him much, and why should he? Finn had seen the jealous glare in Cal's eyes whenever he'd looked at Moss. Either way, this boy would have to help him.

'We need to leave,' he said firmly. 'Now. Even if Moss doesn't come back.'

Even if it was dark outside. Even if sailing away on a strange boat might be the hardest thing he'd ever do.

Cal glanced towards the hole too. When the tunnel shuddered again, sending down dust, Cal nodded.

'We go. But we find her first.'

'Course the dark-eyed boy wouldn't leave her. Maybe she was the only friend he'd ever had; maybe that was why they were so close. Another rumble came, tumbling shards of stone down around them. To sail out of an unknown land in the dark? From a place that'd wrecked their own boat already? It was worse than crazy, it was a death wish.

But then, so was staying in a cave while a volcano erupted.

Finn stood. 'No point hanging around. Show me the boat and I'll see if I can sail it.'

'No "if".' Cal's eyes actually seemed to glint. 'You must.'

There were sharp points of rock – stalactites – not far above Tommy's head. If the rumbling came again, could they fall down on to him?

Cal nodded towards Tommy. 'I can carry.' He placed his palms against the wall as if feeling for vibrations. 'I done it before.'

Finn narrowed his eyes. How much could he trust Cal? It could be a trap, leading him and Tommy into some hole. Cal might want them away so that he could stay with Moss alone. But then, why would he have gone to so much trouble to save Tommy in the first place? And surely if there was a boat, it was worth a shot – might be their only shot. He wondered if Cal would come with them, back to his home town . . . wondered how on earth he'd fit in with the guys in the pub, with his school friends, with anyone! Even thinking of Moss fitting in was hard enough to imagine.

Tommy moaned, and Finn was at his side immediately. 'You

with us again, mate?'

He'd been coming in and out of it ever since Moss had gone.

'Don't leave me behind,' Tommy murmured.

Finn shook his head firmly. 'I won't.' Finn would do whatever it took.

He lifted his friend into a sitting position, wiped his moist brow. When Tommy gasped for air, Finn kept him straight.

'He's getting sicker,' he told Cal.

Cal nodded. 'The island not helping him.'

So Finn started asking – the island, and God, and Buddha, and any other deity he could think of – to keep his friend safe. He watched Cal flex his fingers in and out, frowning when the tattoo-like pattern on Cal's skin seemed to disappear again, then come back.

'Put Tommy on your back,' Cal said. 'I will help.'

With Cal helping, he got Tommy to stand. As Tommy gripped the walls, Finn hiked him up in a fireman's lift over his shoulder.

'Ready to find a boat, mate?' he asked Tommy's legs, now hanging beside him.

'Just don't put it on another reef.' Tommy's voice came back muffled.

Finn smiled to hear it. Then more shards of stone fell down, making Tommy groan.

'Quick,' said Cal.

Cal blew the fire out. Just like that. It extinguished in a second. Finn wanted to ask him how he did it, watch him do it again, but this was no time for party tricks. He was shaking from the weight of Tommy and with the tension of holding him still. The rumbling in the rock got worse.

As they climbed out of the cave and on to the path leading down, Finn stumbled. He wrenched his shoulder painfully as he reached to grip the rock wall. He breathed hard. These walls might as well collapse! Climbing down this path, like this, was impossible. He couldn't even see where he was going!

Cal backed up. Until Finn could feel his shoulders pressed up against him, inviting Finn to lean.

'Am strong enough,' he said. 'Trust. We carry together.'

Finn leant forward, trying it, and put his free hand on Cal's shoulder. With Cal taking some of the weight, it was certainly easier. Perhaps Finn *could* trust him. They made their way slowly, not stumbling now.

Soon something began to glow, hundreds of somethings, all the way down the edges of the narrow path. It was like fairy lights at a party, illuminating the way. Finn followed gladly. As they climbed down, Finn saw them properly: they weren't actual lights, not even fireflies or glow-worms. Here were hundreds, maybe thousands, of those flowers he'd seen all over the island – those stormflowers – and they were open and growing out of the dark, damp rocks, without even any sunlight. They were glinting! Like Moss said they did. Were they helping them to get down easier? Or leading them to their doom?

As he got down further, Finn heard a kind of humming noise too. Also the flowers? *Different rules*, Moss had said. *A magic island.* Maybe now he believed it. Either that, or this was all a seriously strange hallucination and they were all on it, tripping hard.

He touched a flower as he passed, and it buzzed louder. Buzzed at him?

Perhaps it wasn't such a jump to see how a person might change to something different here. Become something unexpected. Like Moss. Or Cal. Become something stranger, like Pa. Become almost ... magic?

'The flowers want you gone,' Cal said. 'They're showing how, lighting the way.'

Finn saw the whole path the flowers were lighting now, on either side like tiny beacons. All the way to a boat. *The boat!* He saw it clearly. It was so similar to the *Swift* – the make and everything! – it could have been the very same. He squinted to see it better. If it weren't for a few different letters on the side and its faded colour, he might not have even known the difference.

An escape! If Finn could just get them past the rocks and the reef ... was he good enough to do it? He'd have to sail with skills he wasn't sure he had.

Finn touched the petals of a flower growing from the wall. He watched as another flower stretched out to brush against Tommy's legs, dew from its leaves settling on the skin between his mate's ripped trousers. And as Finn passed, for an urge and reason he didn't quite understand, Finn found himself saying ... 'Thank you.'

ACT FOUR. SCENE TWENTY.

The rumble came again, like there was a huge beast in the rocks, waking up, about to push through. Moss circled her finger in a spiral against the dusty wall . . . circling in, circling out. *Circle, cycle . . . spiral.* Till she was calmer, less sick. Tethered. *Real* again.

They needed to go, that was clear. She should grab Pa and push him out of the cave. But there was another urge inside her, too, stirred up from the fire images. What else could she make visible there? What would this wind inside her create? It might be her final chance to see.

If Pa refused to remember . . .

If he had true-forgot . . .

If he wouldn't say . . .

The flowers in the cave sang back.

'True images,' she murmured. 'Memory images.'

Secrets, secrets . . .

Quick-fast, she felt heat against her face, the flames reflected. She splayed open her outstretched palms. Wind whooshed around her, smashed something from the table. Pa made a sound that could've been a cry or maybe a laugh. Adder howled and the fire grew bigger. Hotter.

From somewhere far away, she heard Pa warning. 'No, Moss, no . . . You don't want this.'

Then the image came clear.

She stepped back to feel the cave wall against her.

And there he was once more.

That angry man.

Here again. Only a few paces away, taunting in the flames. Somehow, she'd thought he might be.

He was clearer than the other images Pa had made earlier, so clear he might step from the fire. Come closer. She wanted to shut-tight her eyes. She wanted to run, hare-quick. She made herself stay. *Watch.* This was what she'd asked for, wasn't it? An answer. A truth. She'd expected this. As she faced him, his mouth opened to a shout. Like it had in her dreamings. Like when he'd found her at the bottom of the sea. Like in Pa's cave.

She gripped the rock wall tight. But she would not turn away, not like she'd done every time before. This time she had to know who he was.

She locked eyes on him and he came, right out of the fire and into the thick syrup air. Moss slid down stone till she was crouched. Still, she watched. Heard!

Useless!

The word came from somewhere. Flower song? Memory-thought? The man?

You ruined it!

She trembled with the cave walls. This was only a vision – a part of her knew that. An image on the flower-smoke . . . come because she'd called it.

Had she called him those other times, too?

She made herself look. Made herself see.

His hair was curly as well as dark. And his eyes were green – shocking green. Green like hers.

She heard other words. Words that made her crouch – *shiver* – away.

Not good enough!

Will hit you if you do that again!

The man's arm was raised as if he might. She could feel where he would. On her face. Near her ear. It would go sting-paining.

She pressed into the wall, away from his pointing finger. Leant back so hard the wall stabbed her instead. And then . . .

Another memory!

Jab-fast!

She shut her eyes.

She was running. And he chased with brown boots. Towards a wooden deck where boats bobbed, following behind a black-and-white feathered dog tail. Running towards where Pa sat waiting, watching. On a boat. On the *Swallow*.

Moss gulped air in the smoke-thick cave, couldn't get enough.

She knew who that angry man was. Knew it, but couldn't let herself think it. Not yet.

She could feel Pa's hands on her arm, trying to soothe her, saying something she couldn't understand. Could Pa see this image too? Did he know what it meant?

'Course he did!

The picture in his book . . . *he'd seen!*

She could not look at him. But she did not want to look at the angry man, either. She was caught between them both. She pressed harder against the stone, wanting to go so far into it that she was part of it. Part of anything that wasn't this.

Was this why Pa dreamt of floods? If the rest of the world was flooded, they couldn't return. The bad places would be gone, the bad people too. They'd never see this angry man again. Maybe she wanted floods too.

'Moss!' She could hear Pa's voice, feel his fingers on her arm, shaking her. When she turned to him, when she could blink and focus a little, she saw his wet, pale eyes. Blue eyes. Nothing like her eyes. His hair was so pale and straight and different. His face long and bony. Such high cheekbones. He was seabird while she was dog. He'd been wrong to call her Moss-bird all these seasons.

Nothing like her.

Not the same.

Finn had been right. He'd seen it straight away.

'Who are we?' she said.

Pa shook his head, backed away, his chest shuddering like the rock.

She trembled too. The angry man was there, still, at the corner of her vision. But she couldn't look at him. Could only look at Pa.

'Who are you?' Her voice cracked. 'You're not really . . . not really . . .?' She gasped as if there were no air left.

Why hadn't she ever questioned it full? Wondered why she was so different?

But he had told her stories. Had healed her wounds. Taught her how to fish and stitch clothes and make drawings seem real.

He had told her lies.

'It was what you wanted,' he murmured.

Moss touched her ear where she still felt the sting, the throbbing

259

from where she'd been hit as a Small Thing.

Hit.

This time, she didn't need to look at images in the flower-smoke: the memory was already there, inside her, pushed up to the surface ... Now, when she shut her eyes ...

She was the Smallest of Small Things again, smaller than she'd ever been on this island. She was running through a dark wooden house, skidding around corners, screaming. There was an anxious twisting in her belly, a feeling urging her faster. That angry man was chasing her. Shouting. Getting close. She tried to hide behind someone else, soft and spice-smelling; used that woman's skirts to cover her face.

The Angry Pa came anyway. He dug his fingers into her shoulder. Wrenched her so hard from the skirts that Moss tore them. She took those skirt pieces in her hand as she spun away. It made the Angry Pa worse.

You did it on purpose!

She did not have time to duck. She felt pain spread across her face like something spilling. Felt throbbing in her ears.

Then there was no sound at all.

Just the pulsing of blood.

She looked at the brown carpet. Any moment she might fall into it. Maybe she would sink through, get away.

To a quiet place.

Gone.

Far from him.

Then the sounds came back. So much shouting. She curled away.

You never know when to stop! Always one step too far! Sneaky brat!

She ran to the door and pressed at the handle. It would not go down. And the Angry Pa came closer. She pushed, and pushed, and the Angry Pa reached out his huge arm. He would hit again. Hit harder.

Now you'll get it!

His fist came close. She pushed on that handle. Push-push-pushed until . . .

She was running again. Fast-breathless. Till she was chasing a dog with a black-and-white feathery tail. Passing trees and houses and sandy roads. Finding a harbour. Seeing a red boat, bobbing in a line with others.

Until she reached a different man, one who listened when she told about storms coming. Who never yelled or hurt. Who did not think she was sneaky or bad. Who looked at her like she was . . . magic.

Who was sick.

She blinked. Looked back.

Pa had Jess in his arms, standing with her above the fire as if wondering whether to put her there.

Now a different image was on its flames. No angry man any more, but still . . .

An image of Moss, as she was as a Very Small Thing. She was curled in blankets on a boat deck, with Jess tight beside. A younger version of Pa stared at them both. He gave Moss a biscuit and she halved it with the dog.

Moss remembered this too. Another memory.

She had stuck her tongue out, all covered in crumbs. And that Pa who was not yet her pa had tickled her until she laughed hard, and Jess had spun and barked.

'Go home, little moss-eyed girl,' he'd said. 'I need to find some-thing – somewhere far away. Can't take you with me.'

And Moss had stuck her chin out, stubborn.

She remembered.

When Moss looked up at Pa now, he nodded. He'd been watch-ing this image too . . . remembering?

He crouched down over his dog beside the fire, head bowed. Wind grabbed his hair; his bare skin beneath the flower colours paler than tern feathers. Despite the flames, he shivered.

'I used to hide in your boat, didn't I?' she said.

Pa curled into himself, stone-quiet, hugging his dog.

'Pa?' she whispered. 'Do you remember?'

As if he were a million years old, Pa nodded.

'I used to play there.'

'You made company with this daft stray dog.' His voice seemed to come straight from his chest. 'I didn't encourage it . . .'

And she remembered this. All this.

And then . . .

And then . . .

Then, one day . . .

'You took me,' she said.

'An accident,' Pa murmured, then added, 'a happy one.' When he sighed, coloured air came from his lips. It hovered before him, circling Jess in a rainbow halo.

'You took me,' she said again. 'I do not belong here . . .'

Maybe she did not belong anywhere, to anyone.

She felt trembles in the stone beneath her. She grabbed Adder to keep her close, mirroring what Pa did with Jess, heard things falling and smashing. What was happening outside their cave?

'Who are you, then?' she asked again.

'Pa,' he murmured. 'Just Pa.'

'You don't have a name?'

Perhaps he had forgotten it.

He had lied.

He had taken her.

He was not her pa.

He did not even know his own name.

There were hot tears on her cheeks, even as she tried to smudge them away. Another thought struck her sharp. What was it he had called her, in the memory? 'Little moss-eyed girl'? And if Pa didn't know his real name . . .

'Am I even called Moss?'

When he didn't answer, she asked him again. She shouted it!

Something else smashed. She turned to see the door covering billowing out. But Pa was deep-down-deep, shaking-broken, not noticing. If she did have another name, perhaps Pa had forgotten that too.

Then the ground really shook.

Lunging, she pulled Pa from a falling rock's path. She clutched him as a gash opened up beside them, right through the rock floor. The cave was true breaking.

'Wait,' Pa said as she dragged him free, tried to drag him from the cave. 'Wait!'

Struggling, he turned back, Jess in his arms, eyes locked on the fire. Moss saw the serious-calm on his face, and then knew what he would do. Her throat went pinched, but what else could he do with her now? Slow-gentle and tear-cheeked, Pa leant towards the fire. There, he placed Jess in the flames.

'Dog dreams for the island,' he said. 'Give something back.'

Moss skidded backwards, not wanting to see Jess burn on her pyre. She clutched Adder tighter so she wouldn't look too. Then, with strength she didn't know she had, she pulled Adder and Pa away. Pa moaned to leave Jess behind, but he came. They all came.

Outside were more gashes in the rock. The whole island was shaking. Everything breaking. Had she done this, like Pa said? By wanting truth? No more stories?

Pa stumbled to Aster, who was skittering on the cliff edge. Smoke was spreading out from the cave, billowing like a colourful skirt above them. Even now, there were images on that smoke, floating into the sky:

Pa giving her food on the boat.

Telling her stories.

Pa with his arms tight around her.

Pa making a tiny wind curl and dance in the palm of his hand just for her.

Making her laugh.

Healing her.

Showing her stormflowers.

She thought of spirals going in and spirals going out. She looked out to the ocean. Bird Island was back again, not flickering at all. Sudden-fast, she remembered what Cal had said on the *Swallow*.

Maybe that land is not the one that's flickering.

Maybe they all were.

Maybe it made a kind of sense.

Pa turned to look at her, his eyes blinking fast – flickering, almost, too. 'The island is breaking, Moss. Get safe.'

Safe.

The word sang on the air.

But there was one last memory, she felt it build. She pulled at it, needed to share it.

'One day was different,' she said. 'Do you remember it too?'

That day . . . Pa was not on his boat when she'd run to find him. But she had stepped aboard anyway, her cheek throbbing, purple-bruised. On mouse-quiet feet, she'd climbed down into the cabin and crawled inside the cupboard where he kept his clothes. She hid. There, the Angry Pa would not find her. Would not know where she was. Not ever. Through a crack in the cupboard door, she'd warned the black-and-white dog quiet with her eyes. She'd waited. Did not crawl back out until the boat had sailed far gone.

Moss felt the cold wind coming in off the sea. The rumble in the rock.

She could remember now, hiding. Choosing this Pa. The Pa who healed instead of hurt. Who'd thought she was magic.

Storm-woke. He'd called her that too.

Pa's hands were on her arm. She touched his fingers. 'Peter,' she said, soft. 'Your name.'

Pa stared at her long.

'You came from England.' As she said it, she remembered sitting with him on the *Swallow*'s deck, all that talking. 'Your grandfather had died and you were sick too. Sick in your mind. You said the storms were getting worse. *The world* was getting worse. You told me stories.'

Pa wiped wetness from his eyes. Slow-gentle, he reached across to touch her face, on the side where her ear still throbbed even now.

'I did not turn back,' Pa said. 'When I knew you were there, hiding on my boat . . . I should have.'

But Moss was thinking of his sketch, of the likeness in it. 'You saw him chase me?'

He nodded.

And that made her certain. 'I did not want to go back.'

And this, she realized, was true. Moss reached up to Pa's hand. 'Saved, not stole.'

Pa was shaking his head. But there was a spark of hope in his eyes now too.

'Miranda,' he said.

'*Mir-an-da.*' She tried it out. The word felt strange, did not feel like her.

She pulled Pa to move. 'I will tell the story. It will be all right. Trust me. It will be fine, returning to the rest of the world.'

Spirals, spirals, moving out . . . coming real.

She would make it all right. They both would.

And Pa nodded. 'OK.'

It was time.

He curled his fingers, beckoning to his horse. He sang the same two-note trill he sang to the flowers. Aster turned her head, ears pricked, listening.

Before he leapt on to the horse's back and held his hand out for Moss, he looked to the wild-churning sea.

'I see it,' he said, gazing at Cal's land. 'It's there.'

ACT FOUR. SCENE TWENTY-ONE.

C al crawled quick-fast back up to the deck after making Tommy safe below. Rocks were crumbling, rain-falling. He untied salt-stiff knots that'd fixed that boat to the cave – set it free.

'Take it gone!' he shouted to Finn.

But from where the boat's steer-wheel was, Cal saw Finn's eyes were as spun-wide as Moss's spiral drawings. The island groaned, sent more stones falling. Cal ducked one the size of a lizard egg, then caught it before it could crack a hole in the boards! He skittered across deck to shake Finn hard, till the boy focused back on the boat and what needed doing.

'We all die if you do not move it quick!' Cal urged.

Finn's jaw was tight-hard; he would do it! There was fierce-calm in this boy now, more strong than Cal had seen before. He pressed fingers to his shoulder.

'Tell me what to do, and I help.'

Finn nodded. 'Push the boat away from the rock sides! Don't let the boat hit anything!'

There was a sound like an animal – like a wild dog's growl – as

Finn made the boat move forward in a leap. Cal stumbled back at the noise, surprised when Finn laughed sudden-sharp.

'Wasn't sure that would kick in!' he shouted. 'Seems this boat's got a magic motor!'

Quick-fast, the boat slosh-whooshed, bobbed close to cave sides. Cal got working. He ran round deck, push-pushing the boat away. When the boat moved fast towards the rock gap out ahead, he took a long paddle of wood to push the sides away sharper. He was huff-puffing hard. The wide-big sea got closer. Still, the boat scraped rock a few times, making Cal stop his breathings. But it held. Everything held.

When the boat got nearer to big waves, flowers sang louder, pushing scents out. Cal felt them cling-long to his nose, buzz-bright in his brain. All around, it sounded like the island was moaning. As they left through the jagged-sharp opening – Cal pushing and pulling and sweating and bleeding to make sure they didn't hit cave sides – he saw lizards. They were jumping from rocks, spreading webbed hands wide as they hit the sea. Stingers were below, also, their pale, soft bodies moving like clouds. Were they scared of the volcano too? Or were they escaping?

Then they were out. Far out. Beyond even the reef. The water was rough-dark, only moon to light it. The sea had stripes, like them zebras from books. Cal had only twice before been this far out. When he washed up, which he did not full-remember. And when he'd tried to leave with Moss on the raft. Both times he'd been pulled in.

Not this time.

Quick-fast, he looked for the Flicker-land and saw it, more solid now.

'Bird Island!' He pointed it out to Finn.

He saw Tommy been right – the land were just rock and birds, no huts or humans. Not the same land where the man from his dreamings lived.

But he didn't have time to look proper. Because the growling noise Finn made from the boat changed, and the boat went true-fast. Waves slapped the sides, made Cal sway. He gripped the long pole through the middle to steady himself. He thought of Moss as a Very Small Thing on this very same boat, and that settled him most. But Cal were not scared – not one weasel-bit!

Finn was laughing when he looked back. Cal came closer to see why.

'Can't believe getting out of there was so easy!' Finn said. 'Where next?'

Cal pointed to where the cove was. Finn steered the boat – it went tossing and turning, but he kept it moving straight. Cal squinted for Moss in case she was already on this shore, sent thoughts out on the winds about where they were. Then, far-high, he saw smoke, like there were a thousand fires on top of the volcano. Flower-smoke! It were like branches stretching down – clawing, grasping. It came sinking 'cross the island.

Was there moving fire with it too, underneath-sneaky, coming for Moss and Pa? Coming for Jess and Adder and Aster, and the wild dogs, and all the lizards that did not jump?

Finn kept the boat level with the shoreline of Western Beach. They were far-further out than that day on the raft. And maybe it were that, and maybe it were not, but Cal were remembering – long-ago thoughts were coming clear. Stories about Flower Island, different ones from what the Pa had told: ones from a time – *place*

– other than here. Stories about beings forgetting what they came knowing.

'What the—?'

The shout startled him. Cal looked across to see Finn with his mouth wide. Seems he'd seen volcano smoke too. Cal didn't explain it: he couldn't. 'Cause understanding this island were a bit like knowing Moss – he were never sure he got her complete-right, never saw her all in one easy look-see. Cal couldn't explain a thing like that.

As smoke came thick and more coloured towards them, so did the singing. Flower-singing. So much louder now.

'Seriously,' Finn said, 'what the hell is this place?'

Then the boat moved sharp. It were like something grabbed it, twisted and spun it. Like there were a whirly-pool right under. The same pulling feeling as when Cal and Moss had been on the raft. Like something did not want them to leave.

'Hey!'

A shout. Tommy on deck now too, risen bleary from the cabin, holding firm to its door. Looking. Frowning. Staring. *Standing.*

Cal smiled. *Well!*

Finn's grin came fast, too. 'What're you doing up here?' He spun the steer-wheel hard, fighting with the boat and trying to make it go. 'Do you feel all right?'

Tommy stared at the island, full-confusion on his face. 'What's the pull?' he said.

Finn pushed at the steer-wheel, and still the boat would not go forward.

Tommy was baffle-faced, watching. 'It's like when we wrecked,' he said. 'The same feeling. That pulling in.'

ACT FOUR. SCENE TWENTY-TWO.

Moss's hair was tangle-knotted, the wind near-pulling her from Aster. She held on to Pa and they galloped. Drumming in her ears and through her body. Hooves and rumbling. Aster was on wings, flight-fast.

She whistled again for Adder, hoping her dog was keeping up and dodging the falling debris. There was noise, everywhere. Wind hissing. Trees cracking. And, behind everything, a roar. Loud-fierce. The volcano. How long did they have before it swallowed them up? She knew Cal was waiting. She felt that bone-deep inside her. She heard his voice.

Western Beach . . . come fast . . . come now-now . . .

Still, she felt tension in Pa. Felt his doubt in the stiffness of his spine against her chest.

Through the pine forest, faster. The sea whirled fierce, calling to them as it always did, but louder now. Adder barked: still here, still close. It was too dark in the trees to see her proper. Everything was moving. The whole island shifting, swaying, dancing, trembling. And Aster galloped, lightning-fast. Racing for the sea, to be gone. A shudder brought branches down around them; Aster dodged them all. Even now, the island was beautiful-wild. Like Pa, Moss had an ache inside her when she thought about leaving.

But soon they were out of the pine trees and on to the dunes. Fast . . . faster . . . quicker than ever before. Here, the wind was lizardlike, biting and clawing. Sand whirled into their eyes, stung their faces. And there was the sea, full-huge and writhing. There was Bird Island, full-solid.

And, stuck on the reef, spinning and struggling, was Pa's boat. The *Swallow*.

Moss cried out as Aster reared. It took all Moss's concentration to stay clinging to the horse and to Pa – to keep thinking kind-nesses to quiet her.

Pa's boat whirled like Aster. 'Can you see it, Pa?' she said, pointing.

He saw it, she knew: she saw his faint smile in recognition. 'Back again,' he murmured, then looked to Bird Island too.

'All back.'

She remembered Cal's words on the wind. *Come now-now.* 'Maybe they were trying to get to us in the cove and got stuck here instead.'

But Aster wasn't stuck. She set off running again, getting closer to the ocean, closer than she'd been when Finn had sent her racing. Moss felt her shaking: a volcano underneath her, twice now. Moss put her hands around Pa's waist, keeping steady. She turned to find Adder. There was ash in the air. Burning petals. So much smoke. Orange and red, pink and gold. Flower-colours. The air was so thick, in moments they couldn't see, couldn't breathe. Aster skit-tered sideways to the water. Moss thought of Jess, back in Pa's cave. All alone! Burning. She touched her fingers to Aster's salt-crusted

272

skin as she got to tide's edge. Would she be leaving Aster soon, too? Was that what the horse wanted?

'We'll need to swim, Pa,' Moss said. 'If we want to get to the boat.'

When Pa looked at her, his eyes were yearning-sad. Moss thought she knew why: he wanted to stay with his horse, with his island. Even if it meant drowning. Or being burnt. As Aster dipped fetlocks to water, her hooves disappeared in the swirling sea. Did Pa realize that the horse wouldn't come? Did Aster know it too?

'But my success . . .' he whispered, winding up her mane with his fingertips.

'Not your only one.' Moss gripped his hand.

'You too?' He raised eyebrows. When he looked at her, she grinned.

'Come on, Pa. It's time. We have to leave now.'

Keeping hold of Aster's mane with her other hand, she got down from the horse. The water was shock-cold, the wind against her legs making it full-colder.

Pa reached out to tap the end of Moss's nose. 'There's magic all through you,' he said. 'As much as in Aster.'

Moss gripped harder on Pa's hand and pulled. Aster had to stay. Couldn't have a horse on a boat – she'd sink them all. But would Pa go without her? Would Aster be all right? Moss felt the ache in her heart too.

'She wants to be in the water,' she said to urge them both, but knowing it was true also. 'She wants to be here. Wants to stay.'

Like Pa did.

Like a part of Moss did too. And this part was splintering her.

She brushed her hand against Aster's neck, as she had when the horse had first arrived.

'I can feel it,' she said. 'It is the sea you want, isn't it?'

And Moss did feel this urge – through the horse's muscles and movement – that urge to dive to the water, to skitter on sand, to gallop in pines. To stay! This island was her; she was the island. Wherever else Cal had come from, Aster was from here. Flower-made. Moss knew this, bone-deep.

Could Pa leave that?

He watched his horse, deciding.

When Aster reared again, he came from her, tumbling to Moss in the shallow sea. His head snapped back to Aster straight after, an invisible cord between them.

Aster tossed her head, and flower petals swirled around her like a coloured crown. So many buzzing, all wanting to be with her. She was rainbow-haired. Prancing and high-stepped, she went further out, until the water was nearly up to her stomach, her tail risen and proud. She did not look back to either of them.

Pa sang to her like he sang to the flowers, the two-toned trill. Then he whispered something too soft to catch on the wind, and Aster's ears flicked backwards, listening, pausing, prancing . . .

Pa breathed in, air rattling in his throat. And Aster dived away, straight and sharp. That huge horse as elegant and streamlined as a seabird. Down, down into the ocean, and a wave took her under. Moss saw her for a moment more, diving as a dolphin might, curved and pale as a wave tip herself.

Waterhorse.

Water.

Gone.

Like how she'd arrived.

Pa breathed out.

After a moment, Moss did too. Maybe it would be all right now. Maybe Pa had released whatever hold still attached him to this place. Maybe the island would go calm. Pa would too. Soon, they would swim out and get the boat free: leave. A new start for them both. It *was* what she wanted, wasn't it?

'Come on, Pa,' she said.

But the cliffs were still rumbling and shifting. There was still so much ash in the air. The ground still shook. When she tried to search for the boat on the reef, smoke blinded her. She grabbed Adder, clutched her tight-tight. Whatever else happened, she would not lose her dog. Pa clutched Moss tight-tight too, shielding her from the wind.

'We *have* to leave, Pa,' she said.

He tightened his arms around her, looking back to the volcano. 'It doesn't want to lose our stories,' he said. 'Remember ... when the island catches stories, it stays hiding. But when the stories leave ...'

'The island comes real.' She finished it for him. 'Comes back.'

And maybe it was true. Pa's truth, anyway. Maybe he'd made it that way.

'It's not Bird Island that been flickering,' she said, remembering again Cal's words. Maybe Pa's stories, and the stormflowers, were what had been keeping them hidden. Or, hidden until now.

She grabbed Pa's hand, pulled him another step into the water. 'Time for us all to be real. We've all been flickering.'

And that felt true too.

The smoke was so thick, making them cough, making their eyes tear. As they went further into the sea, Adder howled. Moss grabbed her scruff and pulled her. She heard voices now, too, shouting from the boat, urging them on. They'd seen them!

'Come quick,' she said.

They tumbled to swimming, the water flint-sharp. She let go of Adder and swam strong, the waves sloshing. She pulled Pa with her, even when he spluttered for air. Seaweed tangled around their feet, trying to pull them down, pull them back.

They swam hard.

But soon, Moss felt Pa sink. He was snagged on something. Slipping! For a moment, she lost him. She went back. Salt water in her throat, in her ears.

'Pa?'

She searched for him in the waves, treading water. She saw a shape through the thick flower air. He was face down, spinning, whirlpool-frenzied. He was water-full.

Grasping her arms around him, she yanked and kicked. But he was tangle-tight on weed, buffeted by currents and waves, caught. She couldn't do it! She bobbed at the surface. Called for Adder, who'd gone too. Called for anyone!

Was this how it ended, drowning? Going back to the sea like Aster? Never ever going beyond the reef!

No!

She pushed at Pa again. Cried out with the effort of flipping him to his back. But she did it . . . *she did*! His eyes were still open. He saw her. They blinked.

'Breathe, Pa!'

He coughed and spluttered. But she was sinking too as she held him. Spluttering also.

No!

She screamed it out, louder than anything, her noise bigger than the volcano. This wasn't their end!

276

And someone heard.

Quick-fast, something else was swimming with them. *Someone.* Moving as easy as the water itself. Eel-fast.

Cal?

Hands grabbed her coverings and pulled her up. She felt Pa coming too now, grabbed to her tight. Up, up, up, towards the surface. She gasped at the cool salt air. The ease of it. At Cal beside her. Swimming! At how he did not seem afraid, not of water or anything. At how he smiled like pure light.

ACT FOUR. SCENE TWENTY-THREE.

Cal did not think clear when he jumped: only of Moss, of her swirling down deep. Not coming with!

But the water had not stung him – had not taken him sink-down and turned him over like storm treasure.

He had swum fast-free till his fingers clasped solid around Moss and he pull-pulled her up. She gulped air, and he did too. Gasped deep. Then she were looking at him with wide-eyes. Reaching to touch his skin.

It were changing. He felt it. He saw it too.

But quick-fast, he were swimming her back to the boat, to where them two boys grabbed and took her from water. And he went back for the Pa. Even when he did not right want to! Even when it were only for Moss that he did!

The Pa were heavy with sea, but Cal kicked and pulled hard. He got the Pa to the boat's side and pushed him to the boys. Gasping hard, he pulled his own limbs over, too.

There, he held his hands in front. Looked at what Moss had seen in him. What he knew to be true.

As the water dripped from him and settled to the boat, his skin

278

were true-different. As water left him, so, too, did his scale-sheen. It faded gone! Flicker-flicker-gone! Disappeared! No more inside him! Cal saw it make patterns in the puddles before it faded complete.

And Moss had seen it. There, in the water. There, in the cave. This were not just his imaginings.

When he looked across again, he found her eyes, saw her gasping still. At him! His changing!

He held out his hands and shook them to make the water go faster. And – *there!* – the webbings between his fingers felt different, too. Fading? Going? He shook-shook his hands and his webbings seemed to . . . flicker. And again! He shook-shook-shook till the water – till the webbings – disappeared. Till his fingers were naked-normal. Smoothed! Cal went deep-deep-diving for air. Breathed! Watched! Made sure!

It were real. Now his scale-sheen and webbings . . . gone! Like they'd never even been. Their disappearing hadn't even hurt. Not one weasel-bit.

When he looked up this time, it were the Pa who were staring: his mouth open like a chick begging food. Sudden-quick all the anger Cal had towards him came back. Like a fire fresh-lit. Like a burning-bright.

Cal had saved the Pa.

Should he?

The Pa had pulled him by the foot, long ago, back when he were a Small Thing. Took him from another place. *Stole him.* Storm-flower-magicked with webbings and scales. Said he came from a fish!

Cal should have let the Pa go water-heavy! Should have let him kiss seabeds! Let him drown!

And the Pa did not even look grateful.

Cal strode towards him, stood in front. 'You took me,' he said. 'You lied.'

The Pa shook his head, looked away, but he knew. *He knew!*

'You said I were fish-made! Said there were no land. You lied hard!'

Cal held his hands up as proof, shoving them to the Pa's face. He could push them inside of Pa, push till there were no Pa, grab and twist his insides nasty. He could push him over the edge, back into the ocean. But even now, he felt Moss's eyes, fast-steady. If he pushed the Pa, he pushed her, too. Even now, still, she had carings for the sick man.

'I am sorry,' the Pa murmured. 'I did not mean, did not know, did not fully understand . . . I thought the flowers, maybe Moss . . .'

'You knew I were not made from flowers! Always knew it!'

And again and again, the Pa shook his head. 'Never meant for you to come,' he said. 'Just Aster. You came . . . by accident. I never knew who you were.'

'Still don't!' Cal spat at his feet. Turned from him. 'I should push you over. Should let you die.'

Because Cal were remembering. Cal had other ones, somewhere. Cal had been pulled from that. Cal had another voice.

Maybe it had been an accident that Cal came. But he would not hear the Pa's sorry, either. 'Cause Cal had saved Pa while the Pa had taken him!

Though, Cal knew it also – without that taking, Cal would've found no Moss. He moved from the Pa quick-fast and went to Finn instead. 'Sail the boat gone,' he said firm. 'Now.'

He did not look back at the sick man. Let the Pa suffer in the new world, just as Cal had suffered in his! He would come back to Moss, instead.

ACT FOUR. SCENE TWENTY-FOUR.

Moss felt the boat's deck beneath her, and the shake and lick and warmth of her dog. *Adder!* She heard voices she knew. The other boy – Tommy – was staring at her. Was he the one who'd pulled her over the side from the water? He looked at her, concern through his face. Full-sure, he was alive. Healthy, even.

His smile was bigger than Finn's, and there was mischief in his eyes. 'I can see you properly now, out of that cave! Odd-looking, sure, but . . .!' He winked, full-cheeky. 'Cal said you glowed, but you glint brighter in person!'

There were still dark circles around his eyes, and ghost-paleness to his skin, but he no longer looked so sick as if he were about to die. Maybe the island had let him go, too: released him.

She looked past him for Cal again, still not quite believing what she'd just seen happen in his skin. He was beside Finn, watching her right back. She wanted to touch him, go close, but she could only gasp air and wait.

Behind Cal and Finn, the island was a blur of smoke. Groaning and rumbling. It was a living thing, a monster thing . . . a bright burning thing in the dark. Above it all, its flowers were singing.

Stay. Play. Swirl with us. Dream.

'Let's get this boat going again,' Finn called across to his friend. 'Get it gone before the smoke swallows us. It'll be easier now, with you back in the land of the living.'

Tommy half smiled at her again before he squeezed her shoulder and went. 'Still bossy, then,' he grumbled at Finn. 'One little shipwreck's not changed that.'

Moss smelt smoke, and felt it – still crawling into her lungs, still so sweet. She leant back into the boat with Adder clutched-tight, not wanting to see the island, or feel this tearing pain from looking. Because that's what this leaving was. Like a volcano inside, ripping her. Exploding. She could only imagine what Pa felt.

She looked across the deck again. They were there, all of them; everyone but Aster and Jess. On a real boat. Going away after so long. Maybe they were about to forget everything. Who would she be then? A brave new person? Maybe.

Cal crawled over, and she reached to take his hand. There was no silver sheen to his skin. The faint tattoo of scales – all gone. The webbings between his fingers gone too. Now she held a normal hand, a boy's hand . . . was it really so normal as that? She pressed his fingers to her lips, kissed them warm.

Behind her, Finn and Tommy discussed how to get the boat from the reef. She heard groaning and scraping, then something like a loud roar. Slow-slow, the boat came free. The island was letting them all go. Maybe it was. Something inside her still felt tethered though.

'Did you see the horse again?' Finn called across to Tommy. 'There in the water? I saw what you meant in the cave, Tom! She was swimming, diving! The exact same horse as before!'

Aster? She sat up to ask Finn what had happened to her. Where had he seen her go? Was she alive? Was she . . . *anything* . . . any more?

Tommy coughed. 'A horse out here? In the sea? Finn, mate, you've been drinking too much of the funny juice.'

Finn stayed quiet then. She watched him go to the boat's side and lean over, maybe still looking for Aster. Why hadn't Tommy seen her? Or had he, and he'd just forgotten her already? Perhaps Tommy had passed the forgetting line Pa talked of. Perhaps that line wasn't make-believe like she'd hoped.

Close to Moss, Cal smiled. He'd been listening too.

'Aster-spirit,' he murmured. 'That one is flower-made.'

Moss nodded. Cal hadn't forgotten anything. 'Dreamt from the deep.' She paused as she realized it. 'From Pa.'

Pa still looked across the ocean, watching for Aster too. Moss felt an ache to see.

The boat moved, lurched sudden. Were they leaving? Moss swallowed, gripped Cal as the boat moved again. She could feel herself swaying, tipping to dream. But she did not want to be sleeping now. What if, some far-off day in the future, she woke and remembered nothing? The panic struck her sharp as pike teeth. She could not forget! Not anything. The island was part of her: her growing-up. She felt its buzz inside. She needed to write it all down – *everything* – so she could always remember. Now, before the forgetting line.

Quick-fast she was up, stumbling across the slick surface of the deck and down into the cabin below. She took out Pa's other scrapbook from under the bed where she'd left it, and turned to its final page. The hand-drawn map fell out. She turned it over.

And she began to write.

There was a shout up on deck. Sails were going up. She crawled out from the cabin and to where Pa was standing. Still here then, still with them.

She saw all of Western Beach now, nearly the whole of the island, all the way from the finger-point of the Lizard Rocks to their little cove. The volcano still spewed smoke. Pa watched it, silent. She slipped her hand in his. The island was exploding with fire and colour, strange-beautiful. Wondrous-strange. Still, the flowers sang.

'You found it, Pa,' she said. 'The island that was not meant to exist, the one that came to you in dreamings. You made it live.'

'For a time,' he said. 'We both did.'

She saw it all so clear – how the island was visible now because she'd made it so. And she saw, too, that Pa could not let go of it. Would he always be staring out from whatever new place she put him in? Always wanting to be back? Would he get true-sick again, would he get sicker?

Flames leapt from the volcano into the sky. And Pa was looking and longing, so hard, so heart-strong. She shivered when a sudden wind took them faster gone.

'Do you think we forget it all, Moss?' he murmured. 'Do you want to?'

She couldn't answer, not right away. Because if she did forget this island, who would she be? A beaten-up daughter of an angry man? Just that? Would she remember Pa properly from her time here? Would she remember the flowers? Pressing her lips to Cal's on a beach under moonlight, and then, later, in a cave? The beauty of the cove at dawn-break?

'No,' she said true. 'I do not want to forget.'

'I wonder if the island will live,' Pa whispered, 'without us. I wonder if we'll be able to come back.'

Moss knew what he wanted. Flower Island was his exile. Away from the bad people in the rest of the world. Away from the mind-illness he'd had proper back there. But she could not let him stay. He might die like that. And besides, she would miss him too much . . . wouldn't she?

Though, back in the rest of the world . . .

'Will we be together?' she asked. 'Where we're going? They won't take me away from you?'

She had no idea, after all, how it worked. Reading about something like countries and governments was not quite the same as knowing it, seeing it true. He looked at her sad-long.

'They won't believe me, you know,' he said. 'They've never believed me about a thing, where we're going.' He sighed at the sea. 'My world has never . . . quite . . . been the same as theirs. No one's ever . . . quite . . . understood.'

His smile was fleeting-thin.

She didn't know who the *they* were, but she understood something of what he said. Pa had always been in a slight different place. Maybe his *real* was like another person's dream.

'They might think you stole me?' she asked, remembering what he'd said before.

'They will know it.' His hands gripped-tight the boat rail. 'I'll be locked up away. You'll be back with your angry man.'

Her ear throbbed again with just the thought.

When she looked back at the ocean, she frowned. There was a white-wave horse again, racing close to the boat. Was it Aster, sea-made? Was Pa's longing keeping her close, even now?

She wondered about being in this new world with Pa, and yet without him too, about him being locked away. No one could be free like that.

'Maybe you should stay,' she said, releasing his hand, 'like you want. Keep the island hidden like that. Stay with Aster. Keep it for us.'

It hurt knife-sharp to say. It felt right too.

'But you'd never forgive...'

She nodded. 'I would.' She'd be grateful instead. For the island. For Cal. For the buzz she still felt inside.

Besides, without Pa, she was brand new. No one would know her history. It would hurt, but it was clean-hurt. Knife-sharp-clean.

A smile breezed on him. But his eyes went clouding after.

''Tis OK, Pa,' she said.

He stared for a long time to the sea. He was watching Aster beneath, she knew it. He was wanting to be there. Wanting to be with Moss, too. But, this time, he could not have both.

'Go,' she whispered. She half grinned. 'Maybe I could come back to visit sometime?'

He squeezed her hand. 'Yes!' Quick-fast, he leant forward and kissed her forehead. He took a stormflower petal from her hair and pressed it to her tongue.

'I'll keep it alive,' he whispered. 'Ready for when you return. *Please* return.'

Maybe, one day, she would. If she did not forget. If the flower-buzz stayed inside her. If she kept hold of Cal and her dog. She tried to ignore the pit inside her, opening wider each time she imagined not seeing Pa again. It was possible, wasn't it, that she wouldn't? Perhaps sometimes it was better not to think thoughts like that, to live like Pa in dream.

Pa touched the end of her nose. 'Greatest experiment.' His tears slipped down his cheeks. 'Thank you.'

Behind them, the island burnt bright, a million flower petals glowing orange as a lizard's eye. Pa looked over to Cal. He raised his hand, though Cal did not look or wave back.

'Look after him,' Pa said.

And if Cal heard, he did not say anything. He only spat at the deck.

Pa climbed on to the boat's edge. 'Goodbye, my magic Moss. I'll send flowers on the wind so you won't forget.'

'Goodbye.' She was tear-choked too now.

Pa dived into the ocean.

Gone.

Moss clung to the side of the boat and peered over. She saw him swimming, spinning on to his back to look up at her, then across to Cal, too, even when Cal, still, would not see. Then he was waving goodbye.

Perhaps he would not survive, stranded with only the flowers and Aster to tether him. Perhaps he would become as real as a spirit himself – made only from dreams – churning his stories back into the island. But he would be happy like that, at least; away from the darkness he saw in the rest of the world. Exiled free. Where he'd been trying to get to all along, before Moss had hid with him and made his stories grow bigger.

When Moss looked over at them, Tommy and Finn did not even

seem to notice he'd gone. Cal still stared determined-strong in the other direction.

As Pa bobbed from the boat and towards his land, the stingers came. They billowed out around him as water-clouds. Pa swam backwards, and the water got rougher, waves slap-slapping against him. Around him, it began to glow luminous-bright, sparkle-bright . . . wondrous-bright.

Even so, Moss saw her – swimming underneath, down in the deep dark of the sea, sparkle-shone. Aster, come back for him. Moss breathed out slow. Pa's waterhorse would swim to shore with him, keep him safe; she'd help him dream some more. Adder whined as he went, howling to the rising moon. Moss felt like doing it too.

The last image Moss had of Pa, he was smiling at her, *glinting*, the fire from the island reflected in his skin. He was sinking back into the water, to where Aster was, to where coral and flowers bloomed.

And the island went calm.

Simple. As. That.

It went back to dream.

Moss shook her head. Even now, she did not understand its magic. If it was even magic. If that island was even there at all. But she felt it. Felt Pa there too.

She could not forget.

And Moss hadn't forgotten anything yet. She still tasted the flower-buzz on her tongue. Maybe the island would stay inside her. Anything was possible, wasn't it?

Though, each time she looked back at their island, it was further away. They hadn't gone much further when it began to flicker. Until it was like how Bird Island had first looked when Moss had seen it from their cove: flickering, then solid, then flickering again. Soon, she was looking at it from the sides of her eyes. Squinting to see.

She went across to Cal and took his hand.

'Coming up, going down,' she murmured, pointing it out for him.

Was it disappearing? Fading from reality? Any moment now, would Moss be forgetting? Might they all?

'I risk it with you,' Cal said, soft. 'Wherever you want to go.'

He leant his head on to her shoulder and his lips brushed against her neck. She shiver-smiled.

'See it all?' she asked. 'The whole world?'

Cal nodded. 'We find your home and mine.'

She turned to him. His skin was sunbeam-glinting. He was storm-woke bright, and *hers*.

She leant forward and caught his smile. She kissed proper – all the real of him and all the magic parts too. Kissed him hard! She did not care if he was boy or spirit or something in between, just cared that he was Cal. She felt his arms come round her, holding her limpet-fast. Like this they were yin-yanged. Birds on a branch. Storm-woke both. She kissed until she no longer felt so tipsy-spun. *Tethered*.

The island was still there when they turned.

Just.

Finn and Tommy billowed the sails out full. And they left. Sailing towards the real world and its answers. Towards Miranda, and towards who Callan was, too. And she would see it true.

ACT FIVE
SPRING

The Scene: At Sea

Current

ACT FIVE. SCENE ONE.

Finn woke from a dream. A glorious dream. A kick-ass one. He tossed and rolled in the belly of his boat. If he kept his eyes closed, he could remember her face . . . just. Those green eyes, so cool he could drink them up. He'd been lying on the sand, holding her close. *Gorgeous.* He went up on deck to tell Tommy.

'Another dream!' he shouted to his mate. 'A hot girl this time! Wild and stormy!'

'Yeah?' Tommy barked a laugh. 'Sounds like a cocktail!' He made a sobbing noise as he thought further. 'But we don't even have any rum!'

'Maybe that's why we've been dreaming.' Finn laughed with his friend. 'We've had no booze for days . . . weeks! They should send people who need to sober up out on these things.'

Tommy flipped Finn the bird. 'You might be in luck; think there's land coming.'

'Finally!'

Tommy had the rudder under control, so Finn went to sit up at the bow. He looked out with his feet dangling. They were tacking left and the sails were far out. The full sun was in his face, obscuring any land that might be there. He shut his eyes again. He could go back to sleep right there on deck. He could dream of that girl again; she was still in his mind. She'd had petals threaded through her dark, braided hair. Perhaps she was an angel.

How many days since they'd seen land now? How much longer until they could get a drink? See a real girl? Act . . . *normal*?

The sun was turning his eyelids fire-red. He turned away from the sun, and his eyes fell upon the dog, still here, still black and white and goofy-looking. He reached out to scratch her silky ears and copped a lick to the face. She must have wandered on to their deck in the last port, maybe when they'd been drunk one night . . . the last time they'd been drunk. Probably the same night they'd repainted their boat with a different name and somehow lost half their stuff. Either way, Finn was pretty sure that the dog was a stray, but still . . . He really hoped he hadn't stolen anyone's pet by accident.

'Amy?' he tried again. 'Sally?'

The dog stared blankly back. None of the names had stuck.

'Woofmaker? Bones? Snapper? Big Tongue?'

On cue, she lolled her tongue out. Then licked him again with it.

Finn shut his eyes once more. There'd been flowers in his dream, too. Beautiful flowers. Ones that smelt like the sweetest honey, or the strongest ganja. He hadn't told Tommy that. So weird! It must be something about sailing – it made him dream so vividly. Either that or he was going nuts with the boredom of the endless ocean. Cabin fever! Salt madness! Here, there was nothing else to do but remember dreams.

He went back down into the cabin, the dog trailing behind.

'Not come to take over steering, then?' Tommy said as he passed.

'Nah. Back to bed.'

'Shithead.'

But when he lay on the hard bunk, he couldn't sleep. Not even when the dog curled up close to him and gave him her warmth. Those flowers from the dream! They were all he could think of. Them and that dream girl's eyes. The petals in her hair.

He started rifling through drawers and cupboards, looking for paper. Under the bed was an old sketchbook, with a few blank pages at the end. Where'd he nabbed that from? *Who?* He flicked to one page, found a pencil, and started to sketch.

As he drew, he could remember more about the flowers from his dream. They had been singing to him, promising him things. He'd wanted to eat them.

He smiled. He was definitely going nuts.

But he still couldn't stop looking at the picture he had drawn. He wasn't much of an artist usually, but this sketch was good. It looked just like one of the pretty little flowers he'd dreamt of, one he could almost . . . touch.

He snapped the book shut just to stop his endless staring. And a different piece of paper fell out. There was an old hand-drawn map on it. On the back were words, in handwriting that was not his or Tommy's.

You won't remember. It will all just be something unreal, wild and strange. But dreams can be real too. And reality can also be just a dream.

Take my dog as proof of it. Her name is Adder. Remember it! And

295

don't let her soft touch fool you. She is fierce. Fiercest thing I've ever known. She comes from a wild, free place. Yes, sometimes, untamed places do exist. Sometimes mysteries do too.

Let them.

Let your dreams be dreams.

Remember them. Try to remember the very edges of the things that aren't there.

Because that's where the island lies. Flower Island. Maybe you'll go there again some day. If you remember. If you can find it.

But, you know . . . I think Adder might remember that place anyway. Can you see it there, in her glint-wise eyes? She is half islander, after all. One day she might be able to get back. I'll follow her. Back to Pa. Back to half of myself . . . back to dreaming . . . back to that spiral cycle of appearing and disappearing too. Maybe one day I will . . .

With a snap of her teeth, the dog took the paper from Finn's hands, chewed it up, and swallowed.

'What the—?' He laughed at her goofy expression, then called up to Tommy. 'The dog's crazy! It just ate paper . . .'

But already Finn was forgetting the words written on it, forgetting, too, where they had sailed from. Remembering all of it only as a vague, distant dream. A glorious dream. A kick-ass one.

He leant back into his balled-up sweater pillow. Perhaps he wasn't ready to go home just yet. They had to refit Dad's boat with all the stuff they'd lost, for one thing. But perhaps there was more to see out here on the ocean anyway, more to find. The place where the flowers from his dream grew, for one thing. He turned his face towards the dog's snout.

'Adder,' he whispered.

That sounded . . . just right. Suited her, even. And the dog licked his chin almost like confirmation. She smelt of fish, of rotting oysters, and of the wide, wild sea.

'What are we going to do together?' he said. 'What would you show me?'

Then Finn was turning over, shutting his eyes, forgetting even that dog. From somewhere far away, he heard a whistle, and then a distant voice he – almost – recognized . . . but it was already part of his dream, part of his sleeping, part of his dropping deep-down-deep . . . And already, the dog was shifting away, bounding gone . . .

And Finn was dreaming.

* APPLAUSE *

EPILOGUE
SPRING

THE SCENE: AT SEA

Moss waited, till beyond the very edge of Bird Island. If they were going to forget, it would have happened by now, like how it'd been for Finn and Tommy.

But . . . Moss and Cal had remembered, still they did. All of it. Felt like all of it, anyway. Maybe they'd never be full-sure. They'd remembered while the two boys forgot. They'd whispered about it, heads bowed close.

The flower colours. The glow-blue water. Pa.

It was all still inside.

Maybe she'd had enough stormflowers to be an islander; maybe Cal had too. Or maybe it was Pa, after all, sending out his thoughts on the petals, ever experimenting. But she still felt that flower-buzz if she concentrated full-hard. She still felt that tiny wind inside.

She waited until new land appeared, one that wasn't flickering this time. When Adder had raised her head too and looked in its direction, only then had she poked Cal in the ribs.

'Now,' she whispered. 'Let's go now.'

Moss had dived. The water had been sparkle-full with fish and sunlight, and it had moved to let her inside it. She swam fast through it, wiggling like the mermaid from her dreamings so long past. She swam to leave sadness behind, too . . . the letting-go ache from leaving Pa and Aster and Jess. Leaving the island! The flint-sharp ache even from leaving Finn and Tommy and the boat called *Swallow*. If she let it, she could drown in sadness like that. Get taken right under and stay in those deeps.

Cal joined her. Adder would come soon, she wouldn't forget. Adder had been born on that island, after all; she was half wild dog, half dreaming, herself. But her dog liked Finn full-deep and needed time to say goodbye. Moss let her.

Soon, bobbing on the ocean with Cal, Moss whistled for her. She smiled big as the dog raced up from the boat's cabin, nails scratching against the wood, and leapt over the side towards them. Cal laughed as the dog took a belly slap.

'Knew you wouldn't stay,' Moss said to her. 'Wouldn't leave me yet.'

And Moss was full-glad, ruffling her dog's wet fur. She murmured her thanks into Adder's silky ears.

Moss swam and swam, and swam faster again when Cal, and then Adder, moved up beside her. They swam until they were like fish in a current. Until stingers joined them, too. She reached across to take Cal's hand, moving her legs like a mermaid's tail. Swam, swam, swam . . . from one dream to another. From colour to dark. From sad to light. Who knew, really, where to?

She led them all to the land ahead. She wasn't scared. She told herself she wasn't, anyway. She told herself she was happy to raise her head above the water and swim towards what she once might have been, back to whatever answers lay waiting. To have Cal and Adder beside her, and a buzz inside. She told herself that she had not forgotten Pa, but she would be more than him, too. She told herself she could go back, if she wanted. Like this, she would be the happy and sad, the light and dark . . .

She would be the dreaming, and the real, in one.

Exit.

ACKNOWLEDGEMENTS

I wanted the process of this book to be about play and exploration. That kind of process takes time, and patience, and gentle nurture. Thank you to everyone who gave me that. In particular . . .

Thank you to my publisher, Chicken House, for being so long-suffering and dedicated. Thank you to Barry. Thank you to Siobhan for the careful edits. Thank you to the brilliant Scholastic team, also. Thanks, Sam, for 'getting it'!

Thank you to my agent, Nicola.

Thank you to the writers in my life – those of you I write with, and those who read drafts. Special thanks to me ole spleen, Melvin Burgess, and to generous Marcus Sedgwick. Thank you to Fox Benwell for always being so positive. Thank you, Derek Niemann, for reading an early draft. Thanks to Joe Ducie for reading several drafts! Thank you, especially, to Andy D. – who inspires me to 'write joy' always. Thank you, also, to colleagues and students at Bath Spa University – you all inspire me, but especially Julia Green.

Thank you to friends and family. Adrian, I might not have ever started this book without you. Catherine, I couldn't have continued it without you. And, Johanna, I wouldn't have understood this book without you. Thank you to Lon for support and reading. Thanks, Pen-Pen, for the Scotland shenanigans. To Jennifer for original 'Moss inspiration'! Thank you to 'the Christopher Clan' and to Great Aunty Anne for general life inspiration! To Larch (of course!) for dog inspiration!

Thank you to Eleri and Geraint at Gwernan Hotel who stoked the fire and made sandwiches while I tried to finish a draft.

Thank you to Mum for always being so positive about the book and so willing to read it (even when it's bad!). And thank you to Dad and Barb – I couldn't write a book about the theatre without it being for you!

Lastly, thank you, Raj. You are wonder-bright and lovely.

ALSO BY LUCY CHRISTOPHER

STOLEN by LUCY CHRISTOPHER

It happened like this.

I was stolen from an airport.

Taken from everything I knew, everything I was used to. Taken to sand and heat, dirt and danger. And he expected me to love him. This is my story.

A letter from nowhere.

A vivid new voice for teens.
MELVIN BURGESS

Tautly written and hard to put down.
INDEPENDENT ON SUNDAY

Paperback, ISBN 978-1-908435-75-0, £7.99 • ebook, ISBN 978-1-908435-18-7, £7.99

26.4.18

BETTWS

ALSO BY LUCY CHRISTOPHER

THE KILLING WOODS by LUCY CHRISTOPHER

E mily's dad is accused of killing a teenage girl.
She's sure he's innocent, and is determined to discover
the truth of what happened. But her journey leads her to
discover that dangerous games are being played in the woods at
night . . .

*Original and thrilling, this is another cracker
from an author to watch.*

THE SUN

*A gripping, heartbreaking, emotionally substantial
look at war wounds and the allure of danger.*

KIRKUS STARRED REVIEW

Paperback, ISBN 978-1-906427-72-6, £7.99 • ebook, ISBN 978-1-908435-70-5, £7.99